MISFIT GIRL

DEATH OF THE BLUE FLOWER

Misfit Girl Suspense
Thriller, vol. 1

ROXANN HILL

Translated by:

PAUL WAGLE

For Eva and Paul

Ich suche die blaue Blume,
Ich suche und finde sie nie,
Mir träumt, dass in der Blume
Mein gutes Glück mir blüh.

I search for the blue flower,
I search but never find it,
I dream, that in that flower
Happiness would bloom for me.

Joseph von Eichendorff (1788–1857), "Die Blaue Blume"
("The Blue Flower")

AUTHOR'S NOTE

Several Holms—they are called *Halligen* in Germany—exist on the North Sea—some larger, some small— a few have only one house, others a little village, even fewer remain uninhabited. The Hallig islands boast a total population of just over two hundred people.

The first Halligen were formed during the devastating storm surge of January 16, 1362, the so called, *Die Grote Mandränke* (the great drowning). Large parts of the mainland were swept away in what is considered to be the birth of the Halligen. Further storm surges over the centuries continued to shape the Halligen. Many of them disappeared completely. At the same time, by depositing sediment the tides gradually created the Halligen as we know them today.

Fifteen to twenty times a year, the Halligen are flooded by salt water so much that only the buildings erected on the highest elevations protrude from the sea. Life on a Hallig is fundamentally different from life on the mainland. The inhabitants of the Hallig are much more exposed to the forces of nature and have to accept restrictions. But they have adapted to this. They live with the tides and are always prepared to provide for themselves if they are cut off from the mainland—be it due to strong easterly winds that make it impossible for supply boats to reach the Halligen, during storms or in winter, when ice floes form.

The name Kronsoog is fictitious.

PROLOGUE

Sonja, Marko and Sven

The first rays of sun fought their way through the black of the night. A pasty gray crept in. The street seemed deserted, run down. At this hour, there was hardly any traffic.

A nearly empty transit bus drove past, followed by a delivery van from some bakery chain. Otherwise, the city slept.

"Are you sure we have the right address?" Marko asked. He straightened up and turned around in the front seat of the parked car. He was tall with brawny shoulders; his face was smooth, almost expressionless. He had celebrated his twenty-fifth birthday three weeks earlier. That made him two years older than Sven, who was huddled over in the passenger seat. Sven was not really a morning person. He complained every time they had to work so early. But that was his only flaw. He always did what he was told and did not talk much. You could rely on him one hundred percent. A good partner to have.

"Of course. I'm positive," Sonja retorted. She sat in the backseat, nursing a Diet Coke as usual.

"How is that possible? Every corner in this giant city looks exactly like the last one."

"Have I ever led you astray?" Sonja's voice rang calm, almost bored, lacking any trace of enthusiasm.

Marko shrugged and looked back at the rows of houses with viewless windows. Sonja was their leader. She was always on top of things. Thanks to her precision and diligence, she had never made a mistake. What she said went.

"How much longer do we have to wait?" Sven bellyached.

Sonja brushed her dark, almost black hair out of her eyes and looked at her watch. "Seven minutes. He'll leave the house at five."

"So early?"

"Twice a week before work, he delivers flyers."

"Very industrious," Marko noted.

"You could say that." Sonja sipped her Coke.

Sven snickered. "Our surprise will do him good. He really deserves this reward."

"Have you decided who gets to deliver the surprise?" Marko asked as casually as possible, in hopes of downplaying the gravity of the situation. Both he and his friend vied for Sonja to select them for this task. This was, after all, the best part of the job: to walk right up to the people and hand them their reward.

"I think . . ." Sonja began. A charged silence followed. She grinned and took another drink.

"Don't make it so dramatic," Marko said.

"Of course." Sonja pretended to concentrate hard. "Now that I think about it, Sven went the last two times. And did a really good job. But . . ."

"But what?" Sven hissed. All of a sudden, he was wide awake.

"But in general, Marko gets along better with the customers."

"That's unfair!" Sven erupted. "How can you even say that? I'm just as professional as Marko."

"Well, yeah," Sonja agreed after some hesitation. "But all the same, today it's Marko's turn."

"That's mean," Sven protested. "He's gotten to do it much more than me."

"Enough already!" Sonja's sharp words ended the discussion.

Sven looked to the side dejectedly. Marko beamed with pride and anticipation.

"Okay," Sonja said. "He'll be the only pedestrian on the sidewalk. Gray hair, mustache. He'll be carrying a satchel full of flyers. The thing is pretty heavy. And since he's not very big, it'll be quite a bit for him to haul." She reached down next to the seat, produced a plastic sack, and handed it to Marko. "You deliver the gift, make sure that everything is all right, and come straight back to the car."

"I'm not a novice," Marko muttered. His hand trembled a little as he grabbed the bag. It was visibly difficult for him to contain his excitement.

He got out, quietly closed the driver's door, and waved briefly to his team. Then he set off.

A few blackbirds were chirping loudly. Soon their song would be lost in the morning traffic.

His footsteps echoed dully across the asphalt, and he quickly spotted a man in the distance. He looked exactly how Sonja had described him. Only he did not carry one, but two heavy satchels. A veritable beast of burden. Today was clearly this guy's lucky day.

Marko had to force himself not to speed up. Slow and steady, he proceeded along. When the man noticed him, Marko smiled broadly. After a moment's hesitation, the gray-haired man returned his smile.

Marko stopped short, raised his hand as if to wave.

The gray-haired man just stood there, seemingly bewildered.

Marko's smile grew warm and genuine. He reached into the plastic bag, keeping the man in sight. His hand found its way to the grip of the semiautomatic pistol equipped with a silencer.

He let the empty bag fall, brought the unlocked weapon into position, and shot the man at point-blank range in the face. A faint pop resounded, followed by a metallic clatter as the discharged shell danced across the sidewalk.

The gray-haired man fell backward like a wet sack. His arms and legs were still moving slightly. All the winners did this.

Marko stepped a bit closer and shot two more times. Now even the twitching stopped.

A dark fluid spread out from under the man's head.

Done.

Marko turned away. He bent down and picked up the plastic bag. He scoured the ground for the bullet casings. The first two he found quickly. The third was hidden in the gutter. He carefully tucked all three into the pocket of his jacket before he returned to the vehicle. Haste makes waste.

Sven, who had moved over to the driver's seat, looked away with feigned anger as Marko climbed into the car.

Marko nudged his friend's shoulder amiably. "The next one is yours—if Sonja has nothing against it."

Sonja laughed. "Why would I have anything against it? I think it's great when you two get along. A good team should share everything."

That was true, with the exception of sex. Sven was not allowed to get in on that.

Sven started the car. They drove down the street at a leisurely pace. As they passed the dead man lying, right in front of the door of someone's home, they didn't even look. That job was done.

"It's going to be a beautiful day," Marko noted.

"Yep," Sven concurred. "Seventy-seven degrees and sunny. Super beach weather."

"First, couldn't we . . .?" Sonja said.

Marko avoided looking back. Sven acted as if he were concentrating on the nonexistent traffic in the side-view mirror.

"Oh, come on," Sonja interjected.

"Don't you love it when she begs?" Marko asked Sven.

"It's great," Sven answered.

"You know—down by the river, just outside the city limits? The little park bench we drove past?" Sonja said.

"You can't let it rest, can you?" Marko said.

"Of course, Sonja saw it. Did you think just the two of us noticed?" Sven grinned.

Sonja leaned forward between the two front seats and made her irresistible pouty face. "Oh, come on. There's got to be time for a little fun."

"Who's the one who said work has to be the most important thing in life?" Marko tried to sound serious, but as soon as he finished, all three broke into roaring laughter.

"It really won't take long," Sonja insisted.

Marko sighed dramatically. "No one can refuse you anything."

In the meantime, they had nearly left the city. They drove past high-rise apartments, and then the buildings grew sparse. On the right side, you could now see trees and the river beyond.

Soon they were parked at an abandoned rest stop. All three got out.

Sonja held a small canister in her hand. She danced around like a mischievous kid. Her eyes sparkled. She was in a good mood. "You can come along," she offered the two men. "Then you can enjoy it up close."

"You don't mind?" Sven asked.

"My mother always said, 'A pleasure that's shared is a pleasure that's doubled.' And there are three of us, so it's fun times three." Without waiting for a response, Sonja hurried along. Her two friends followed hot on her heels.

Although it promised to be a warm day, a dilatory fog lay on the water. The air smelled cool and clean. Dewdrops glistened on the grass and the lower leaves of the bushes. The river splashed quietly and continuously on its long odyssey to the sea.

From the park bench, one had a magnificent view of the sleepy storybook valley. Sonja crept cautiously toward her destination. When she reached the bench, she opened the canister and poured its contents generously over the man curled up there sleeping off his inebriation.

The bag of bones stirred uneasily but did not wake up.

A zippo appeared in Sonja's hand. She rolled her thumb across the flint wheel, and a small yellow-blue light danced to life. With her head cocked sideways, she lowered her arm and let go.

Instantly, an unearthly glow spread over the body of the sleeping man. Flames shot up—initially reserved and timid, and then blazing and destructive.

Sonja jumped back a few steps and watched spellbound as the man suddenly regained consciousness and sprang to his feet. Now he began to scream. He screeched and yelled almost inhumanly, and flailed like a madman, while the fire leaped a meter above him. Then his voice failed. He ran toward the water, but they all knew that he would never make it that far.

Sven followed the spectacle with fascination.

Marko, on the other hand, only had eyes for Sonja. She was never more beautiful than in moments like these.

1

I was back in the sea. Water on my body. Water on my face. With every stroke, my arms, coupled with the power of my legs, shot me forward. Nobody could hold me back. I was in my element here. This was my home.

Whenever I stretched my head up to get air, I could hear the cries of the seagulls above me. Their melancholic wailing, as timeless as the sea, swelled, only to retreat and rise up again. The gulls were on the hunt. I knew how they would dart down to the water and—if successful—surface with fish hanging from their beaks. They went about their business, single-minded and completely focused, just as I did—lost in this perfect moment when body and mind find themselves in unison, when there is no ambiguity, no questions, only peace.

I had already covered more than five hundred meters. Kronsoog, my island, my *Hallig*, was far behind me.

Soon it would get dangerous.

I knew the exact spot. They appeared here, the currents. If I didn't pay attention, they would rip me out to sea with them. Just one slipup and even the best swimmer wouldn't have a chance. The North Sea showed no mercy when it came to any kind of weakness. She'd abduct her victims and never return them.

I took a breath and dove as deeply as I could. Death pulled on me with its icy fingers. I could feel it. It lay in wait for one mistake, one thoughtless move. I had to manage twenty-five—or better, thirty—strokes. Extended, unwavering, and consistent. The urge to get air grew stronger. A burning pressure built up in my chest and expanded until it was nearly unbearable. Muscles began to ache, and my pulsating head pounded every thought into pieces.

Then the danger zone was behind me. Panting, I came to the surface, felt the hard wind on my face, and greedily sucked in the smell of the salty water.

I continued on my course. Calm and steady, my body plowed through the waves that obligingly allowed my passage.

The sun peeked through the clouds. Its rays broke in the whitecaps and blinded me.

I would never be happier.

I did not feel alone. A certainty accompanied me. The certainty of being watched by my grandmother. She never admitted it, but every time I swam toward the mainland, she casually came down to the shore and observed me. She put her hand to her forehead, and her blue eyes, which despite being buried in the deep wrinkles of her face had lost none of their youthfulness, followed my every move. She remained motionless until I doubled back and put the currents behind me a second time. Then, with a resolute gesture, she'd pull her fair hair up and disappear into the house or the barn. She worked constantly. She never took a break. There was certainly no lack of chores on our Hallig.

It was the height of summer. The North Sea glistened like polished lead. It had retreated, and the land around our farm rose formidable and peaceful out of the cold waters, resembling an oasis. The salt marshes shimmered green. Their fine blades danced excitedly in the wind. But it was the gentle blue that reigned.

Sea lavender.

It grew everywhere and bathed everything in a surreal blue glow. Its delightful scent mixed with the fragrance of the cold, salty sea.

My home.

My fingertips came across something solid. I steadied myself and grabbed the metallic ladder. I held on for a moment and caught my breath before I placed my foot on the bottom rung.

Grooved surface, so no one would slip.

Reluctantly I pulled myself up; the water let me go freely. A lot was left behind in it. Too much. The memory of another time, in a different place. Certainly, with other dreams. Everything had changed. And me? I had also changed. But not in ways I would have wished.

Anguished, I exhaled.

An elderly woman in a flowered swimsuit was looking down at me. She waited until I was standing on the tiles before pushing past me and lowering herself carefully into the water.

The odor of chlorine reached my nose.

I blinked, blinded by the stark florescent lights from the arsenal of lamps on the ceiling. Almost simultaneously, the typical noises of an indoor swimming pool grabbed hold of me. Children laughing and cheering. Mothers chatting, their conversations echoing from clear across the pool. Someone jumping into the water. A coach's whistle cutting shrilly through the hall.

I went over to the bench, slipped into my flip-flops, grabbed my towel, and laid it across my shoulder. The white terry cloth made a striking contrast to my dark skin.

I had not inherited my grandmother's complexion. Her skin had always been pale, virtually colorless, like every Frisian. I, on the other hand, got my looks from my father. He was African American.

I checked the clock. Forty laps in an hour. Two kilometers. That wasn't bad, but I would need to be able to cover eight kilometers at a good pace, and not in this bathtub but outside in the North Sea. I had registered for the long-distance swim from Norddeich to the island Norderney. I was going to take part in the race and place in the top ten—my ultimate goal. And then . . .

Suddenly, I felt exhausted and drained. What had gotten into me to exert myself like this before my shift even started?

I would be back tomorrow.

2

I placed the dishes on the cart, poured the rest of the coffee into a bucket, and made my way to the next room. The door was ajar, but I knocked anyway, opened it without waiting for a response, and entered. The patient sat in an armchair, reading the daily paper. She hadn't touched her cake and had taken a couple of sips of her tea at best.

"Should I come back later?" I asked.

At first, I thought she had not heard me, because she did not answer. But after a moment, she said without looking up, "No, take them with you." She turned the page.

I collected the tray, moving it as carefully as I could, so as not to bother her. Nevertheless, the cup bumped up against the newspaper, and some tea sloshed onto the saucer.

"Be careful," the patient said.

I bit my lip. "Nothing spilled. Do you need anything else?"

"Not now." Once again, she didn't lift an eye toward me. "Maybe later you could bring me another tea."

"Gladly," I said and turned back toward the hall. This time, I closed the door.

Outside, I was greeted by distinguished tranquility. The hall appeared clean and new. Everything shined immaculately. Plants as high as the ceiling provided splashes of green. Scattered seating accommodations, arranged casually around floor-level windows overlooking Lake Starnberg, ensured an inviting atmosphere. It didn't even smell like a hospital.

I pushed my cart to the next room and repeated the question-and-answer session. If I hadn't known better, I would have thought I was in a hotel. Ultimately, that is what it was: a high-end hotel. A five-star residence. A night in this clinic easily cost what I made in a month. If you could afford to stay here, either you were very well insured, or you had cash to burn. Or both.

One of my colleagues came down the hall. She was probably fifteen years older than me. I guessed her to be in her early forties. Like all of us caregivers, she wore white pants and a light-yellow blouse—to match the color scheme of the clinic, as if we were part of the decor. "Sybil Kaufmann" was engraved on her name tag.

She seemed relaxed and in a good mood. Maybe someday I would manage to enjoy working here too. At present, I found it monotonous and boring.

She looked me up and down. "Alicia, how is it going?" She had adopted the condescending tone of the patients.

"Good," I replied.

"Are you almost finished with your rooms?"

"Twelve more."

She raised her eyebrows. "You still have to do twelve rooms? That won't leave you much time before dinner."

I did not answer but just stared at her until she looked to the side. "Well . . ." She coughed uncomfortably.

"You're new. You don't have the routine down yet. If you want, I can help you. Then it'll at least go a bit faster. You'd only have to do me a small favor."

"What?"

"You use few words." She attempted a smile but succeeded only moderately. "Well, if you take Mr. Winkler, I'll finish your rounds for you."

I took my time with the answer. She brushed a curl off her brow nervously as she waited for my response. She had wonderful hair. Copper strands flashed in the light and fell over her shoulders. I always kept my unruly frizz cropped short, or else it was untameable.

"All right," I said. "Where can I find him?"

"Twelve fourteen. Down the hall on the left."

Placing my hands on the cart, I started walking.

It didn't take long before I was at room number twelve fourteen. I went in.

No lights. Stale air. This time, I could distinctly smell antiseptic. My eyes couldn't see a thing in the darkness. I blinked.

"What's the matter?" I heard a voice. It was scratchy and irritated.

"I've come to collect the dishes," I replied.

"You?"

"Yes, me." I remained in place.

"What are you waiting for?"

I began to adapt to the dim light. On the bed sat a broad-shouldered man, maybe mid-thirties. He looked like an athlete. Strong, muscular arms, slender hips. His hair fashionably short—no. It had fallen out and was beginning to grow back. Obviously, the result of chemotherapy. He was looking straight at me. His light eyes glistened faintly. He raised his hand and motioned toward the bedside table.

"There," he said.

I went over and was about to stack the plates and cutlery together when he coughed. A wicked and audibly painful hack. He lurched forward. I got scared that he would fall off the bed and started toward him.

He raised his hand once more, ordering me to stay put with a silent yet unmistakable gesture. I waited until he managed to breathe normally.

"Are you all right?"

"That's a dumb question." He reached with his left hand, picked up a small rubber ball from the bedspread next to him, and began kneading it in his palm.

"Can I bring you anything else?" I asked.

"The food I got for lunch was wrong."

"Wrong?"

"I ordered a different meal. One of your moronic colleagues brought me fish. But I had wanted the steak."

"Are you even allowed to eat that?" I let slip.

"I eat whatever I want, you nincompoop. Imagine that."

"I only meant—"

"Maybe you should at least try to think before you open your mouth."

"It's not my fault," I said.

"That you're incompetent?"

"No. That you have cancer."

He inhaled sharply. "Ha, quick-witted. Dense but quick-witted. What a combination."

I took the tray in my hands and started to leave the room.

"By the by," he said, "tonight I would like to have a mineral water. And a cold one, for a change. Maybe you could get it out of the refrigerator and not off a sunny windowsill."

I turned back to him. Now I could see him rather well. His face was striking, albeit pasty and with deep shadows encircling his eyes. He might have actually been an attractive man before this.

"Is there anything else I could do for you with my limited intelligence?" I asked.

He remained silent and focused his attention on the hand that kneaded the rubber ball incessantly.

I stood watching him for some time before I left the room.

3

The empty corridor greeted me with its elegant indifference. I was pushing my cart toward the kitchen when I heard, "Alicia, how'd it go?"

Sybil ducked out from a room and blocked my path. She examined me with blatant curiosity and a distinct trace of schadenfreude.

I shrugged.

She smiled knowingly. "Come on, that Winkler is beyond words. The guy hates the whole world. Some people get like that after chemo. There isn't anything you can do about it."

She was probably expecting me to pour my heart out to her. "It doesn't bother me in the least," I responded.

Her grin disappeared; she frowned and lowered her gaze. When she looked back up, there was a sharp glint in her eyes. "Then you can take care of him from now on. You two are made for each other."

She reached into her cart, retrieved a tube of ointment, and studied it contemplatively. "Oh! I did the rest of your rounds, and it was a good amount of work. So, you have to do something else for me."

I didn't answer, just waited for her to continue talking.

She held the ointment out to me. "Ms. Morgenroth. In front, by the filthy rich. In suite C."

I made no move to take the tube from her.

"Congenital defect that's only detected with advancing age."

I still didn't budge.

"It's her skin. You'll need to apply this ointment. And in return, no one will find out that you don't get your rounds done on time."

I took the tube out of her hand. "Suite C?"

She nodded. "But hurry! I have no desire to deliver your dinners for you too."

In the front section of the building, the corridor widened. The paintings on the walls were originals. I knocked on a door embossed with a golden *C* and entered.

Handcrafted furniture. Expensive rugs. A magnificent view of the lake.

A frail white-haired lady sat in a gigantic wing chair. She was reading a small booklet with a black cover. As soon as she noticed me, she snapped it closed, looked up, and smiled. Countless wrinkles and pale-blue piercing eyes that reminded me of someone. Someone who had left me behind years before.

"Yes?" she said.

At least she had a different voice than my grandmother.

I cleared my throat and held out my hand to show her the ointment.

"Ah," she said. "My cream. But," she added with a knowing smile, "if it's too much for you, I can do it myself."

"No," I said.

"No, what?"

I walked over and stood before her. "I don't mind applying your ointment. You just caught me . . ."

Those old blue eyes scrutinized me keenly. "Do I remind you of someone?"

Now I had to smile. "Yes, of my grandmother."

"Was she nice?"

"Annoyingly so."

The lady made a strange sound. She was laughing.

I helped remove her cardigan. The finest cashmere. Her blouse was made of silk. She opened the buttons and slipped out of it. Her arms were thin, wrinkled, traversed with bluish-black veins. The skin was scaly, rough, and cracked in places. She had to be in pain, even if she didn't let on that she was.

I carefully applied the ointment and gently rubbed it in. She stretched out her other arm for me. I repeated the procedure. She moved her hand, and on the inside of her forearm, I noticed a six-digit number. 135763. Crude and ineptly tattooed, faded over the decades.

Out of the corner of my eye, I could tell that she was watching my reaction. Conscientiously, I finished my work and went into the luxurious bathroom to wash my hands. On the way back, I brought a white light cotton bathrobe with me and placed it over her shoulders.

"Is there something else I can do for you?"

The old lady shook her head almost imperceptibly. "You're not from around here," she said.

"How can you tell?"

"While you were applying the cream, and even before, you kept glancing at the lake."

"I like the water," I admitted.

"Does it remind you of home?"

"The North Sea."

"What brought you from so far away, to Starnberg?"

I tried to appear indifferent. "Mobility. Globalization. I had to go where I could find work."

"Whatever," she said. "That's a bunch of tripe. You're homesick. Admit it."

This time, I grinned.

"You know what I do when I'm longing for a time gone by or the place where I grew up?"

I shook my head.

The old woman indicated the little booklet she had been reading earlier, which was now lying on the chest of drawers in front of her. "I read poems."

"And that helps?"

She thought about it for a moment. "Yes. Really. If you want, we can try it together tomorrow."

"That would make me happy," I said without hesitation.

"By the way, what's your name?" she asked me.

"Alicia. Alicia Petersen."

"A nice Frisian name."

I had to laugh. "The Frisian part of me really shows."

"They say you shouldn't judge a book by its cover, don't they?"

"Precisely."

"By the way, my name is Miriam Morgenroth. But you can call me Miriam."

"Good," I said. "See you tomorrow, Miriam."

4

I closed the door behind me. My quarters in the dormitory were not especially large—five meters deep and just wide enough for a single bed. The room had built-in drawers covered with Formica—practical, not to mention easy to clean. Past the cabinets to the right was the bathroom.

Residents weren't allowed to air out the dorms when they weren't there, so a stifling mugginess filled the room. I walked over to the window and ripped it wide open. My gaze fell on backyards, garages, and trash cans. *Typical Lake Starnberg*, I thought sarcastically with a pained grin.

The walls were paper thin. I could hear the footsteps of other residents in the hall. Next door, a shower ran.

Home sweet home.

I sat at the one-chair table, facing the whitewashed wall. The minuscule tabletop was also Formica. I wondered if I was hungry. I had some granola in one of the cabinets, and I could go get my milk out of the communal kitchen. Along the way, I would surely meet some very nice people who would want to engage me in a conversation and who would be excited to hear about my workday.

But I had absolutely no interest in any other human. I did not want to see anyone. I had had enough of my colleagues and patients for one day.

Gradually, the room grew cooler. The evening sun timidly peeped through the window. Its rays had already lost their strength.

A picture frame stood on the table, its back to me. I hesitated and deliberately exhaled before I turned it around. An island surrounded by gray water. The sky a color that made you feel the cold. The waves rolled against the land that rose only a few meters from the sea. In the distance, I could make out a thatched farmstead. Its weathered bricks gleamed red. The grass near the house appeared tender and fragile, yet it defied wind and sea. Among its blades grew countless little plants. Inconspicuous at first glance but in their numbers luminous and brilliant, like a galaxy of blue stars. Their scent, bitter and sweet at the same time, formed an inimitable mixture with the smell of the salt water.

I stared at the picture for a long time. I forgot my work, the clinic, and my squalid living quarters. The sea began to roar, the wind raked across my face, and I heard the cry of the seagulls as they rose triumphantly above me.

5

Sonja, Marko and Sven

Sonja squeezed her way past the patrons of the nightclub. Standing crowded together, nearly everyone faced the dance floor. They held glasses in their hands, drank, and yelled at each other, trying to be heard above the loud music.

As she pushed through the crowd, Sonja smiled. The men mostly made attempts to return her smile; the women begrudgingly made space for her to pass.

Sonja looked good in the low light. Her pallor seemed privileged; her painted black eyes, extravagant; her dark-red mouth, inviting and sensual. Her impossibly short mini-skirt barely covered her ass and was so tight that it resembled a second skin.

She reached the ladies' room and went in. It suddenly got a lot quieter. The thumping bass was now only a faint pulse.

A young woman, about twenty, stood in front of the mirror and combed her golden-blond locks.

Sonja reached into her handbag, fumbled around for her mascara, and pushed up next to the woman. The blonde didn't show the slightest inclination to budge even a little to the side. She threw Sonja a cursory glance in the mirror and kept combing her hair. "You'll need to be patient with me for just another moment," she said condescendingly.

Sonja hesitated. Then a grin crept across her face, and she rammed the woman hard with her shoulder.

The blonde lost her balance and staggered to the left. "You stupid bitch! Are you crazy?" she screamed as she rubbed her upper arm. "That hurt like hell!"

Sonja's grin grew broader. Her eyes took on a strange glow. She reached into her makeup bag and grabbed hold of her assisted-opening pocketknife. In a single motion, she flipped the blade out and cut the blonde's throat with it. Blood welled up instantly.

The woman clutched her fingers around the open wound on her neck. Her eyes were wide with silent terror. She wheezed and gurgled.

"Hold your trap," Sonja ordered, and slapped her in the chest. The blonde stumbled backward toward the open stall.

Sonja shoved her one last time. The girl smashed into the door and fell over the toilet. Her head hit the wall, and she slid to the floor.

Sonja used her foot to shove a stray leg into the stall and shut the door. She went to the sink, cleaned her pocketknife, snapped it closed, and tucked it back into her purse.

She searched calmly for her makeup kit. Her eyeliner desperately needed another coat, and her lips could also use some more color.

After finishing the touch-ups to her satisfaction, Sonja examined herself in the mirror, carefully stowed everything back into her handbag, and left the room. Meanwhile, a dark pool had formed between the toilet stalls and was continuing to spread.

Outside, Sonja was greeted by the smell of alcohol mixed with sweat and the blaring music. She stopped for a moment and looked around for Sven and Marko. She spotted them at the bar. Marko raised his arm and waved.

With a spring in her step, she moved through the crowd to the rhythm of the music and rejoined her two partners. Marko held a cocktail glass against his chest. Sven drank a bottle of beer.

Without asking, she took Marko's glass and emptied it with one swig. She set it down on the bar, leaned forward, and screamed, "This is the lamest club we've ever been to."

"What did you expect?" Sven replied just as loudly.

"Sven likes it. There are tons of women," Marko said.

"There are women in other places too," Sonja said. "We're getting the fuck out of here. And anyway, the toilets are disgusting."

6

A woman around thirty. Tall, with a great figure. Her hair dyed the obligatory golden blond. Made up but not too trashy. Expensive apparel. The entire package screamed hubris and wealth.

Sybil, who was always abrasive and direct with me, affected an eager, subservient face and chirped, "Might I be of assistance to you?"

Blondie stopped walking and looked at Sybil obligingly. She completely ignored me. Before she answered, she conjured up a smile, but I could clearly see that it did not reach her eyes. "I'm searching for my fiancé." When she realized that this information was not sufficient, she added, "Inspector Winkler."

"Oh, Mr. Christian Winkler," Sybil repeated. "Of course. Room twelve fourteen. Right down the hall on the left-hand side."

"Thank you very much," the blonde replied and swung her hips as she walked away.

She was hardly out of earshot when Sybil snickered. "What I would do to be a fly on that wall right now."

When I gave her an inquisitive look, she said, "Winkler got completely screwed up by the chemo. He can hardly control himself. He's going to take his bad mood out on that shitty, pretentious blonde. And who knows if the stupid bimbo can handle it." She grinned.

"I couldn't care less," I said.

"It doesn't interest you at all? Not even a tiny bit?" Sybil scrutinized me meticulously, and when she didn't get a reaction, she cleared her throat and said, "You really are odd. But that doesn't matter. You still have to get all your rounds done today. So"—she grabbed a few patient reports and filed them away with an authoritative motion—"don't mess about again and leave half your rounds to me. Yesterday was the exception."

I remained silent.

"And this morning, Ms. Morgenroth called the head office and requested that in the future only you should take care of her. It's a mystery to me why she would want this, but it's also none of my business."

"Then that's one more patient for me," I assessed.

"It might well be."

"With Winkler, that would make two."

Sybil wet her lips and avoided my eyes.

"If I take those two, you have to do two of mine."

"It's not that simple, sweetheart," Sybil snapped.

"Au contraire," I retorted. "It is that simple."

I left Sybil behind at the nurses' station and made my way to Miriam's suite.

Miriam sat in her armchair, dressed in a bathrobe. "I've prepared myself," she said in place of a greeting. "So, we can get the cream out of the way more quickly."

She rolled her sleeves up. I took the ointment out of my apron and went to work.

A fresh pot of tea and two cups stood on the coffee table.

Miriam followed my gaze. "You do drink tea?"

"Sure," I said. "I won't touch coffee."

The left arm, with the tattooed number 135763, struck me as a little more red today. I gave it a great deal of attention.

Eventually, I finished and went to wash my hands. When I returned from the bathroom, Miriam had filled both our cups. It smelled like jasmine. She noticed my hesitation and smiled conspiratorially. "I told them in the office today that you should give me a massage. And that takes at least half an hour."

"Should I give you a massage now, Ms. Morgenroth?" I asked.

"What do you think, Alicia? Now we're going to read together, drink tea, and have a good time, like two girlfriends."

"Girlfriends?"

"If you want to be friends with an old fogy like me, then yes."

I laughed and began to pull up a stool.

Miriam raised her hand, alarmed. "Not the stool. My friends always sit in an armchair, just like me."

I sat down in the chair opposite her, and Miriam leaned forward to offer me a cup of tea. "And please stop addressing me so formally. I already feel ancient enough as it is. Miriam is fine."

We drank. Neither of us said a word.

Miriam set her teacup down on the table. The fine china clinked softly. She took the small book she'd been reading the day before and leafed through it a little. The lines in her face deepened as she did this. After a few moments, she sighed, smoothed the page flat, and glanced up, clearly having found what she was looking for. "I love novels. Really big tales loaded with many lives. But here"—she made a sweeping gesture—"I'm constantly being interrupted. There's a steady flow of every kind of doctor popping in and trying out ridiculous therapies on me. So, I read poems. They're short, yet contain everything that I so desperately require."

I nodded as if I understood her.

"I'm going to recite one of my favorite pieces for you. It's best if you close your eyes and let it sink in, and afterward you can tell me what you felt."

"That's silly," I said.

Miriam laughed. "Silly, maybe." All of a sudden, she sounded very young. "But you should try it once, if you dare. Or are you afraid?"

"I'm not afraid." I leaned back and closed my eyes.

An ever so slight chuckle resounded. "So, this poem," she started, "was written by Joseph von Eichendorff, who happens to be my favorite poet. And it's called 'The Blue Flower.'"

For a moment, a painful memory bored its way into my heart, and I had to force myself not to open my eyes.

Miriam began:

"I search for the blue flower,
I search but never find it,
I dream, that in that flower
Happiness would bloom for me."

Her voice intensified the strange melody of the words. A mixture of melancholy and glee swept over me, coupled with a longing that threatened to rip me apart.

Miriam continued:

"I've wander'd already so long,
Have long hoped, trusted,
But ah, still nowhere have I
The blue flower detected."

Miriam fell silent.

I blinked and looked into her eyes. "That's not true," I said. "About the blue flower."

Miriam cocked her head a bit, a few more wrinkles appeared on her forehead, and she said, "Of course, the blue flowers do not really exist. They represent everything that we long for. What we wish for from the bottom of our hearts but also that which we will never acquire."

"I understand that," I said. "But the blue flowers . . . They actually do exist."

"Oh?" Miriam arched her eyebrows high in astonishment.

"Trust me. I've seen them myself. On the Hallig where I grew up."

"You really come from a North Sea island?" she said.

I nodded. "Nothing special. Less than an acre on the sea. Quiet and peaceful in the summer. But in fall and winter, all hell breaks loose. Storms and floods . . ." I babbled on until I suddenly caught myself, glanced to the floor, and cleared my throat bashfully.

"That's your home?" Miriam asked.

I nodded again. "And that's where the blue flower grows. A thousandfold. They start blooming in the summer, and eventually the entire Hallig is overrun with a blue luminescence. And it smells . . ." I couldn't find the words to describe it. "It's the most beautiful place in the world."

There was a knock. Sybil stuck her head in from the hallway. Her expression darkened when she saw me sitting idle in the armchair. "Excuse me, Ms. Morgenroth, but I desperately need Alicia." Turning to me, she added, "They're starting their rounds, and your patients' files aren't filled out yet."

I rose immediately but waited until Sybil left and the door had closed behind her.

"Did you like the poem?" Miriam asked.

"He has something," I answered. "This guy."

"Eichendorff," Miriam said, and we both laughed.

"Are you coming back tomorrow?" she asked.

I leaned down and straightened her bathrobe, though it didn't really need it. "Of course," I said.

Miriam squeezed my arm good-bye. "And tomorrow, I'll say you have to bathe me. That will give us at least another half hour."

Sybil looked at me disapprovingly when I returned to the nurses' station. Without a word, she handed me the papers and a pen. "You've had a long enough break. Now hurry up. I don't want to get in trouble with the doctors because of you."

The rounds were scheduled for eleven. I still had a good quarter of an hour. Plenty of time.

A loud noise disturbed the posh silence of the corridor. A door had been slammed. High-heeled shoes landed so hard on the floor that even the expensive carpeting was unable to swallow their thunder.

Blondie strode angrily past us, her face bright red. Now she didn't spare a second of her precious time for us subordinate beings. Instead, she thrust the glass exit door open with a hard jolt. It smashed against the wall, rattling in its frame. Through some miracle, it remained intact. Then Mr. Winkler's fiancée disappeared from our sight.

"Wow," Sybil exclaimed. "What an exit!" She slapped the file she had been working on closed. "If I'm interpreting this correctly, Mr. Winkler is up for grabs again. And his mood will probably be even lousier than before. If that's at all possible. Have fun with him!"

7

Without exception, the doctors addressed us formally, and when they did have to speak to us, they always stared intently at our name tags. They made no attempt to look us in the eye or to get to know us in any way whatsoever. To them, we were simply support staff—faceless and interchangeable.

Nevertheless, Sybil always endeavored to make the best impression. She presented the patients' files with a deferential manner, explaining one or two of the entries. I remained in the background, preparing the cart that I would use to deliver lunch. I took some drinks out of the refrigerator and placed them in their allocated holders.

The doctors departed as quickly as they had come. They floated down the corridor in their white smocks, sharing quiet conversation and exuding auras of self-importance.

"Was everything all right?" I asked Sybil when we were alone.

She was sorting documents. It was obvious that she had a soft spot for administrative duties. "The doctors were very satisfied"—she frowned—"but I'm just now noticing we're missing Mr. Winkler's chart. Is it possible that you misplaced it?"

I had finished loading my cart. "No. I did not."

Sybil sighed. "Then we left it lying in his room."

"Seems so."

"Would you be so kind as to go get it?" Sybil's fingers drummed impatiently on the counter. When I didn't immediately jump, she added, "Winkler is yours now. We've settled that."

"That's why you're taking two patients of mine," I replied.

Sybil reluctantly nodded and made an agitated hand gesture in the direction of Winkler's room.

I left the prep area, walked down the hall, and cautiously knocked.

No reaction. Maybe I had gotten lucky, and he was asleep.

I carefully opened the door.

The curtain was drawn; semidarkness prevailed. His bed was empty.

He sat in one of the armchairs, chin propped up on bent arms. No, that wasn't it. He had an object in his hand that he was holding in front of his face.

My eyes adjusted to the dimness, and I could see that he had placed the barrel of a handgun in his mouth. His finger was on the trigger. Although he was completely absorbed in his intent, his eyes moved. He had realized that he was no longer alone.

I needed a fraction of a second to catch myself and decide how I should react. I lifted my hand in a wave and accompanied it with a naïve and loud "Hello."

I busied myself searching for the missing file. To help, I switched on the overhead light. Brightness filled the room.

Winkler's eyes glared with fury; he removed the pistol from his mouth. In the process, the metal loudly struck his front teeth. He kept the gun in his hand, resting it on his right knee. He audibly inhaled a couple of times before he said, "Can't a guy ever get any peace around here?"

"I knocked," I responded as I moved a few magazines, still pretending to look for something. I had long since spotted the missing file.

"And then you march in here, just like that?"

"Exactly. I needed your chart. The doctor forgot it during his rounds."

With the muzzle of his weapon, Winkler shoved the folder that lay in front of him on the coffee table in my direction. I grabbed the papers without taking my eyes off him.

"What are you staring at?" he hissed.

I shrugged.

"I bet you'll be the first one who runs down the hall snitching on me to the doctors."

"I don't snitch on anyone. Not even on a cop, though you all deserve everything you get."

"Well, look at that!" The expression on Winkler's face suddenly changed. Now he seemed wide awake and completely focused. "The young lady knows what she's talking about. Probably has even done some time."

"You're a good detective."

"I was," Winkler remarked, and then he laughed. It was a laugh filled with bitterness. "That's over. Like so many other things."

I motioned to the pistol in his hand. "You call that a good idea?"

"It's my decision. But probably not for much longer. I don't believe you're not going to blurt this out to everyone the minute you leave the room."

I shook my head. "You're mistaken."

"Then you'll blame yourself for the rest of your life, when I do eventually pull the trigger." The green of his eyes came across cool, though they also seemed to contain an enormous amount of vulnerability.

"No, you won't," I said.

"No, I won't what?" he snapped. "You don't believe I'd go through with it?" He raised the gun to his face and stared at it.

"You enjoy your self-pity too much," I said. "But if I'm wrong, someone else will have to clean the mess up, anyway."

His anger was displaced by astonishment. "You're impossible," he finally managed to say.

I grinned. "I do my best."

8

Sonja

Marko accessed the premises via the back alley-way. After a little looking, he parked the car in a space that bore the inscription "Customer" in big white letters.

Sonja climbed out, walked the few steps to the building, and opened a side entrance. At two desks, employees sat facing computer monitors, gray bibs over their clothes. A plastic sign suspended from the ceiling read "Repairs."

Before any of the staff could react, Sonja said curtly, "I have an appointment with Mr. Wiegand."

The automotive mechanic gestured to a corner office on his left. "The boss just got in."

Sonja crossed the showroom, passing a few brand-new cars with virgin paint and shiny chrome. She opened the door to the office and entered. Double-paned glass sealed in every noise that threatened to seep out.

A fifty-year-old man, small yet corpulent, stared at a computer screen. As Sonja walked in, he briefly looked up, nodded, and pointed at one of the chairs in front of his mahogany desk.

Sonja sat and waited until the man finished his work. He clicked the mouse, clearly sending an e-mail. Now he turned to Sonja. Through the rimless glasses, his eyes appeared enlarged and almost compassionate.

"You have the car here?" he asked.

"It's right outside," Sonja replied. "We swapped the last one at the other location."

"Good." The man nodded.

"And, Mr. Wiegand," Sonja said, "is the client satisfied?"

The man took his time answering; he moistened his lips before he spoke. "With the end result, completely. But the means . . . How many shots were fired? Four?"

Sonja raised three fingers.

"Isn't that a bit excessive?"

"No. My colleague just wanted to be certain."

"If you say so." Wiegand opened a drawer and removed two envelopes. One he shoved across the table to Sonja. The other he kept.

Sonja didn't touch the package lying in front of her. Instead, she smiled.

"Twenty thousand," the man said. "In fifties and hundreds. Unmarked and nonsequential bills."

"All right." Sonja grabbed the envelope and stuck it in her inside jacket pocket.

"Don't you want to count it?" the man asked.

Sonja smiled again.

Wiegand tried to return the smile but didn't succeed. He cleared his throat and tapped the edge of the second envelope a couple of times on the highly polished wood.

Sonja looked at the package pensively.

"This here," Wiegand explained, "must be handled quickly."

"What do you mean by 'quickly'?" Sonja said.

"Within the week."

"Everything's in there?" She gestured at the manila envelope in his hand. "Habits, map, photo of the target, and anything else we might need?"

Wiegand nodded. "I verified it myself. The file is complete."

"Usual procedure?"

"No," Wiegand answered. "The client has made a special request."

Sonja leaned back in her chair and folded her arms in front of her chest. "Special request? Special requests cost extra."

Wiegand stretched his arm out and placed the second envelope within Sonja's reach. "How much do you want?"

Sonja thought for a moment. "Fifty percent more."

The expression on Wiegand's face did not change. "There is thirty thousand in the envelope."

Sonja stood and picked up the dossier. "It's a pleasure doing business with you."

Wiegand also rose. "Have fun with the contract. This time, you'll be working where others go on holiday."

"Oh."

"Lake Starnberg. Have you ever been?"

"No," Sonja said. "And I don't give a shit. I only spend my vacations on Majorca."

9

The most expensive Egyptian cotton. The highest grade of plush. All embroidered with the insignia of the clinic: a graphic of waves underneath the name "Starnberg." I rolled up the towels and stacked them on my cart. Those plump things had a lot of uses.

The glass door at the end of the hall opened, and a red-headed woman walked toward me. About my age, maybe two or three years younger. She wore jeans, a T-shirt, and a blazer. While she approached, she kept her eyes fixed on the signs mounted next to the doors to the patients' rooms.

"Are you looking for someone?" I asked. "Might I be of assistance?"

The woman stood still and adjusted the strap of her shoulder bag. She probably had a laptop stowed in it. "My name is Beck. I'm looking for Ms. Morgenroth," she said.

I think I eyeballed her a touch too long. She laughed tensely, as if my gaze made her uncomfortable. "I'm in the right ward, aren't I?"

I laid the towel I had just rolled up with the others and leaned on the cart. "Ms. Morgenroth is in suite C." I motioned farther down the hall.

When the young lady silently walked past me, I grabbed hold of her arm. "But you can't go in right now."

She frowned. "Why?"

"Rounds. The doctors are with her right now. They can't be disturbed."

The young lady glanced at my hand, and I let go of her arm.

"Excuse me," she said, "but I've been waiting weeks for an opportunity to speak with Ms. Morgenroth. How long do you think the doctors will be with her?"

I looked at her until she lowered her eyes. "You'll have to wait a few minutes."

"Okay," she said. "I think I have that much time." Her smile didn't seem genuine.

"You're not related to Ms. Morgenroth," I surmised.

She shook her head. "No. I'm working on my doctorate at the University of Munich, and Ms. Morgenroth has kindly agreed to grant me an interview. It's very important to me. She's a rare historical witness."

"Interview? What's the topic of your thesis?"

At that moment, a door farther down the hall opened, and a group of men in white coats appeared in the corridor.

"Are those the doctors?" Ms. Beck asked.

"Yes." I walked in front of her, leaving my cart. "I'll go with you."

"You don't need to trouble yourself."

"The staff is only allowed to admit people to the patient's room if the visit is approved," I said over my shoulder while walking.

I stopped in front of Miriam's suite and knocked softly. "Please wait in the hallway while I confirm your appointment," I instructed Ms. Beck before I opened the door and entered.

Miriam sat on her bed, buttoning up her blouse.

"You have a visitor," I said.

Miriam frowned at the young woman who, despite my clear instructions, had pushed her way into the room behind me.

"Ms. Morgenroth?" she said. "Ms. Miriam Morgenroth?"

Miriam nodded. "And may I ask who you might be?"

"My name is Beck. Franziska Beck. We've spoken twice on the telephone."

Miriam turned pale. Her hand began to tremble.

"You said," Ms. Beck continued, "that it would be all right if I asked a few questions in person. I already interviewed your nephew, Dr. Vogt. He was extremely open and very cooperative."

"Miriam, if you don't want to, you don't have to speak with anyone," I stated quietly yet firmly.

Ms. Beck gave me a look of astonishment and opened her mouth to respond. At the same time, Miriam raised her hand. "It's all right, Alicia. We'll be fine." She got out of bed. As I started to rush to her aid, she shook her head almost imperceptibly. She stepped into her slippers and walked over to her favorite chair to take a seat. She sighed. "Not that I enjoy giving this interview. I really don't. I voluntarily recall the horrors of the past as seldom as possible. But soon, very soon, no one will be alive who can still tell what happened. And I think I have a responsibility to speak about all the dreadful things."

"Should I stay?" I asked. I had never seen Miriam this upset.

She shook her head insistently. "No. That won't be necessary. I can get through this alone. But I would be happy if you looked in on me later."

"I'm free around six," I said.

Miriam glanced over at Ms. Beck. "We'll surely be finished by then, won't we?"

"I think so." The young woman opened her bag and pulled out a laptop adorned with a large Hello Kitty sticker.

"Alicia, I'll see you later, around six. But don't you have to train?"

I smiled. "Not until eight. At that hour, I practically have the lanes to myself."

Ms. Beck cleared her throat. "I don't want to rush you, but . . ."

"I'm off," I said and walked out of the room. The last thing I saw was Ms. Beck sitting on the opposite chair and flipping open her laptop with determination.

In the corridor, I was greeted by the usual tranquility. *No*, I thought, *this is not tranquility. Everything here is sound-proof. Not a tone escapes. We're isolated from the world and from life.*

I returned to my cart, grabbed several towels, and set off for Mr. Winkler's room.

Like last time, he sat in semidarkness, with his curtains drawn. And he was kneading his ball again. His fingers relentlessly squeezed the hard rubber. He didn't say anything to me.

I went into the bathroom in silence, swapped used towels out for fresh ones, and straightened up his effects.

Before I left him, I pushed the curtains back and pulled the window wide open to let in some fresh air. He followed me with his eyes, and I stopped and stared back at him. Finally, he turned away and looked out the window.

"I'll come back shortly and close it," I said.

"Feel free," he answered. Today he sounded calm and collected, but I knew that his demeanor was a façade.

10

Miriam sat in her armchair. The balcony door was ajar. She looked out at the lake, beyond which the sun had just set.

"Sorry," I said, "but I couldn't come any sooner."

She did not respond.

"Miriam, is everything all right?"

She turned her head to me. "Alicia," she said. "Have you been here long?"

"No," I said. "We were scheduled for six. But I had so much to do. I really couldn't get here any earlier."

"Oh, my dear, that doesn't matter."

"It does matter. You were looking forward to it."

"Oh well. That university student needed a lot more time, anyway."

"I don't understand why you even spoke with her. She was so unfriendly."

Miriam laughed. "You're so wonderfully young. That's when you're *schnell fertig* with words, as Schiller said."

I furrowed my brow.

"*Schnell fertig.* You know how it is: you don't take any lip, and then render a judgment about others too hastily."

"Well, that may be true," I said. "But all the same, I noticed that you didn't want to talk to her."

Miriam sighed. "You're right. And it took more out of me than I expected."

I examined Miriam more intently. Her cheeks were sunken, her skin wan. "If you'd like, I could scrap my swim. Then we'd have a lot of time."

"No." The shake of Miriam's head was barely detectable. "I'm worn out. All the memories have consumed my strength. I'll lie down soon. And you—you are going to exercise."

"If that's what you want." It proved difficult to hide my disappointment.

"Are you so excited about spending your precious free time with an old lady like me?" Miriam smiled, and a trace of life returned to her eyes. She straightened up. "Tomorrow," she said. "We'll see each other again tomorrow."

11

This time, it was Miriam's turn to listen. She had laid her head back and closed her eyes. As if by magic, the countless lines and wrinkles on her face disappeared, and her features exhibited an almost unearthly serenity. She waited.

"I can't do it," I said.

"Giving up before you've even started? That's not very smart," Miriam said softly yet poignantly.

I swallowed hard, opened the book on my knee, and said, "But if I mess up, you can't laugh."

"I won't. I swear."

"Who exactly is this Storm?"

"Theodor Storm? I think you'll like him. He comes from your neck of the woods, and he loved the sea."

I resigned myself to my fate. "All right, I can at least give it a try. But if I don't like it, I'm going to stop."

"Deal," Miriam promised.

"'Seashore,'" I read aloud, and added superfluously, "That's the title."

Miriam remained quiet, and I began. The words were cold, impersonal, and strangely foreign. But after a few lines, images started to rise up before my inner eye. Images so familiar that they belonged to me like my breath or my blood.

"Gray fowl scamper
Along the water be . . ."

had just passed my lips as a faint squeak announced the opening of the door. A tall, slender man stood in the doorway. Apparently, he had heard my last words; without hesitating, he completed the verse:

"Like dreams lie the islands
In mist on the sea."

Startled, I looked at the text. He had recited the poem perfectly, without having the book in front of him. Just like that.

The man grinned. He must have been around fifty, but in some peculiar way, he struck me as being rather youthful. "Theodor Storm," he said, "my favorite poet."

Miriam leaned forward in her chair. "Georg! It's nice that you came! This is an unexpected pleasure."

"I have some business in the neighborhood, and between appointments, I thought that I could quickly fly by and see my favorite aunt," he said.

He went over to Miriam, wrapped an arm around her shoulders, and kissed her on the cheek.

Miriam held him tight. As she hugged him, she winked at me. "My nephew, an extremely handsome man but unfortunately already spoken for."

The man straightened up and took Miriam's hand. In the process, he glanced over at me.

"Georg," Miriam said, "may I introduce you to my friend Alicia? Alicia Petersen. My dearest and only nephew, Georg Vogt. Actually, *Doctor* Georg Vogt. That title cost us a stack of money, didn't it?"

Miriam and her nephew laughed heartily. It sounded congenial and intimate.

"To be perfectly honest," he said, "I needed several years to finish my doctorate. But I neither plagiarized nor had anyone else write my dissertation for me. Only a little help from Miriam," he confessed.

"He has a PhD in German literature. It's of no use in our business, but it made a cultivated man out of him." Miriam caressed his arm approvingly.

Dr. Vogt held his hand out to me. I took it. His grip was firm.

"I'm pleased to make the acquaintance of one of Miriam's relatives, Dr. Vogt," I said.

Dr. Vogt pulled up a stool and sat down. "Alicia—may I call you that? You're a friend of my aunt, and I'd like it if you'd simply call me Georg."

I hesitated, not knowing what to say.

"Well, we're not actually related to each other," Miriam said, coming to my rescue. "I only raised this young gentleman. And for his entire adult life, he's run our mutual banking and real estate business."

Miriam's explanation did not really make me more comfortable, but I tried to give the impression that I was used to running around in the same circles as bankers. "Well then," I said. "It's nice to meet you, Georg."

Georg laughed complacently and turned to Miriam. "You were floored, weren't you? That I still knew the poem from Storm."

Miriam pursed her lips. "Not really. You had always liked it very much. And for Alicia, it has an even more special significance."

"Oh yeah?"

Miriam nodded. "Alicia comes from the North Sea. From a small island on the sea."

"A Hallig?"

"Exactly," I said. "I know I don't look it, but I'm a real Frisian."

"Then you no doubt love the water as much as I do." Georg looked at me with renewed interest.

"I swim almost every day."

"Alicia is training for a long-distance swim from the mainland to an island," Miriam said. "What was it called? Nordstrand?"

"No, Norderney," I said. "The course runs from Norddeich out to Norderney."

"That's easily ten kilometers," Georg said.

"Eight," I corrected him.

Again, he observed me intently. Then he nodded. "That's a hard stretch in the open sea. I have some idea of what I'm talking about. I was a fairly respectable swimmer when I was young."

Miriam clenched her tiny shriveled hand into a fist and punched her nephew sidelong in the ribs. "Don't talk such nonsense. You were part of the Olympic swim team and held your own."

Georg shrugged his shoulders in apology. "That was years ago. I know you can't see it on me, but I train at least an hour a day in the pool."

"On the contrary," I replied. "It's very evident."

A silence followed my words that, strangely enough, didn't make me feel awkward.

Eventually, Georg looked at his watch. "Oh, damn it. How time flies! I have an appointment at the notary public at half past."

Miriam laughed and gave him a small shove. "Then you better hurry. Our business shouldn't suffer because you fritter away your afternoons with your old aunt."

Georg stood and sighed. "Next time, I'll plan more time. I'll bring one of our polished employees along to take care of business. Those guys could do something to earn their money for a change."

Again, he took Miriam in his arms, and this time, he held her longer. He turned to me. "Alicia, I'm happy my aunt has found a good friend here. And especially one that loves the sea and can swim."

We waited until he left us, closing the door on his way out.

Miriam adjusted her chair, found a comfortable position, and leaned her head back, smiling. "By the way," she said, "I've thought up something very special for us to do."

"What?" I asked.

Her smile widened. "I think next we should read a novel together."

"Won't that take too long? You said the other day that you were constantly being disturbed here."

"An old woman can always change her mind. And I have to stay here another three weeks. I'm sure we can finish it in that time. So. We'll read Storm's *The Rider on the White Horse*."

"I can't stand stories with ponies and horses."

Miriam snickered. "You'll be amazed. I'm thoroughly convinced that you're going to love this book. We'll get started tomorrow."

12

Sonja, Marko and Sven

Sonja gingerly opened the little ziplock baggie and shook the contents into her Coke. The white powder dissolved, bubbling. All the same, she stuck her forefinger in the liquid and stirred it impatiently.

She eagerly licked her finger before taking a long swig.

Marko was one step ahead of her. His eyes had already become glassy. He was half lying on the bed in the mobile home, staring vacantly at nothing in particular. Loud music pounded out of the speakers.

Sonja's glass was empty. She refilled it and pulled out another baggie. This time, she didn't go to the trouble of dissolving it in her drink. She leaned her head back, let it trickle into her mouth, swallowed dryly, and flushed it down with the Coke.

"Are you sure this is really dope?" she asked. "It tastes like an old Pixy Stick to me. I don't feel anything at all."

In response, Marko grimaced.

"I don't know where Sven gets this stuff," Sonja continued. "I've told him a dozen times, buy good dope. We don't need to save there. But still, I think he runs around until he finds the cheapest shit available, composed almost entirely of wallpaper glue."

Sonja stretched, and walked up and down the few steps that the narrow space allowed. "This RV is really cool," she said. "I told those stupid guys we'd leave the Opel with them in exchange for this old beater. You chug along the highway, not making much progress, but when the night comes—*bang!* You have everything you need. A cool house on wheels. Even a kitchen. For those who want to cook." She looked at the kitchen, which was covered with dirty dishes, half-emptied cans, and other trash.

"Really comfortable," she said. "Like home. When we get back, we should buy our own RV. Only larger. Much larger. So, *vroom!* On weekends when we're so inclined, we can just climb in and take off. You know, going nowhere fast."

Sweat built up on her brow, and her breath quickened. She clapped her hands. "I'm not hungry at all. I haven't eaten a thing since early this morning, and I don't need to. Can you follow me?"

Marko laughed immaturely. "I couldn't eat either. Man, this music is the worst shit. It sounds totally wrong. Listen closely: no bass. They forgot the fucking bass."

The heavy metal that droned out of the speakers sounded very distant.

Sonja grinned. "This stereo system is super. But we're surrounded by complete imbeciles. If we really turned it up, some granny with curlers in her hair would immediately show up, complaining. Then we could just smack her in the kisser."

"Or Sven could shoot her in the face!" Marko made the mandatory hand gesture as if he were shooting an imaginary target with a gun. His finger pulled a nonexistent trigger. He laughed his head off. "Imagine what would happen then. All the idiotic campers and cops running around. As if you'd kicked an anthill."

"Or"—Sonja chuckled—"we just take a little gas. And when they're asleep, we pour it all over their trailers. You think that wouldn't put a smile on their faces? The smell alone! Can you say *barbecue?*"

Marko was silent for a while, and then said, "It sure would look cool in the middle of the night. We should really do that some time."

Someone knocked. The blows on the flimsy door echoed in the small space.

Marko reached back and pulled a pistol equipped with a silencer out from under a pillow. It was still stashed in a plastic bag, but he could aim it quite easily at the entrance.

"If that really is a granny, promise me that you'll put a cap in her!" Sonja shouted hysterically.

Marko did not answer. He used his free hand to wipe off the beads of sweat that had rolled down his forehead into his eyes.

Sonja positioned herself next to the small entrance and bellowed, "Who's there? Are you our neighbor? Do you need to borrow some sugar?" She put her hand up to her mouth and burst out laughing.

"Cut it out," came a voice from outside. "It's me, Sven."

"And you expect me to believe that?" Sonja giggled. "Are you sure you're not our neighbor?"

Sven knocked again. "Come on. Let me in!"

Begrudgingly, Sonja pulled the bolt back, and Sven climbed into the cabin. He was carrying a large package. He didn't know what to do with it, so he set it on the small table, carelessly pushing empty bottles and cans out of the way to make room. Several clattered to the floor.

"What's that?" Marko asked. "Presents?"

"Maybe it's all of our birthdays! Or at least Sven's." Sonja cheered and sang, "Happy birthday to youuu."

"Man," Sven said. "This sucks."

"What sucks?"

"You send me off to get the package and don't even wait for me; you just start getting loaded without me."

"Don't be a party pooper." Sonja opened two baggies, shook their contents into her empty glass, and poured Coke on top of it. Foam bubbled up over the edge and dripped next to the package on the table.

Sven licked his lips, snatched the drink, sucked off the foam first, and then emptied the glass in one slug.

In the meantime, Marko rose clumsily and began to tear at the tape on the package.

"Wait a second," Sonja ordered. She reached into her pocket, pulled out her knife, and fumbled with it awkwardly.

"Should I help you?" Sven stuck his hand out.

Sonja slapped it away. "Stop it. You're making me nervous."

Sven grinned guiltily before pulling his arm back.

It didn't take any time at all for Sonja to unsheathe the broad, tapered blade. She sliced once across the cardboard box. The sharp knife glided effortlessly through it.

Marko pushed Sonja to the side and ripped the package completely open. He reached in and produced a piece of clothing, wrapped neatly in clear plastic. "What the fuck kind of shit is this?" he snorted.

Sonja gave him a shove, grabbed the yellow blouse, and took a quick look at it. "Duh, you moron: clinic clothes."

"How come? None of us are sick," Sven said.

Marko found this so funny that he doubled over with laughter.

"The clothes are for the staff, not the patients, you bird-brain," Sonja hissed. The joking was getting on her nerves now. She couldn't stand another second of it.

"'Starnberg' is written on it," Marko said.

"And why the waves underneath? Do people there have to piss all the time?" Sven asked. In the meantime, his face had gone slack.

"That's a river," Marko said. "Am I right, Sonja?"

"Almost. It's a shitty lake. A shitty lake where only shitty rich bastards live."

"Can we take a few of them out?" Sven said.

"One. And yes. We're gonna take her out."

Sven staggered a little.

Sonja reached into a storage box and retrieved three small packets, which she held up for Sven. Her eyes had taken on that special luster.

"Oh no," Sven begged. "Not again. Please."

"Oh yes," Sonja persisted.

"I won't look. Honest. I'll turn the other way."

"When Marko and I screw, you're outside. We're among upstanding people here. So, go fly a kite."

Marko grinned and pulled his T-shirt over his head.

Sven grabbed his dope, a Coke, and a blanket before he set off for the outdoors. This would take a while.

13

I opened the glass door...

People I do not know are running everywhere. Jumbled voices reverberate. Up ahead I see doctors standing around talking in huddled groups. There is no trace of the distinguished tranquility that otherwise prevails. Uniformed police officers, patients, visitors, and the nursing staff in yellow and white dispersed throughout. Everyone seems to have gathered here...

I took a deep breath and looked for a familiar face. Sybil was talking with a man who, even from a distance, I could tell was a plainclothes cop. He wrote down everything she told him on a notepad.

As inconspicuously as possible, I wove my way through the crowd, careful to avoid making eye contact with anyone. A few steps away from Sybil, I paused and watched her as she continued to jabber at the officer. When she saw me, she pointed with her arm stretched out in my direction, and then tapped the policeman on the chest with her other hand.

His eyes swept through the crowd and came to rest on me. He waved me over.

"Here she is," Sybil said.

"What's going on?" I asked.

The policeman was about forty, was in good shape, and wore a short-sleeved shirt. "Are you Ms. Petersen?"

My answer consisted of a nod.

"I'm Officer Schneider. May I ask where you've just come from?"

"You may."

He frowned. "Funny. Are you trying to be funny?"

I shrugged.

"This week her shift begins at eight." Sybil spoke for me.

"And you've come directly from home?" the police officer asked.

Again, I did not answer.

"Did you meet someone on your way in?"

"Whatever happened," I explained, "I had nothing to do with it, nor is it any of my business."

Sybil's eyes narrowed. "Don't talk like that. You were rather tight with the old lady."

The police officer threw Sybil a disapproving look. Turning back to me, he said, "You haven't seen Ms. Morgenroth today?"

"Miriam?" I asked, feeling a sudden chill. "I last saw her yesterday evening. She was doing just fine. Did something go wrong overnight?"

Officer Schneider studied me intently. "We don't know."

"You don't know?" I exclaimed. "Then why are you all here? Why is . . ." Until now, I had not noticed that the door to suite C, Miriam's room, was standing wide open. Two officers entered it.

Without thinking, I started toward it, but Officer Schneider grabbed my arm and held me back.

"Let go of me. Immediately!" I hissed.

"You shouldn't go in."

"If Miriam isn't doing well, she needs my help—a person she trusts. Someone she knows. She's old and weak."

Officer Schneider did not release his grip. "You're not allowed in there right now. You'll disturb the collection of evidence. And anyway, it's more than likely that nothing happened."

"I don't understand," I said.

"When Ms. Kaufmann"—the officer tilted his head in Sybil's direction—"entered Ms. Morgenroth's room this morning, the bed was messed up, and Ms. Morgenroth was missing."

"Missing?" I repeated.

"Yeah," Sybil frantically interrupted. "First, I looked in the cafeteria and then down in our little park. But after I couldn't find her anywhere, I contacted the clinic management, and they called the police."

I couldn't believe it. "You think she got up last night and simply walked out of the building?"

Officer Schneider cleared his throat. "Ms. Petersen, don't quote me on this, but old people have a tendency to do irrational things. Things that are beyond our comprehension. Ms. Morgenroth's jacket and shoes are gone. Do you understand what I'm getting at?"

"But not Miriam," I protested, horrified. "Miriam isn't suffering from dementia."

"Ms. Morgenroth was, among other things, in geriatric care. She was very old and senile," Sybil remarked with a schoolmasterly tone.

"Just because she doesn't like you, doesn't make her senile!" I snapped.

The slender figure of Miriam's nephew appeared. Two other policemen were with him. Without hesitating, he walked straight over to me. His face was pale, which made the blotches of red that had formed on it all the more prominent. His hair was disheveled. He nervously smoothed it flat.

"Alicia. Thank God you're here," he sputtered. "You must know where Miriam is."

"No. I have no idea," I said, his nervousness beginning to infect me.

"But you're her friend. She trusted you. She would have told you if she had wanted a little . . ." He paused and pinched the bridge of his nose.

"What do you mean by that?"

"Well . . ." Georg hesitated again. "Maybe she needed to stretch her legs a little. On a whim. And then . . ." It seemed difficult for him to continue speaking. "Sometimes she doesn't find her way back."

"You're Dr. Vogt, Ms. Morgenroth's nephew?" Officer Schneider said.

Georg nodded. "Yes. I came as soon as I heard."

"Did I understand correctly just now that your aunt has previously gone missing?"

Georg cleared his throat, took a deep breath, and said, "Yes. Once before. Well, to be honest, it's happened more than once."

Officer Schneider smiled but couldn't conceal his irritation. "Then I don't understand all the commotion. I was told that you personally called the commissioner and . . . How should I say it? Energetically insisted that we thoroughly investigate what has gone on here. But now it seems very likely that we're dealing with an elderly lady who's become disoriented and lost her way."

"Miriam doesn't get disoriented," I interrupted. "She knows exactly what she's doing."

Georg shook his head slightly at first and then ever more decisively. "Unfortunately, not, Alicia. Miriam is highly intelligent. But from time to time, she gets these inclinations. But right now, our bank is at a pivotal juncture, and I can't afford to neglect any detail."

The detective pricked up his ears. "Detail? Which detail could be neglected?"

Georg looked around the group as if searching for help. "I can't say, exactly. In my business, it's no holds barred. Sometimes we're dealing with obscene amounts of money. Fortunes are at stake. I want to be absolutely sure that she hasn't . . ."

"Hasn't what? Been kidnapped?" Officer Schneider asked. "That's why you set this entire extravaganza here"—he gestured to a few of his colleagues—"in motion?"

Georg nodded with a guilty expression.

Officer Schneider appeared to withhold his immediate response and then eventually said, "To some extent, I can understand your anxiety. We'll follow up on every shred of evidence we find. But it seems to me, we're not dealing with a crime here. Your aunt will most likely come back soon or be picked up in the immediate area. I'll ensure that every patrol car is on the lookout for her."

"Maybe we could also consider making a radio announcement. I'll pay for it, of course," Georg said. He seemed to have regained his composure.

"That's a good idea," the officer replied. "But it would be best if you brought that up yourself with the commissioner."

"I'll do that immediately." Georg sounded relieved.

No one was paying attention to me anymore, so I headed toward the door. I needed to get away.

"Alicia!" Sybil's shrill voice stopped me.

I froze in my steps and slowly turned around.

"The work's not going to get done on its own! Where do you think you're headed?"

"You'll have to do without me today," I said. "I'm looking for Miriam."

14

Five days passed. Five long days and not a trace of Miriam. With growing concern, bordering on despair, I had scoured the entire neighborhood for her and spoken with residents and passersby. Nothing. Miriam was still missing.

I had an appointment at 3:00 p.m. The bench I was sitting on was surprisingly comfortable. They had even laid out some pamphlets: instructions on how to protect your house from burglars, ads for the public awareness of alcohol abuse and other such nonsense. The police: to protect and to serve. Lost in reflection, I flipped through the brochures. *Just like in prison*, I thought. *Everything is neat and orderly, everyone is friendly, and behind the façade is indifferent, cold-hearted brutality.*

A door opened, and Officer Schneider stuck his head out. "Ms. Petersen?" he announced and disappeared.

By the time I had followed him into his office, he had already taken a seat behind his desk. With a polite gesture, he offered me a chair.

I sat down in front of his desk, which was covered in an endless mess of pens, files, and papers.

"What can I do for you, Ms. Petersen?" Officer Schneider inquired. He looked at me carefully, his face relaxed and attentive.

"Miriam Morgenroth," I said.

Schneider waited for me to continue speaking. When he realized, I wasn't going to, he chuckled softly and said, "Well, Ms. Petersen, I can fully appreciate that you're concerned about the matter. But"—he lifted his hands apologetically—"unfortunately, since you're not a family member, I can't share any information with you regarding the progress of our investigation."

"Miriam is my friend."

Schneider leaned forward, opened a black file, and cast a glance at it. "Alicia Petersen," he read aloud. "Born November twelfth in Hamburg. Is that you?"

I nodded.

"Convictions for assault, larceny, and"—he leafed through a few pages—"drug abuse." He looked up.

"What does that have to do with Miriam?" I asked him.

"No idea. You tell me."

"I did my time, finished my education. I exercise a lot and keep my hands off drugs. And Miriam is my friend."

Schneider slapped the folder shut with a decisive motion. "Ms. Morgenroth is at the tail end of her eighties. And you, you're not even thirty."

"And?"

"Ms. Morgenroth is extremely wealthy. Your salary is around thirteen, fourteen hundred euros per month?"

"Twelve hundred seventy-six."

"Your concern seems excessive to me. I've ascertained you only met Ms. Morgenroth shortly before her disappearance."

"How long do you have to know someone to like them?"

Schneider leaned back in his chair and folded his arms across his chest. "Why are you really here?"

I could have given him so many answers but none that he would have understood.

"I can't escape the feeling that something has happened to her," I finally explained.

"Mmhmm," Schneider mumbled. He didn't move a muscle. "That's all?"

"Isn't that enough?"

"The way I hear it, your attendance at work has been spotty. You've searched the area several times."

"Maybe," I said.

"But you know what, Ms. Petersen? Old people do these things. You're going to have to accept that."

"What things?"

Schneider waved his hand. "Sometimes they're overcome with restlessness and just march off. It takes place particularly in nursing homes. You can secure the building like a prison, but some of them will still get out."

"Do they?"

"And how! They have a sudden desire to visit their children, unregister their car, or simply want to go shopping at two in the morning."

"Miriam wasn't like that. That's not the case with Miriam."

"How exactly do you know that?" Schneider asked. "Usually, nothing arises. They're taken into custody somewhere, brought back, washed, combed, and parked at the next exercise class. But sometimes, things do happen to them."

I looked at him in anticipation.

He sighed. "They have accidents. They stumble, fall down, break a leg, wrist, a hip, and by the time we find them . . . Well, sometimes they're sadly no longer alive."

"I would have found Miriam if she had fallen. I really searched every nook and cranny."

The detective did not seem to like the direction the conversation was taking. He leaned forward, placing both elbows on the desk. "I probably shouldn't say what I'm about to tell you. So, we're talking in general terms here. Although quite rare, it does come to pass. Some seniors leave the clinic or nursing home with a very specific goal."

"What goal?"

"They're old, sick, and feel useless. That gets them depressed."

I didn't understand what he was trying to say. Apparently, he saw that in my face.

"They retreat somewhere and take their own lives."

"You think Miriam committed suicide?"

Schneider laid his hand flat on the desktop. "Speaking in generalities, seniors who want to kill themselves usually hide. It takes a long time to find them."

I thought about Miriam, her voice, and the book we wanted to read together. "Miriam would never kill herself," I heard myself saying.

"How are you so sure?"

I looked straight at him. "I just know."

"The only alternative would be a crime. But"—he tapped his fingers emphatically—"there was no sign of struggle in her room. There's no evidence of a kidnapping. The family hasn't received any demands for a ransom. The only other logical conclusion is the one I've just painted for you."

"And that will be included in your report?"

Officer Schneider nodded slightly.

"You know that I can't accept this," I said.

He smiled. "I can tell, but I can't do anything about that."

15

I rang the bell and looked into the camera mounted above the wrought-iron gate. A loudspeaker next to me crackled, and a voice said, "Dr. Vogt's residence. May I help you?"

"My name is Petersen," I said. "I have an appointment for five o'clock."

"Petersen?"

"Yes. Alicia Petersen."

The crackling died down, the lock made a buzzing sound, and the door swung open. I went in.

It was two hundred paces to the house. On the left, I could make out a garage. Two dark sedans were parked in front.

An elderly woman appeared at the entrance to the main house. Judging from her expression, she was trying her best to ignore my clothes. Most likely, no one had ever shown up here in jeans and a T-shirt before. And certainly not with my skin color.

As soon as I was close enough, she asked, "Ms. Petersen?" Her voice sounded somewhat skeptical.

"I called Georg yesterday. He told me he would have time now," I said.

She swallowed and tried to smile, which came off as tense. "Franke," she said, introducing herself. "I'm in charge of housekeeping. You'll need to be patient for a moment. Dr. Vogt will be down in just a little while."

She allowed me to enter and then led me through a foyer that was tastefully decorated with a lot of gold and carpets into which my Nikes sunk deeply.

She opened a door. A typical study: a desk with a computer and three telephones, shelves lined with files, a conference table with half a dozen seats, and a set of leather chairs.

"Please make yourself comfortable," Ms. Franke said. "May I bring you something to drink while you wait?"

I shook my head. "That won't be necessary."

"Something to read?"

"No, thank you." I sat on a chair and crossed my legs.

Ms. Franke stood there indecisively for another moment. She gave me that tense smile again before she disappeared. She left the door open a crack. Presumably, she was afraid I would abscond with the computer.

I waited. Waiting is not hard for me. Being alone is something that I am used to, and life on the Hallig had taught me how to deal with time.

"Alicia, nice that you could come." Georg stood a few feet away from me. I hadn't heard him approaching. "I'm sorry that I'm late," he added.

"Don't worry about it." I waved it off. "Ms. Franke was very courteous."

Georg nodded absentmindedly, before he visibly pulled himself together and looked at me. "Do you have any news about Miriam?" he asked.

I shook my head. "No. That's why I wanted to see you. I'm absolutely convinced that she has been a victim of foul play."

Georg sat in the chair opposite me, loosened his tie, and unfastened his top button. "I just had a business meeting. I detest having to run around in a suit all day. Miriam," he said, returning to the matter at hand. "The police can't tell me anything. They don't have the slightest bit of evidence that suggests a crime has taken place. The investigation has led nowhere. You haven't found her. I'm also starting to think something has happened to her. She's been gone for five days now. And it's driving me crazy. She's probably fallen and is lying somewhere hurt . . ."

"I don't think so. I've searched everywhere. I would have found her."

"But then what could have happened?"

I looked around and made a vague hand gesture. "She was kidnapped. Somebody did the unthinkable to her."

Georg's gaze was penetrating. His eyes betrayed profound horror and, at the same time, disbelief. "There haven't been any demands for a ransom. No one has contacted me or the police. Everybody knows how rich we are—a kidnapper would have made contact. Even if . . ."

"You mean, if she resisted and . . . is no longer alive?"

Georg avoided my eyes. "Even then they would try to get our money. Miriam and I are very close. I would pay any sum."

We fell silent. Both of us mulled over our own thoughts.

"I can't let it go, Georg," I began again. "I *have to* investigate. I'll leave no stone unturned until I've found Miriam. One way or another."

"How do you intend to do that?" Georg's expression was more than a little skeptical.

"I don't know. I'll come up with something."

Georg drew a deep breath, ran his hand over his eyes, and said, "Okay, I'll support you. I'll speak with the clinic administration to get you relieved from your duties, if need be."

I looked at him in silence.

"And you're going to need money," he continued. "Believe me, if I wasn't so tied up right now with our bank and this damned real estate business, I'd drop everything and set off with you on the search."

One of the telephones rang. At first, Georg ignored it, and then he threw a sidelong glance at his desk, stood up, and went over to it.

He picked up the receiver. "Vogt."

He listened silently for a while. Once he said "yes" and then "hmm." After some time, he sat down at the desk. "Well," he began, and his voice took on a metallic tone. "I understand you perfectly. But let me tell you something. Contracts are there for a reason. Our bank manages very sound financial reserves. You assured me that you would make a payment on the interest this month. I'm going to hold you to that. Collateralized reinsurance or not. That is not my concern. You incurred a liability. You entered into a contractual commitment with us. And if you can't live up to it, I'll be forced to take legal action. It's as simple as that."

Again, he listened to what the other party had to say and concluded, "Good that we made that clear. We have an agreement." He hung up.

With a distant look in his eyes, he sat in silence behind his desk.

"Is everything all right?" I asked.

Georg turned his attention toward me and forced a smile. "I'm sorry that you had to listen to that. And . . . where were we?"

Before I could answer, he said, nodding, "I wanted to give you a check."

He grabbed a fountain pen, took out a checkbook, opened it, and began to write. "Do what you can. Follow up on every lead, no matter how unlikely. You and Miriam had a special connection. If there's anyone who can find out what happened to her, it's you."

I got up and walked over to the desk. Georg ripped out the check and handed it to me. I waited.

"Ten thousand euros," he said. "If the money runs out and you're still looking for her, you let me know."

"All right." I took the piece of paper.

16

For a change, his room was brightly lit this time. He deliberately turned away from me when I entered, acting as if he were looking out the window. At first, I remained in place, before I took a deep breath and made myself known with a little cough.

"Don't you have anything to do?" Winkler asked.

"Not at the moment," I replied.

"What do you want?"

"I'm sure you heard about Ms. Morgenroth."

Winkler reached over to the coffee table and grabbed his rubber ball. It squeaked quietly as he began to knead it. "I couldn't avoid it. Everyone else shares their opinions, has their theories, and my lovely colleagues from the department didn't have anything better to do than ask me questions."

"And what do you think about all of it?"

Winkler glared at me. "Who the hell is interested in my opinion?"

"I don't know too many people who work for the police. Maybe you've had similar cases."

"I worked in homicide."

"Oh," I said.

His only response was to squeeze the ball harder. The muscles on his forearm bulged.

I stayed put.

Winkler moved the ball to the other hand, and the kneading game began again. "It's been five days since she went missing."

"Six," I said.

"The chances of finding her alive now are approaching zero."

I forced myself to breathe calmly and regularly. "In your opinion, what might have happened?"

He snorted dismissively. "Who cares? Maybe she slipped on a banana peel and flew into the lake. Or a psychopath snatched her. The end result is the same. And I'm sure it's all the same to you."

"But it's not," I said hotly.

Winkler looked interested. "What kind of obligation do you have to her?"

I went over to him and sat down on the empty chair. He didn't protest.

"She's my friend."

"That's nice," he said, his green eyes remained cold. "Then you can be certain that you have one less friend now."

I folded my hands together and rubbed my thumb over the back of my other hand. "If you wanted to find out— just hypothetically speaking—what happened to her, how would you go about it?"

He furrowed his brow. "Hypothetically?"

"Yes. Hypothetically."

Now he gave me a curious look. He was rather handsome, in his own way. Distinct chin, prominent cheekbones, expressive eyes of the rarest green—like the sea shortly before a storm. He waited for me to drop my gaze, and when I didn't, small smile lines formed around his mouth. They disappeared just as quickly.

"Well," he said. "If her body doesn't turn up in the next couple days, or some jogger finds her by chance under a park bench, then I'd be inclined to think a crime has taken place."

"I see. And?"

His hand stopped abusing the ball. "A crime is always committed for a specific reason."

I looked at him inquisitively.

"Cui bono," he said.

"What does that mean?" Once again, I had the impression that he liked our conversation. He probably enjoyed talking down to me. But I didn't care.

"In contrast to what television shows suggest—that multiple half-crazed serial killers are running wild—reality looks quite different." Winkler sat up and leaned toward me. "None of us really likes to kill. You do it, but only when there are no better solutions—as a kind of last resort."

"And this bono stuff?"

This time, I was absolutely sure that he smiled. "Every crime benefits somebody. They want to cover up an abuse, appropriate money, stay in power, or gain power. When you discover whom Miriam's disappearance benefited, then you've found your culprit. And when you get him, he will tell you—"

"What he did with her or her body."

"Exactly."

"Then I should investigate along these lines?"

Winkler leaned back again. His smile faded. "Sure. Go on and investigate. Maybe you can even find the poor bastard who did something to the old bat out of desperation. But you know what? I'll tell you. It won't bring your friend back to life. She'll stay just as dead as before. The whole solving of crimes, the attempt to establish such a thing as justice, is doomed to fail from the start."

I remained still, trying to process what he had just told me. Then I said, "For a cop, you have a pretty crappy view on fighting crime."

"Ah?" He grabbed his ball again. "You forget that I've been locked up in rooms like this one for months. I lost everything that I had and that I was proud of: my job, my hot fiancée, my identity. And this body, ravaged by cancer, doesn't really belong to me anymore. All that loss will make a guy start brooding. And I've realized that everything I've done, everything I've accomplished, was entirely insignificant."

I stood up abruptly, went to the exit, and placed my hand on the doorknob. "No," I said. "I'm sure it wasn't insignificant. But I can see that the sickness has destroyed you completely. Clearly, you no longer want to help anyone."

17

I liked the night shift. First, I would go from room to room, dispensing pills and drinks. Next, I would be called in individually by patients who needed help getting into bed. As soon as this storm had passed, tranquility returned. Darkness crept through the windows from outside, and the lights in the corridor automatically dimmed to their lowest level.

I sat in the nurses' station, finished my paperwork, and drank tea. I placed the last completed file on the shelf behind me, organized the pillboxes for the next day, wiped the countertop clean, and once again took a seat on my swivel chair.

One thirty in the morning.

I turned on the computer and pulled up Google. I typed *Miriam Morgenroth*. Several results for various Miriam Morgenroths appeared, but they all dealt with strangers. No matches.

I checked under "Images." Again, no success.

I tried it without *Miriam*, just *Morgenroth*. There were hundreds of thousands of hits, but after reading through several pages, I had to admit that I wasn't going to get anywhere this way.

After a slight hesitation, I typed in *Dr. Georg Vogt*. Vogt Bank Munich dominated the page. I clicked on their website. It was divided into three categories: private banking, commercial real estate, and residential real estate. Going by the photos, their services were available to a very exclusive clientele.

I struggled through the next pages on the site: articles on monetary appreciation, tangible assets, offerings of stock, and company meetings, along with corporate videos. Utter boring crap.

A few shots of Georg in a black suit, looking very authoritative. He had the serious number down pat.

Under the "About Us" tab I finally read:

When Leopold Vogt and Adam Morgenroth founded their bank, they followed a simple yet sound business strategy: to impress their customers with the personal commitment and professional know-how that only a private bank could offer. We have faithfully lived up to this code until the present day, because we are bound by tradition . . .

Blah blah blah. I lost interest.

It seemed that this Adam Morgenroth was Miriam's father. I looked for more details about him but couldn't find any.

Frustrating.

A slight noise made me jump. Christian Winkler leaned on the counter and looked contemplatively at me. He wore a T-shirt; his biceps were well-defined. In spite of the chemo, he must have worked out a lot. Under the low lights, he appeared genuinely handsome. Especially when he kept his mouth shut.

I glanced at his face and noticed that he was examining me in much the same fashion, albeit completely uninhibited. Judging from the expression in his eyes, he liked what he saw.

"What is it?" I asked abrasively. "Do you need a bedpan?"

"I don't need anything," he replied.

"Then why are you creeping through the corridors in the middle of the night?"

"I couldn't sleep. And thought I—"

"Would come and provoke me?"

He grinned. "Are you chatting online?"

"I wanted to find out some things about Miriam. But I'm not really getting anywhere."

"No? Then you should let a pro have a go at it."

I motioned invitingly at the straight-backed chair next to me. He walked around the counter and took a seat. I slid a bit to the side. He pulled the keyboard closer and began typing with lightning speed.

He smelled good. Not at all sickly.

At first, he had as little success as I had had. But then he pulled up an article on the monitor: "Falk Real Estate Consortium Scandal—Serious Accusations Brought against Vogt Bank."

Winkler whistled through his teeth. "That sounds pretty interesting."

I read the report: Maximilian Falk, the head of a real estate consortium standing on the verge of insolvency, blamed the Vogt Bank board of directors for his financial misery. Miriam was also mentioned. For the first time, I saw her name in print. Maximilian Falk held her personally accountable; Miriam had allegedly made it crystal clear in an interview that Falk Consortium would not receive any more funds from the Vogt Bank because she doubted their creditworthiness. The consortium eventually filed bankruptcy over a nine-digit sum.

"Wow," I said when I had finished reading.

Winkler had leaned back. He was done before me.

"I had no idea that Miriam was involved in such big business," I said.

Winkler bent toward the screen and nodded slightly. "That's more than a thousand million."

"That's called a billion."

"A billion reasons to kill someone," he said. He scrolled up and down the screen. "But look—this article is already three years old."

He leaned back again and glanced up the hallway, an idea playing across his face.

"What is it?" I asked after a while.

"I believe . . ." he began and then fell silent.

"What do you believe?"

"That we should pay this Maximilian Falk a visit."

"We?"

Winkler returned from distant rumination. He directed his undivided attention to me. "You and I," he said. "We ask this shady Mr. Falk some questions. Let's see what we can learn from that."

"But there's no cui bono," I said.

Winkler smiled. "You learn fast. Mr. Falk wouldn't benefit directly if he killed Ms. Morgenroth. But revenge is a motive. As a matter of fact, it's a very strong one."

"And where do we find this Falk?"

Winkler typed the name into the computer. We waited a few seconds, and he pointed at the result that appeared on the monitor. "If this is right, he has a house in Berchtesgaden."

"Berchtesgaden?"

"Less than two hundred kilometers away. We could make it in two hours by car. What do you think about driving up there tomorrow?"

"I don't have a car."

"Well, go figure—I do."

"And what about your rehab?"

"It only goes for a couple more days. So, I can afford to take off for a few hours."

I looked at him dubiously. "You think you're fit enough?"

The light in the nurses' station was not particularly strong, but I had the distinct impression that he blushed. "I think I'll just barely be able to manage the two hours," he said sharply.

18

The motor purred quietly. I was lying in my seat more than sitting. In the rearview mirror, I saw a compact car approach from behind, veer to the left, and pass us.

"I don't understand," I said.

"Hmm?" Winkler said. He wore jeans, a knit shirt, and a light suede jacket. It suited him well. He rested his left elbow on the interior panel of the door and casually steered with one hand. His right hand laid across his thigh.

"I don't understand," I repeated.

Winkler threw an amused look in my direction. He seemed different today—relaxed and in a good mood, for a change.

"Why do you have such an outrageous car"—I knocked on the dashboard—"when you creep along like an old granddad?"

"I don't creep along," he said with an amused grin.

"No?" I asked. "The speedometer goes well past three hundred kilometers per hour, and we're barely doing a hundred and ten, hundred and twenty."

"What do you want? I'm enjoying the ride. Leave the speeding to others."

"A Porsche really fits your driving style."

"I didn't buy this car to break speed records. I liked the design. I love sitting here watching the surroundings pass through this one-of-a-kind panoramic windshield."

"Yeah, that is cool," I admitted. "No doubt expensive, though."

"When I bought the car, I wasn't thinking about the price. And," he added, "back then it was the car that was important to me."

On either side of us, mountains emerged from green meadows like waking giants—at first stooped and trying hard to hide, then slowly lumbering upward, until finally, monumental and unyielding, they towered over the landscape. The sky above us was a bright blue; the few clouds created the impression that they were artistically hung there by an adept interior decorator. An almost kitschy arrangement.

"How did you actually become friends with Ms. Morgenroth? Did you know each other before?" Winkler asked.

"Miriam?"

"Yeah. You seem to have an uncanny attachment to her."

"I met Miriam in the clinic. About two weeks ago."

He looked at me with a creased brow. "Really? Just two weeks? I had the impression that the two of you had a rather intense relationship."

"So, you picked up on that? I thought you were busy with hiding in the dark, squeezing that ball, and . . ." I swallowed the rest of my words, so as to not mention the pistol, but we both knew what I was about to say.

"I am, or rather *was*, a good investigator. I notice things that escape others. That's my special talent."

"Aha," I said. "Talent is what they're calling it these days, when you're good at snooping around in someone else's affairs."

To my astonishment, Winkler laughed. It seemed out of place. I wondered why, and decided it sounded odd because I had never heard him laugh before now.

"So, how does an almost ninety-year-old banker's wife become friends with a young, drop-dead good-looking nurse?"

"Hey," I said.

"What now?"

"As soon as you get a few kilometers away from the clinic, you think it's all right to hit on the help."

"Excuse me," he said. "That was not my intention."

I sighed and immediately got angry with myself, because if truth be told, I did not like his answer.

"We read together," I hurried to explain, in hopes of stifling the imminent embarrassment.

"Read?"

"Miriam is an authority on German literature. She's familiar with many books and loves poetry."

"Poetry?"

"Are you always going to repeat me? Let up on the therapist crap. I know the shtick and really can't stand it."

Winkler glanced at me. "Sorry. I was trained in this manner of speaking for my job, and it's sometimes hard to shake. But poetry," he continued, "I have always found utterly boring."

"In school, I hated it too. Which isn't saying much, because I hated everything."

"Who didn't?" Winkler changed lanes to overtake a semi. It seemed like he only tapped on the gas, but the Porsche sprang forward in such a way that the acceleration thrust me back into my seat.

"Her favorite poem is *The Blue Flower*," I remarked.

"Who wrote it?"

"I forget. But I really liked it."

"Drivel!" Winkler said sardonically. "There's no such thing as the blue flower."

"Miriam explained that to me. The flower represents everything we want but can't reach. You know what I'm talking about."

"Yeah," Winkler answered after a while.

"Somehow you don't sound convinced."

"Oh, on the contrary. Over the last couple of weeks, I've had a lot of time to think about what I might still"— he searched for the right words—"like to live to see."

"Let me guess. You want to become the chief of police and carry a really big gun. That's what all you cops want."

Winkler shook his head resolutely. Without addressing my jibe, he said, "Definitely not. For a while, it seemed like I wasn't ever going to leave the hospitals or rehab clinics. And then it quickly became self-evident what was important to me."

I thought about my prison cell and my room in the nurses' dormitory. I understood him all too well.

"I want to travel," he continued. "Visit distant countries. Backpack through the Himalayas or paint New York red for two or three weeks. Then fly to Tokyo and eat sushi. Not staying anywhere too long, always on the move, always a new goal on the horizon. That's what I want."

I did not respond. He wasn't even speaking to me but was rather thinking out loud. He had dreams, he longed for a different life. And what did I want? I could not answer that question.

The all-oppressing mountains disappeared before my eyes, replaced by an endless gray surface on which waves swelled slowly and majestically, in harmony with the seagulls' calls.

19

We crossed through the very heart of Berchtesgaden. Clean and tidy streets, houses painted with Alpine motifs. All the trim work—shutters, gables, and showy balconies—was intricately carved out of dark wood. Geraniums without end. Very touristy.

The GPS guided us to a private drive, which became steeper as we drove up it. The houses along it started to thin out; the yards grew progressively larger.

We came to the end of a cul-de-sac, and Winkler parked his Porsche next to a driveway.

"You have reached your destination," declared the galvanized computer voice.

I leaned forward dubiously. Behind a tall wrought-iron fence and a dense hedge, I could just make out the contours of a stately manor.

"How did you actually get this address? From Google, as well?" I asked Winkler, who was in the process of unbuckling his seat belt.

"What do you think? I still have my contacts," he said.

We got out. Winkler came around the car and inspected me critically.

"What?" I asked.

"You should put your jacket on."

"Should I?"

Winkler ignored the sarcasm. He nodded.

I pulled my cotton jacket out from the backseat and slipped into it. Once again, Winkler looked at me for a while, and then he stepped forward.

I started to back away automatically, but he held up both hands in a half pleading, half demanding gesture, and I stood still.

He took my collar and pulled it gently into place. Our eyes met. Winkler laughed after a pregnant pause and restored the distance between us. He examined his work, visibly satisfied.

"And?" I asked.

"Passable," he said.

"Passable?" I tried to be angry, but for some reason I couldn't. Instead, I said, "You are truly congeniality incarnate. Do you want to tie my laces as well?"

A corner of Winkler's mouth curled upward. "We need to make a professional impression. And by the way, you can call me by name."

"Well, good, Mr. Commissioner. I'll just go get the car."

Winkler smirked. "For starters, that's good. My name is Christian. But everyone calls me Chris. And what should I call you?"

"Well, what else? Ms. Petersen, of course." I had to laugh. "Alicia is fine."

That seemed to settle the matter for Chris. He left me standing there and started walking along the fence. I followed.

We arrived at the front entrance; a tall gate secured the premises. From atop the masonry posts, two surveillance cameras kept an eye on us; above the buzzer was the obligatory intercom. No nameplate.

"Are you sure that Falk lives here?" I said.

"A hundred percent." Chris rang the bell.

Nothing stirred.

Chris rang two or three more times and finally held his finger down on the button.

A red light blinked on one of the cameras. Simultaneously, a woman's voice came over the intercom. "Yes?"

Chris leaned forward. "Inspector Winkler. I would like to speak with Maximilian Falk."

"Why?" the voice asked.

"It has to do with a criminal inquiry. Further details will be shared with Mr. Falk in person."

"If this is in regards to any of the circumstances surrounding the bankruptcy, I must ask you to contact our lawyer. The legal proceedings have come to a close."

"The bankruptcy does not interest me in the least," Chris replied. "I'm investigating the possibility of a capital offense."

"A capital offense?"

"Exactly. A woman is missing. Ms. Miriam Morgenroth. I'm sure you know her."

It took less than three seconds for the gate to swing open.

20

The front yard was a veritable sea of flowers. Roses, perennials—all in full bloom.

Well before we reached the front door, a woman came out to greet us. Petite, older—I would guess fifty—but still very fit. Light linen pants, a beige short-sleeved blouse. Pearl necklace. Dark hair meticulously coiffed.

"Inspector Winkler?" she began.

Chris nodded while stretching out his hand. "And you are?"

"Mrs. Falk."

"Very pleased to meet you," Chris said. "My colleague, Ms. Petersen. We would like to speak with your husband."

The woman shook her head. "That is unfortunately not going to be possible."

"Is your husband not at home?"

"Well, yes, he is . . . but his physical condition does not permit . . . you understand?"

Chris put a friendly smile on his face. "Mrs. Falk, I'm investigating a capital crime. See it as a concession on my part that I took it upon myself to come to your husband instead of summoning him to Munich. It would be wise of you to appreciate my circumspection and discretion concerning this matter."

Mrs. Falk hesitated and then said, "You mentioned it regarded Miriam Morgenroth?"

Chris nodded. "Only a few questions. It won't take long. Then we'll be done."

"All right," Mrs. Falk conceded after another hesitation. "If you would please follow me." She turned on the spot and walked along an elaborately laid stone path that led around the side of the Alpine mansion. Soon we reached a terrace of gigantic proportions. The mountains before us appeared to rise to the sky, where they fought with the clouds. In the distance below, the houses of the small town in the valley were the size of matchboxes. The river that snaked through the green meadows flashed silver in the sunlight. No sounds of traffic. The chirp of the crickets seemed extremely loud.

"Please take a seat." Mrs. Falk indicated a group of lavishly designed teak chairs, which were covered with colorful cushions. Chris and I chose a bench located in front of a never-ending panoramic window.

Mrs. Falk sat opposite us in a matching armchair. A pergola above us ensured it wouldn't get too bright or uncomfortably warm.

"Your husband won't be joining us?" Chris asked. He pointed to our right. In a shaded area of the terrace, I could just make out the silhouette of a man in a wheelchair with his back turned to us.

"My husband can hear everything we say. I assure you of that," Mrs. Falk replied. "But I will be speaking for him."

Chris looked at the wheelchair and then at Mrs. Falk. "If that's how it has to be. So, Ms. Morgenroth has disappeared. It's been nearly a week now." He paused and leaned back comfortably before adding, "I suspect a crime has taken place."

"And why exactly have you come to us?"

Chris laid his hand on the table and tapped his finger a few times on the wood. "The way I hear it, you haven't maintained the best relationship with Ms. Morgenroth."

Mrs. Falk grunted. Her entire demeanor changed. She appeared disgusted. Almost nauseated. "Not the best relationship? Us and Ms. Morgenroth? That's an understatement if I've ever heard one. That unscrupulous woman completely ruined us."

A sudden wave of anger swept over me as I listened to Mrs. Falk's insulting words. "Excuse me," I interrupted. "But this"—I looked around pointedly—"doesn't exactly strike me as being the poorhouse."

Mrs. Falk winced as if I had hit her. Chris displayed no reaction. My remark seemed to be congruent with his own thoughts.

"What do you know?" Mrs. Falk said, her face flushed. "Our real estate consortium was worth one and a half billion. Due to a major project, we found ourselves in a temporary financial squeeze." She made a dismissive gesture with her hand. "It was nothing special, almost unavoidable when it involves such large investments. We needed to take out an interim loan. And then along comes this Morgenroth and questions our creditworthiness in an interview. She said the Vogt Bank was no longer going to provide us funds because we could not meet the terms of repayment." Mrs. Falk raised her head and looked me directly in the eyes. "Do you know what happened then? No? I'll tell you. Every financial institution dropped us like a hot potato, and the creditors all wanted their money back immediately. That led to the bankruptcy of our conglomeration."

"I can't believe that," I exclaimed. "Miriam would never do such a thing."

This time, Chris acknowledged my remark with an ever so slightly strained facial expression. Mrs. Falk didn't seem to catch on that I had called her archenemy by her first name and had even vehemently defended her.

She leaned forward. "Oh really? Ms. Morgenroth is a ruthless businesswoman. Just because she's so old doesn't make her any less dangerous or deceitful. She and her entire family were always like that. My father had dealings with their bank for decades, and he has repeatedly said that the Morgenroths embezzled millions upon millions before and after the war. They illegally acquired property. Money, gold, and above all diamonds disappeared without a trace. To this very day, none of it has surfaced."

Chris glanced toward the shadows, where the wheelchair sat. "Mrs. Falk, let's forget these horror stories from the old days. I'm interested in the present situation. What happened with your company?"

Mrs. Falk gave a forced laugh. "Well, what do you think? It was dissolved. And a large part of it—in a manner of speaking, the crown jewel—was taken over by the Vogt Bank. We were left with a few crumbs."

Chris looked at Mrs. Falk almost absentmindedly. "You call this palace you live in *crumbs*?"

She shivered involuntarily. "The company was my husband's lifework. He wanted to leave his empire to our children. And that Morgenroth destroyed everything with her stupid allegation. But not only that." Mrs. Falk licked her lips. It seemed hard for her to continue talking. She threw a furtive look to the man who remained motionless in the shadows. "The following proceedings, accusations, and the humiliation weighed on Maximilian to such a degree that he suffered a serious stroke. We found him very late, almost too late. And now . . ." Her head sank.

Chris waited a moment before he cleared his throat. "I am extremely sorry. So, you don't know where Ms. Morgenroth might be found or what might have become of her?"

"We haven't seen that woman in years." Mrs. Falk straightened her shoulders and fought to maintain her composure. "Even during the trial, she only sent her lawyers, under the pretense that she was too old. I'm sorry, but we can't be of any further assistance to you."

Chris stared at Mrs. Falk intently until she looked away. He let some time pass, leaned on the table, and stood up. "Then thank you, Mrs. Falk. If I have any further questions, might I contact you by phone?"

"I'll get something to write on," she said and started for the house.

"That won't be necessary." Chris reached into his pocket, produced a smartphone, and eyed Mrs. Falk expectantly.

"I'll give you my cell number," she said. "So, you can definitely reach me."

Chris nodded, and she started to dictate.

A sound, not unlike a rusty cawing, rang out. The wheelchair spun around and, buzzing, rolled within a few meters of us. The sunlight fell on a slumped-over figure. Grossly contorted shoulders, emaciated arms, disfigured face. Maximilian Falk struggled awkwardly to move his mouth.

His wife rushed over to him, laid a hand on his frail back, and held her head close to his.

Again, we heard the atonal noise. Maximilian Falk spoke with his wife. When he had finished, she stood up and smiled self-consciously.

"May I ask what your husband said?" Chris inquired.

"Nothing," Mrs. Falk replied.

The cawing returned, this time louder and harsher.

Mrs. Falk looked at her husband and took a deep breath. "My husband hopes that this Morgenroth woman was murdered and that she suffered a grisly death. Which is what she deserves."

21

I did not like the mountains. I felt confined, as if I were being deprived of my freedom. I missed the vastness, the infinite void reaching to the heavens. The skinny sliver of sky above us seemed to taunt me.

Chris remained silent, concentrating on the road. I mulled over my thoughts.

"How can someone harbor so much hatred?" I asked at some point.

Chris knew immediately that I was referring to the Falks. "The man is seriously sick. Somebody has to be blamed for it. Somebody other than himself or his wife."

"That may well be," I said. "But Miriam . . ." I shook my head. "She would never do what they alleged."

"They were both adamant that your Ms. Morgenroth set the avalanche in motion."

I thought about it for a moment. "No. They're mistaken. Miriam isn't unethical like that."

"Are you so sure that she's a saint, just because she read a few poems to you?"

"I just know it."

Chris started to answer but ultimately only moved the corner of his mouth. We drove on in silence.

The exit for a rest area came into view. Chris downshifted and turned off the highway. "We're nearly out of gas," he said in response to my inquisitive look. He pulled the car up to a pump.

We climbed out, and while Chris filled the tank, I pulled my wallet out of my purse. "I'm in the mood for some tea. Should I bring you a coffee?" I asked.

"Coffee?" he repeated. "Sounds good."

"How do you take it?"

"Black."

Nothing much was going on in the shop. I filled two large paper cups, carefully sealed them with plastic lids, and headed back to the car.

In the meantime, new customers had arrived. Around a dozen motorcycles: heavy machinery, shiny chrome, extra-wide tires. They blocked my path. The bikers, a troop of hulking guys clad in leather, stood around talking loudly. I tried to snake my way through them, taking care not to spill the hot drinks. Chris was nowhere to be seen. He had apparently finished filling up.

"Uh oh! What do we have here?" The guy had a full beard, and his blond hair was receding at the temples. He stepped in front of me. "Aren't you some real brown sugar!"

His companions became aware of me. At first, they just stared. But then they spread out what at the onset seemed aimlessly, until they had me surrounded.

"Let me by," I said.

"Well, well, *Rihanna*!" the blond jeered. "You have to earn it! A fine young black girl like you must have a few tricks up her sleeve. We're not shy. You can just blow us right here."

"Everything okay?" Chris's voice sounded calm, almost withdrawn.

The blond turned to look at Chris, who had appeared seemingly out of thin air behind him. The two men stared at each other in silence.

"Are you fucking this black bitch?" asked the blond.

Chris raised a hand, took hold of his earlobe, and smiled. "We should go, Alicia," he said.

I squeezed past the motorcycles; the men were no longer paying attention to me. Instead, they all looked at Chris. I stood next to him.

"You got lucky," the blond said.

"Oh yeah?" Chris answered.

"There are security cameras everywhere. If there weren't, I'd have already beaten the crap out of you, and then we would've shown that stupid whore what real men are."

Chris didn't say a thing. He turned away, put his arm across my shoulders, and together we walked to the Porsche. Contemptuous hoots and hollers chased us.

22

We continued on our way at a very leisurely pace. I had the impression that Chris purposely dawdled. After a few minutes, motorcycles shot past us. Like bats out of hell, they came screaming over the pavement. The bikers seemed fused to their hogs. They were soon out of our sight.

I tried to take a sip of my tea. It was still too hot. I set it back in its holder. Chris didn't speak; instead, he whistled softly through his teeth. He struck me as being in a good mood. We drove in silence for a while.

A road sign announced another rest area in four kilometers. The distance steadily shrank away. Eight hundred meters, four hundred. We were almost past the exit when, without warning, Chris slammed hard on the brakes, veered to the right, and turned off the highway. It quickly became clear to me why: he pulled up behind two shiny motorcycles and switched the engine off.

Through the passenger window, I could see the blond from earlier. He had just taken a piss and was zipping up his pants. One of his sidekicks was sitting on a crude wooden bench and greeted him with a can of beer. They obviously hadn't seen us yet.

"I have to take care of something real quick." Chris unbuckled his seat belt.

"Do you think that's a good idea?" I asked.

"Definitely." He paused for a moment and seemed to reconsider. Then he shoved his right hand into his jacket and reached around to the back of his waistband. When his hand reappeared, it was holding his pistol.

I sat up. "Since when do you carry a gun?"

He turned toward me. "Ever since I became a police officer."

"And what are you going to do with it now?"

"Nothing," he said. He reached across me and carefully stowed the gun in the glove compartment.

Chris got out. He slammed the door shut, walked around the Porsche and up to the two guys in leather.

In the meantime, they'd noticed him. The windows in the Porsche were rolled up; I couldn't hear what they were yelling. The only sound that reached me was the constant noise of vehicles as they barreled down the highway, not too far from me.

Whatever it was the men were saying to him, it didn't dissuade Chris in the slightest. He kept on walking toward them.

The blond guy's friend blocked his way. Chris moved so fast that I could barely see his punches. The biker held his hands up to his neck, teetered, and fell forward to his knees.

Now it was just a matter of the blond. He rushed toward Chris with his gigantic fists raised and his mouth open, screaming. Like a dancer, Chris stepped to the side. His would-be assailant's blow landed ineffectively in the empty space where Chris had been standing a split second prior.

Before the guy could respond, Chris nailed him with a hard kick to the hip. The guy spun like a dried leaf in the wind and fell to the ground.

Chris grabbed him by his jacket and hoisted him up. The blond tried in vain to shield his head with his hands. Again and again, Chris's right fist jabbed forward, pounding his face.

My tea had reached the perfect temperature. It tasted pretty good. I drank it in small sips and was half finished by the time Chris got back into the car. He carefully buckled himself in; he had previously cleaned his hands off outside.

"Ready?" I asked.

Chris nodded. "Ready."

"And? Do you feel better now?"

"Much," he said and coughed.

The cough got worse, and Chris doubled over, clinging on to the steering wheel with both hands. His body shook, his shoulders trembled.

When the attack was over, he reached into his pocket, pulled out a tissue, and wiped his mouth. I could see that the tissue was covered with crimson flecks.

I put my arm around his shoulder and hugged him tight for an instant. Then I let him go. "Can you imagine? I've never driven a Porsche in my life."

Chris didn't say anything in response. I acted as if he had. "Yeah, I know you're really attached to your car. But I promise I'll be careful. You slide into my seat, keep an eye on me. And I'll get us home. What do you think?"

Chris's answer consisted of a short nod.

I got out, and Chris climbed strenuously into the passenger seat and leaned back. The skin that stretched over his cheeks shimmered white, nearly translucent.

As I started the Porsche and guided it back onto the highway, I saw in the rearview mirror the two bikers slowly staggering to their feet.

Today Chris had paid handsomely.

23

To my surprise, the Porsche was very comfortable to drive. Like Chris, I didn't feel compelled to speed. Fifth gear, one hundred thirty kilometers an hour, and everything was going fine.

Chris sat next to me without speaking. His relentless coughing fits had eventually calmed down. He seemed to be immersed in thought. As I approached the Starnberg junction, I prepared to exit the highway, but Chris protested. "No. I'd prefer if you continued on till Munich."

"Why?" I asked. "You have to return to the clinic."

"My rehab is over in three days, anyway. I've just decided to release myself a little early—that's all."

"You don't want to know if I think it's a good idea or not?" I shot him a look. He appeared pasty and very tired.

"You got that right."

"Where do you want to go instead?"

"To my place."

"My mind reader has called in 'quit' on me," I said. "I need the address."

"You wouldn't find it anyhow. Just stay on the highway."

Reluctantly, I followed his instructions. The evening rush hour had begun. Traffic became denser and denser, almost gridlocked. After nearly thirty minutes of this, we came to his exit. Stop lights, traffic jams, and with luck, some steady moving. Sometimes, I was under the impression that Chris had fallen asleep. But he always broke his silence in time to give me accurate directions.

The sun was already setting as we pulled up in front of a fancy, albeit soulless, apartment complex. Chris climbed out with exaggerated vigor. However, when I got up next to him, I noticed that he had to hold on to the roof of the car with both hands.

"Where to now?"

"Up ahead," he said. "Third floor."

"Okay," I said. "I don't know where I am. Will you show me the way?"

Chris nodded, paused a moment, then put his arm around my shoulders. We set off in unison.

Initially, it went quite well. But after a few steps, his strength seemed to gradually abandon him. The weight on my shoulders grew heavier and became unwieldy.

We reached the front door. By then, Chris was wheezing as if he had just completed a thousand-meter sprint. Although the sun still hung in the sky, a lamp above the buzzers was already burning. Its pale light made the beads of sweat on his forehead shine.

He awkwardly fumbled in his pocket for his keys, found them after a while, and opened the door for us. Luckily, there was an elevator. Once we were inside it, Chris let go of me, leaned his back against the mirrored wall, and firmly held on to the handrail.

With a jolt, we came to a stop. The door opened noiselessly. Chris pushed himself off the wall. One of his legs no longer wanted to carry him; he almost fell over. I went to his aid. Again, he put his arm around me, and we continued down the hall.

This time, it took him longer to find the right key. The overhead light in his apartment blinked indecisively before illuminating a large, modernly furnished living room. Leather couch, glass table, comfortable reading chair, small flat-screen television. There were even a few books on the shelves. The typical bachelor pad.

Without speaking, we headed for the sofa. Chris eased himself onto it, not able to completely suppress a groan. His chest was pumping hard, and he avoided my eyes.

"Are you hungry?" I asked.

Chris shook his head. "I haven't been here for months. I doubt there's anything edible in the place."

"But maybe something to drink," I said.

"Tea should be in the top cabinet in the kitchen."

"Tea?" I replied, only to remain indecisively in place.

"What is it?" he asked.

"You get situated, while I . . ." I pointed to the open kitchenette.

"Of course. I'm a big boy. I'm sitting on a sofa. What could go wrong?"

My only response was a forced smile.

I went into the kitchen and opened every cabinet until I found a suitable pot. To be on the safe side, I let the water run for a while before I filled the pot and placed it on the stove. The tea wasn't where Chris had said it would be. I fished some out of a drawer—tea bags, a cheap Earl Grey blend. There wasn't any sugar. Nor any honey. Ditto on the milk. The refrigerator was unplugged.

The water started boiling. I took the pot off the stove, threw in two tea bags, and let it steep for a while before I poured it into two large cups and returned with them to the living room.

Chris was still sitting where I had left him. However, his head had lolled to the side, and his eyes were shut. I listened carefully and heard steady, deep breaths.

I set the cups down and went over to him. As gently as possible, I held him by the shoulders and brought him to a supine position. He didn't even notice. I pulled off his shoes and lifted his legs onto the couch. That didn't wake him either.

In his bedroom, the bed was neatly made. I pulled off the blanket and took it back with me to lay over him. Then I sat on the armchair and tried my tea. It was still warm but tasted awful. If I had come to my grandmother with such muck, she would have chased me around the barn. I couldn't help grinning.

So, this was where Chris lived, before he came to the clinic. The furniture was expensive; the oriental carpets seemed high quality. On the walls, I could see a couple of large rectangular spots where until recently pictures had hung. I was reminded of his ex-fiancée. She had obviously come for what belonged to her.

I remembered how she had slammed the glass door against the wall at the clinic. They had broken up that day. Who had instigated it? Chris could get in a mood, the likes of which I had never seen. He could drive you insane.

I looked over at him and watched how he slept. He had a masculine face. Strong cheekbones, determined chin. He could be hurtful, mean, and like I witnessed today, quite brutal. But while he lay there sleeping, he struck me as incredibly sensitive and lonely—a boy who has rowed too far out to sea and suddenly realizes that he has forgotten in which direction the mainland lies.

I stood up so I could pull the blanket over his shoulders. His forehead felt cold. I stroked his face gently. Now I wasn't at risk of being ridiculed. On his cheeks, I felt stubble. I would have so loved to touch his lips. But I didn't dare.

After a while, I sat back down and stared at one of the pictureless spots. Before long, I could hear the ripple of the sea and the cries of the seagulls. And when I looked closely, I could make out a small boat, far out on the horizon. It fought with the waves, restless and alone.

24

I unlocked the door with Chris's key, grabbed my plastic bag, and hauled it to the kitchen. Eggs, steak, white bread. A half pound of really good tea. Milk, sugar, butter, and everything else I needed.

I found a frying pan and immediately got to work. I was insanely hungry.

As I cooked, I heard the water running in the shower. After it died down, the monotonous drone of an electric razor followed. That too went silent.

The door opened, and Chris entered the living room. Fresh pants, an obviously new shirt with iron creases. He was still pale, but in his eyes, the old fire blazed. "That smells delicious," he said, pointing at the stove.

"Are you feeling better?" I asked.

He tried to hide his insecurity with a satisfied smile. I pretended that I hadn't noticed.

"Of course, I'm fine."

He came over and peeked into the skillet. "What you got cooking?"

"It's a surprise." I pushed him softly but firmly to the dining table.

Chris raised his hands in surrender and sat down.

I made each of us a plate of steak, scrambled eggs, and fried onions; poured two large mugs of tea; loaded it all on a tray; and carried it to the table.

"This'll save my life," Chris said. He impatiently grabbed the plate from my hand, snatched up the silverware, cut a huge bite out of the meat, and devoured it almost without chewing.

I sipped the tea. It was just right.

Without looking up, Chris muttered, "Wonderful," and in next to no time, he had finished everything on his plate. He leaned back. Only now did he notice his drink and take a large gulp. He sighed contentedly.

"Tea tastes good too," he said, sounding surprised and not very clever. "I normally drink coffee, you know."

"Aha," I replied. Though now I hurried, I hadn't even eaten half of my steak.

"What are you going to do now?" he asked unexpectedly.

"What do you think?" I said, chewing. "I'm going to enjoy my breakfast."

"I didn't mean that. I wanted to know what your plans were for this Morgenroth thing."

"I won't be able to rest until I've found Miriam," I said. "I don't think that Mr. and Mrs. Falk were telling the truth. I need to dig deeper."

Chris thought a moment before he answered. "I guess you have a point. Something is wrong here. If you'd like, I can keep helping you."

"Wow," I said. "Now that is a surprise."

"Why do you say that?"

I threw him a speculative glance. "You may be a lot of things, but you don't seem like the type of guy that does others—or better said, me—selfless favors."

Chris returned my look. Actually, he stared at me intently. He probably thought I would avert my gaze. But I didn't. I kept watching him as I continued to eat.

We remained silent for a while.

Finally, he cleared his throat. "If I help you, I'm not really being selfless."

I had finished eating. I dropped my knife onto my plate and leaned back as well. "What do you mean?"

Chris made an indecisive grimace. "At first, I thought it was absolutely crazy that you wanted to go search for this gray-haired old lady nobody else really seemed to miss. But I was so bored in rehab, and when I started feeling better, any excitement was welcome. However, yesterday at the Falks's, it became clear that there's more behind this than meets the eye."

"Really?"

Chris nodded. "You've got this outrageously wealthy old woman who just disappears. If I understood correctly, Miriam Morgenroth is still sitting on the executive board of a bank."

"No," I said. "She owns the bank. At least, fifty percent of it."

Chris raised his eyebrows. "Even better. Dubious business practices. Huge sums being transferred. A fleeced billionaire falls by the wayside, penniless. And who knows"—Chris ran a contemplative finger over his upper lip—"this might just be the tip of the iceberg."

"So?" I still didn't understand what he was getting at.

Chris lowered his eyes briefly, took a deep breath, and stared at me again. "I'll have to explain it to you, then. I've solved dozens of cases. I always wanted justice to be served, to ensure that the culprit got his just punishment. I did exactly what was expected of me. But do you know who I always forgot about?"

I shook my head.

"Myself. I've never taken care of number one. But now, after this fucking disease, I'm smarter. I have a case here that's shady as all hell. And if I play my cards right, this time, I can cash in."

"Money? For you it's about money?"

Chris snorted. "Of course. Don't you know the saying? Once in a lifetime, everyone gets the opportunity to become filthy rich. I've thought long and hard about it. Days, weeks on end. I had all the time in the world to do so. In my entire life, I've never had a real chance. And without warning, Miriam Morgenroth enters the picture. And I can practically feel it. I can literally taste it. There's gold in them there hills."

"You're really hot after money?"

"You still have to ask?

"What do you want with it?"

Chris looked at me intensely. And when he realized that I really couldn't understand his motivation, he smirked in disbelief. "If you don't have money, it's like being sick. You can't do what you want to do. Life"—Chris made a swooping gesture with his hand—"passes you by, and you're at best a spectator. If you want to change that, you have to do whatever it takes to carve out your own chunk. And then . . ."

"And then?"

"Then I'll fulfill all of my dreams. I won't skip a thing: New York, San Francisco, Rio de Janeiro. The Maldives and from there over to Hawaii. I'll chase my own personal blue flower."

"That's all that you want out of life?"

For a moment, a look in his eye suggested second thoughts. Then he shed any sign of doubt. "That's exactly right. So, we're going to do everything we can to find your Ms. Morgenroth. And I'll be sorely mistaken if somewhere along the way there's not a large pile of dough waiting to be picked up."

My tea was cold. It was no longer appealing. I set it on the table, grabbed a napkin, and wiped my mouth. "You obviously have a clear idea of what we should do next."

Chris smiled smugly. "Don't forget that I'm a damn good investigator. Of course, I know what we're going to do next."

25

Sven

Three p.m. For Sven, that was a sacred time. Japanese animated films—anime. Right now, his hero was fighting against a formidable rival.

Sven had seen this episode probably a dozen times before, but he liked it as much as the first time. Maybe even more.

His hero grasped onto his belt, took a ball off of it, and pushed a prominently protruding button. Instantly, the capsule expanded, and as he flung it in the direction of his opponent, an ape appeared and started spinning like a fire wheel. Sven shouted out of pure bliss.

A grunting sound came from near his feet, but Sven wasn't going to let anything, or anyone interrupt his favorite show. He kicked brusquely two or three times. The noise stopped.

A second monster, launched by the hero's rival, appeared on the flat screen. A raven with a hat swooped down on the ape. An embittered battle commenced.

Although Sven knew exactly how things would turn out, these duels still fascinated him time and again. He got downright feverish. He cheered for the hero and his cute monster.

Commercial break.

Sven sighed and was abruptly overtaken by hunger. See what the refrigerator has to offer. He stood and damn near fell over what was lying on the floor. He gave it another kick. Then he stepped around it and went into the kitchen.

A bottle of champagne, cheese, tomatoes. A head of broccoli. He would rather die than eat that stuff. A Tupperware box. He opened it. Thinly sliced cured ham. A bit salty but quite good. He took the whole stack. Some motherfucker had inserted plastic between each of the slices. He pulled the sheets out, to the great detriment of the outer appearance. But who cared. In short order, he balled up the small shreds of meat into a thick wad and bit into it. As previously noted, somewhat salty but good.

Sven ambled back through the living room. This time, he sidestepped the obstacle on the floor. He sat down on the couch. Satisfied, he watched the hero win the day, returned the monster to his belt, and walk into the sunset.

Credits. In the meantime, he had polished off the ham.

He operated the remote control. Since his hands were in latex gloves and still a bit greasy from the meat, it proved to be a hassle, but eventually the screen went black.

Sven rose and looked at the floor in front of the glass coffee table. He had spread out a clear plastic drop cloth there with great foresightedness. Heavy duty. On top of it lay a woman in her mid-twenties. Her red hair was disheveled and sweaty. Her mouth was covered with shiny silver tape. Her hands were secured tightly behind her back. Her ankles were also bound.

She grunted like before and jerked back and forth, re-sembling a fish out of water. It was always funny when his victims did this. Nothing ever came of it, yet they always tried it again and again.

Sven glanced at his watch. At around four thirty, he wanted to meet Sonja and Marko at the new campsite. Shit, time was running out. He wouldn't be able to play with the victim anymore.

He knelt down, put his hands around the woman's neck, and squeezed. The woman's eyes bugged out in hor-ror, and she tried to shake him off.

Amused, Sven raised an eyebrow and softly said, "Tut-tut." He freed his hands and showed the victim empty palms as a signal that she had nothing to fear.

Boundless relief showed in the woman's expression.

Sven laughed heartily. The surprise was a resounding success.

Lightning fast, he seized her once again. But this time, his fingers dug mercilessly into her soft neck.

The woman froze up like a block of ice from the pain. Then her legs began to twitch; her heels drummed on the carpet. Her eyes grew larger. They nearly popped out of their sockets.

Sven almost regretted having gagged the woman. When he didn't, his victims' tongues protruded, and that always looked fantastically funny. To die for. But today, it wasn't meant to be.

The quakes of the body subsided until all movement stopped. The smell of urine reached his nose. That's why he had laid down the plastic.

Sven got up. Sonja always said the victims could still hear you for a while and would be infinitely angry if you insulted them now. But he didn't really feel like doing that.

Instead, he rolled the corpse up in the plastic tarp and carefully wrapped the bundle with the duct tape. Now he just had to stow the body well out of sight. With that, his day's work would be done.

26

C hris and I walked out of a parking garage and found ourselves in a pedestrian zone. The structures flaunted beautiful art nouveau façades. Although it was nearly eleven in the morning, the rush was yet to come. The small cafés were still relatively empty.

We headed to a magnificent building. The first floor featured Gothic arches made of granite, above which rose four stories of tastefully whimsical architecture. The mullioned stained-glass windows were most likely the original ones from the turn of the nineteenth century.

The front of the building was embellished with a sign that said "Vogt Bank Munich" in gold lettering.

Chris held the door open and laid his hand on my back as a gesture that I should enter. I thanked him with a smile and didn't let on that he was the first man to ever do this for me.

Inside, we were greeted by a lavish reception area. An elderly lady in an elegant outfit was straightening some papers. She looked from me to Chris and back again. With practiced politeness, she concealed her original surprise and put a vacuous smile on her face. "May I help you?"

"Petersen," I said. "Alicia Petersen. I have an appointment with Dr. Vogt."

This time, the receptionist didn't manage to hide her amazement, so I added, "Georg."

"Of course," she answered and indicated an elevator off to the side. "Fifth floor. Dr. Vogt is expecting you."

Chris thanked her with a nod.

The elevator was paneled with mahogany. The handrails were brass. Even the large mirror on the back wall had a gilded frame.

Fifth floor. The sliding doors opened to another reception area. Again, an elderly lady; again, fabricated friendliness. Finally, we entered Georg's office.

Not an office in the usual sense. An entire story gutted and supported by a few columns. The floor-to-ceiling lattice windows offered an unrivaled view of the area, including Munich's landmark Frauenkirche.

As soon as we walked in, Georg jumped up from behind his enormous desk, ran up to us, opened his arms, and hugged me. "Alicia," he said. "How nice it is to see you."

From the corner of my eye, I noticed the puzzled expression on Chris's face. I must admit, I liked this reaction.

"I'm happy to see you too," I said. "May I introduce Mr. Winkler?"

Georg paused a moment, let go of me, and held a hand out to Chris. "A friend of Alicia's?" he asked.

They shook hands.

"We met in the clinic," Chris answered.

"Oh," Georg said, as if that explained matters and at the same time threw me a quizzical look. When I didn't react to his silent signal, he said, "Where are my manners? Let's grab a seat." He indicated a set of chairs around a conference table. "May I offer you something to drink? Maybe a water or a cup of coffee?"

Chris shook his head. "We just had breakfast. It's really not necessary."

I sat down first. Chris paused at a table on which a sprawling model was assembled. I saw tall apartment buildings, a shopping mall, streets, parks, even a sports complex. Chris stared, mesmerized by the lifelike representation of an urban center with trees, not to mention scale-sized cars and people.

Chris's fascination did not escape Georg. He stepped next to him. His eyes also lit up. "Our latest project."

"Impressive," Chris said.

Georg smiled. "That it is. We're going to breathe new life into an entire city district. Before, this was a derelict factory area, run-down apartments with coal-burning ovens. The sewage system was in disrepair. The entire infrastructure is over a hundred years old."

"But this here"—Chris gestured to the high-rise towers—"looks like the mock-up of the city of tomorrow."

Georg didn't even try to hide his pride. "Jobs, apartments, recreation, commerce. All closely situated, not in competition but rather in harmony. An urban sanctuary. The people will live and work happily there."

"An ambitious project," Chris said.

Georg regarded Chris with new interest. "You seem to have an understanding of the topic. Are you an architect?"

Chris shook his head regretfully. "I once considered that as a career. But I ended up with the police."

"With the police?" Georg's smile instantly faded.

"Yes. On the homicide squad."

"Have you found Miriam? Has something happened to her?"

Chris was about to answer, but I stepped in. "No, no—don't worry. Chris—I mean, Mr. Winkler—has simply offered to help me."

Georg gave a sigh of relief. "Oh, I thought there was bad news about Miriam." Again, he took a deep breath. "You must understand, Mr. Winkler. Miriam is—"

"You don't need to explain," Chris said. "Alicia already told me everything."

"Yes. Then we should really sit down." Without waiting for a reply, Georg turned away from the model and grabbed a chair opposite me. Chris followed him and took a place at my side.

"Have you seen any sign of Miriam?" Georg asked.

I shook my head.

Georg turned to Chris. "You know, Miriam practically raised me. We may not be blood relatives, but she was something like a mother to me. And . . ." He hesitated. "Please don't draw any false conclusions, but her disappearance is not only dreadful on a personal level. From a business perspective, it's extremely problematic. Miriam is a co-owner of this bank. And without her . . ." He broke off again and looked down at his hands, which were clenched on his lap. "Contracts, transactions, policies are all missing her signature."

"That must be tough," Chris said.

"That it is, Mr. Winkler. Alicia was Miriam's friend. Since the police more or less closed the case after a few days, Alicia has tirelessly continued to search for her. But if she doesn't find anything, I'll have to do more. I'll hire an additional private investigator."

Chris took a moment to answer. Finally, he said, "That won't be necessary, Dr. Vogt."

"No?"

Chris leaned forward and stared at Georg with his piercing green eyes. "No. I'll do everything in my power to help Alicia in the search for Ms. Morgenroth."

Georg remained silent at first. Then he said, "But I thought you're with the police. And they've closed the case, essentially."

"I still have a few months off duty. I can use the time however I want. Alicia and I will find Ms. Morgenroth."

"Yesterday, we paid a visit to the Falk family in Berchtesgaden," I said, breaking the subsequent silence.

Georg appeared startled. "Max Falk?"

"Correct," Chris said. "Mr. Falk raised serious allegations about Ms. Morgenroth."

"Did he?" Georg laughed dryly.

"Why does that not seem to surprise you?"

"Falk plays the victim now. But he nearly drove us under with his speculations. Myself, Miriam, our bank, and more than a dozen other investors."

"Mr. Falk painted quite a different picture," Chris said. "He claimed that Ms. Morgenroth is to blame for his misery, because in an interview she—"

"All lies!" Georg exclaimed. I'd never seen him this upset. "We were the main investors then. I trusted Mr. Falk unconditionally. Miriam's assiduous eye for detail was the only thing that rescued us. We realized that we were supporting a practically bankrupt company that was undertaking a huge project just to keep its doors open, which should mount up to be the saving grace of their ailing conglomerate. When Miriam figured this out, we pulled the emergency brake. If we hadn't, everybody that invested their money in this gigantic swindle would have gone under, including us."

Chris nodded. "But still, Mr. and Mrs. Falk hold Ms. Morgenroth solely responsible for their present situation."

Georg shifted uneasily on his chair. "These accusations aren't new. They were also the subject of a court case, and we—I mean, Miriam and the Vogt Bank—were acquitted on all charges. We were attributed absolutely no fault for the Falks's financial crisis."

Chris thought over what Georg had just explained. "Do you believe that Max Falk could be behind Miriam's disappearance in any way?"

Georg shrugged his shoulders. "I have no idea. He's seriously sick and full of hatred. I couldn't begin to guess what he is capable of doing with such animosity."

There was another pause. "Besides the Falks," Chris said, "can you think of anyone else who might have something against Ms. Morgenroth?"

Georg shook his head. "Because of Miriam's diligence, we weren't caught up in the bankruptcy that Falk brought about. Miriam also ensured that the other investors were compensated in full. That was very important to her personally."

"Miriam disappeared a week ago," I said. "If she'd had an accident, I would have found her by now."

"I share Alicia's opinion," Chris said. "I'm nearly certain that a crime has taken place. And there's no one better than me at solving crimes. I always get my man."

The look on Georg's face was contemplative. He drew a hand over his mouth and then ran it through his hair. "If you're going to pursue this, you should also work for me. I'll hire you. Officially. And give you the same rate that the most reputable agency would charge."

Chris was completely unfazed by Georg's words. "All right. It wouldn't have been necessary, but I'll accept your offer."

"Then we have a deal." Georg seemed very relieved. "And as soon as you learn anything . . ."

"Of course," I said. "We'll inform you immediately."

Chris rose. Georg followed his example, and the two men shook hands again—this time with a new intimacy.

"Please believe me," Georg said. "I'd like nothing more than to be out there looking with you."

"We'll find her," I said and hugged Georg good-bye before following Chris, who had already left the room.

27

The elevator door closed behind us, and I had the sensation that we'd been cut off from the rest of the world. We started down toward the first floor. Chris leaned casually against the wall once more. I noticed that the rings under his eyes had deepened. The effort wore on him, but for the time being, he did not seem to be bothered by it. That I could see.

Following a sudden impulse, I pressed the stop button. With a jolt, our ride ended. Chris didn't move. He just looked at me expectantly.

"What do you want to do now?" I asked.

"With every kidnapping," he began after a while, "with every murder, there are certain signs in advance."

"I don't understand."

"Fights, discussions with strangers, peculiar mail, the victim feels threatened or stalked. Mostly small things that we all overlook but that turn out to be very important. And Dr. Vogt couldn't give us any evidence of this happening in Ms. Morgenroth's case."

"No, he couldn't."

"But still, the signs must have been there."

We were silent for a while as I thought over Chris's words.

"*Georg* couldn't give us any evidence of those things," I said triumphantly.

"Who then?" Chris said. "You?"

"Yes."

"And you're just bringing it up now?"

"I hadn't realized that it could be relevant. And probably it's not. Maybe I'm making a mountain out of a molehill."

Chris's intense sea-green eyes held me tight.

I cleared my throat. "Shortly before Miriam's disappearance, she received a visit from a student. And it upset her, even though she tried to pretend it hadn't."

"From a student?"

I nodded. "She questioned Miriam. Interviewed her or something. Miriam spoke with her for nearly two hours, but I know for a fact that she would have preferred not to."

"What was the interview about? The banking industry?"

I shrugged. "I really don't recall. But I don't believe so. I think the student was working on her PhD and was writing her dissertation. Something to do with history."

"She was working on her doctorate in history?"

I tried to remember more clearly. "If my memory isn't failing me, yes."

Chris pushed himself away from the wall. "Can you recall her name? I mean, the name of the student?"

I hesitated. "Becker . . . Beck . . . something like that."

The expression in Chris's eyes changed. In a blink, it became softer, almost compassionate. He moved toward me. He was so close that I could feel the heat of his body. He smiled and stretched out his arm. I almost thought that he wanted to touch me. But he simply pressed the stop button again. The elevator lurched and started down.

"Alicia, you're a smart woman," he said. "And whatever the story is with this student, we'll find her in a flash. Let's see what she frightened Ms. Morgenroth with."

28

I parked the Porsche and turned off the engine.

Chris pointed at a traffic sign directly in front of the car. "You do realize that this is a fire lane?"

"Sure," I said. "But that doesn't matter. When one of your nice cop colleagues comes along to write us a ticket or tow away your little sports car, you simply interrupt your break and speed around the block."

"Break?" Chris sounded irritated.

"Yes, a break. That visit to Georg's bank was exhausting. I urgently need some tea."

"Jesus!" he snapped. "I can't stand this pity trip of yours. Can you just stop? I'm dead tired. And I think I've just sweated out all the pills I've taken over the last six months in one go." Chris avoided my gaze. He made his hand into a fist, as if he were clenching his rubber ball, and hit the passenger window over and over.

When he had calmed down, I said, "I still want tea."

"You're going to Starbucks for tea?"

I grinned. "Tea for me, coffee for you. Is that all right?"

The rage in Chris's eyes slowly disappeared. He began to laugh. "I act like an idiot, don't I?"

I reached over to pat him on the shoulder. "It's nothing new."

My face was very close to his. He didn't say anything and avoided my eyes.

"Okay then, I'm off," I said unnecessarily.

Luckily, the café wasn't packed, and in next to no time, I had returned with two big cups. Chris was still sitting in the passenger seat. But unlike before, he was now busy making phone calls.

I set both drinks on the roof of the Porsche, opened the door, snatched the paper cups, and climbed behind the wheel.

"Officer Hetz speaking," Chris was saying into the phone. "I'd like to talk to someone from admissions."

Apparently, the other party was connecting him to the responsible person. I took the opportunity to give Chris his coffee. *"Hetz?"* I asked.

Chris nodded, grinning, before taking a careful sip. "Yes." He spoke again into his phone. "This is Officer Hetz. I need the address of one of your doctoral students. A woman by the name of Becker or Beck." He listened to what was obviously a long-winded answer and then said, "I understand your concerns about data protection, but someone smashed into a car in your parking lot yesterday and drove off without a word. We've apprehended the suspect. But he claims that he left a note on the car. And that one of your students saw him do this and even spoke with him."

Again, Chris fell silent and listened while calmly drinking his coffee. "Of course. I already told you that I'm well aware what data protection means. But we're talking about a hit-and-run. Not about some student who urinated in a trash can. If you don't give me a name, I'll be forced to summon every employee from the janitor to the dean to come down to police headquarters for questioning." Chris paused dramatically before adding, "Your call."

This time, the response was brief. "Understood," Chris said. "Find someone who can make this decision. I can wait."

He laid his phone on his thigh and looked at me pointedly. "Really good coffee," he said. "But too sweet."

"Otherwise, it's undrinkable," I said.

Chris shook his head and raised the phone to his ear. "Yes, I'm listening . . . Aha . . . and this woman is working on a doctorate in history? Red hair, mid-twenties . . . Thank you. That wasn't so hard." He slipped his phone into his pocket. "Her name is Franziska Beck, and I have her address."

29

A side street with houses from the early nineteenth century interspersed with apartment buildings constructed from reinforced concrete. We left the Porsche in a residents' parking lot and strolled up the sidewalk.

"There it is." Chris pointed to a yellow apartment complex.

As we got closer, we could see that the door stood open. Inside, the stairwell smelled of cleaning agents, the steps were still wet. By all appearances, they had just been mopped.

The buzzer revealed that F. Beck lived on the third floor.

The oak stairs creaked in protest as we climbed them. We didn't run into anybody; the entire third story seemed lifeless and abandoned.

"They've all cut and run," I said.

"Let's try our luck." Chris positioned himself in front of the peephole and pressed long on the doorbell. We could hear the chime ring through the door. We waited. Nothing.

Again, Chris rang the bell. Same outcome.

"They're not at home." I stated the obvious.

"I can see that," Chris said.

"What do we do now?"

Chris looked around indecisively.

"We could wait in the café across the way until she comes back," I suggested. "She has to turn up eventually."

"We could." Chris reached into his jacket pocket and took out two plastic baggies. He handed them to me. Correction—not baggies but latex gloves.

"What should I do with these?" I asked.

Chris's answer was a mischievous grin. He produced a second pair and pulled them on. I did the same as Chris began wiggling a thin pick in the keyhole.

After a moment, the door sprang open.

We entered quickly. Chris shut the door gently behind us.

IKEA furniture, Billy bookcase, a screaming red carpet. An oversized flat-screen television. Warm, stuffy air.

"It doesn't feel like she aired the place out today," I said.

Chris moved carefully, always walking on the carpet. Again, I followed his example.

The living room looked tidy and impersonal; the kitchen clean. No pots on the stove. Chris opened the refrigerator and examined the inside. I glanced over his shoulder. Some cheese, unsightly tomatoes, dried-up broccoli. A Tupperware box, empty. A bottle of champagne.

"Nobody has been here for a few days," Chris said.

"But where did she go?"

"Maybe she's on vacation."

I shook my head. "I don't think so."

"How come?"

"Didn't you notice the empty laptop case? I didn't see the laptop that goes in it."

"Hmm," Chris said. "Good observation."

We moved into the bedroom. It was also clean; the bed was covered with a smooth bedspread.

Chris opened a wardrobe. Sweaters stacked precisely, the T-shirts sorted by color. Jackets and skirts in protective sleeves.

I grinned. "Wow. Somebody is a neat freak. That's bordering on obsessive."

Chris opened the other side of the wardrobe. I sat down on the bed. It felt unusually hard. I tried to bounce a little, but it wouldn't let me. The mattress didn't budge at all under my weight.

"That's strange," I said.

Chris turned to me. "What?"

"The bed. It has no spring. It must be terribly uncomfortable."

Chris tipped his head to the side and studied the bed. Then he audibly exhaled. It sounded strained. "Stand up, Alicia, but do it gently."

"Why?"

"Please, just do me the favor."

I rose and took a couple of steps away. He walked past me and knelt down. He looked under the bed for a considerable amount of time. Then he reached underneath it. He pulled, groaning at the effort, and a large package wrapped in plastic appeared. Really long—almost two meters.

As I bent over to look more closely at what we had found, I could make out a woman's face framed in red hair through the transparent sheeting. Her skin was discolored; her eyes bulged far out of their sockets; her mouth was sealed with duct tape.

I felt sick.

30

"Don't puke," Chris warned. "Or everything will be covered with your DNA."

My stomach lurched again. I gasped for air.

"Are you going to make it?" Chris asked.

I swallowed several times. "Yes."

"Maybe you want to go outside?"

I shook my head firmly and suppressed another gagging sensation as well as I could. "No, I'll be fine."

Chris stared at me for a long while, and only when he was sure that I had it under control did he turn back to the corpse. He got down on all fours, his face just a few centimeters from the plastic sheeting. "Dark spots on the neck," he said. "As far as I can see, someone put his hands around her throat and squeezed with all his might."

He leaned forward to get a different angle. "Most likely the larynx was crushed. There's usually a lot of passion behind such acts."

"Passion?"

"Well, choking is a very personal way to kill someone. Incidentally, she's been dead for some time. Three days, I would say."

"And what does that mean?"

Chris sat up halfway. He motioned toward the bulky plastic package. "That, Alicia, means that we're on the right track."

"What makes you think so?"

"Someone clearly wanted to prevent our dead friend here from talking. Or maybe she was even directly involved in the murder of Miriam Morgenroth."

Something inside me refused to comprehend what he said. Thoughts raced through my head. I hastily spit out my next words. "We can't be certain that Miriam is dead. Nobody can. Maybe . . . maybe she's still alive and is waiting somewhere that I . . ."

Chris started to reply, forced a cough, and then looked out the window. A wave of immense sadness rushed over me as I realized what he wanted to tell me.

"We . . ." I stammered, "we have to notify the police. Straight away."

"Are you sure?"

"Listen. There's a body. A murder happened in this apartment—we know that. We need to . . ."

Chris tried to push the plastic package back under the bed. "Can you lend me a hand?" he said between heavy breaths.

"What should I do?" I asked, shocked.

"Lift the bed a little. The body has already begun to bloat."

"Are you crazy?" I shouted. "That will make us accomplices. I've been in prison once. I'm not going back."

To my great surprise, Chris laughed. "If we call my colleagues in, they'll ask questions. They'll want to know how we got in. Why we were even here in the first place. For days, if not weeks, we'll shuttle from one authority to the next, answering questions. Detectives, prosecutors, psychologists—the whole nine yards."

"So what?"

"Time will get away from us. If we call the police, we won't be able to keep searching for your friend Miriam. Our trail will go cold. The murderer or murderers will escape."

"You want to just leave the body behind?"

Chris shrugged. "She isn't bothering anyone. And she did live here."

Reluctantly, I went to the bed and lifted the frame enough that Chris could shove the long package back under.

"She'll be found anyway, eventually." I tried one last time.

Chris stood up. He made an effort to make his movements look easy, but he didn't succeed. I saw a layer of sweat form on his forehead. "In a couple of weeks at the latest, when her mailbox overflows, someone will notice. Maybe sooner if family or friends begin to worry. Unpleasant odors won't be an issue. Our perpetrator was very careful about that." Chris stopped. Then he grinned. He actually seemed amused. "Man, will they be surprised when they look under the bed."

"How can you make jokes about this?" In my horrified anger, I could barely get the words out.

Chris did not respond. Instead, he looked around the room. "Have you found the laptop yet?"

I shook my head.

"Let's search the living room again."

We moved carefully around the coffee table and the chairs. Chris opened every drawer again and even checked behind the television.

"Nothing," he said finally. "The killer took it."

I pointed in the direction of the bedroom. "She was murdered for a laptop?"

"Not specifically for the laptop. Rather, I'm guessing, for what she had saved on it. And when we find the laptop, then—" Chris broke off his sentence, narrowed his eyes, and whistled through his teeth. "What do we have here?"

He made a few steps and stood in front of the telephone. A red light was blinking on the base station. "Should we see who called the corpse?" He pressed a button, and an automated woman's voiced droned, "You have four new messages."

The first was from the property manager, giving a date when the electric meter would be read. Then an employee from a car dealership, informing her that the car was due for its forty thousand-kilometer checkup. The next message was just a dial tone. Apparently, the caller had hung up without saying a single word.

After the tone, a woman's voice rang out. "Hello, Andy! It's me, Franzi!" she shouted. She obviously did not get an answer, because she continued. "Come on—pick up, Andy! . . . Andy, darling, I have something exciting to tell you . . . Are you really not there? Or did you already leave again? . . . Man, I'm about to explode! I can't even believe it! . . . I just got out of my talk with Morgenroth. And it's exactly like you said. Every word is true." A strange, distorted sound could be heard. Some sort of cheer. "I can only say one thing, Andy. We've hit the jackpot!" Again, a shout for joy, and then she sang, "Twinkle, twinkle little star, how I wonder where you are. Up above the world so high, like a diamond in my eye." The line went dead.

31

We stepped into the hall, and Chris quietly closed the front door. He removed a tissue from his pocket and began wiping the doorbell clean. "That is the only thing we've touched," he explained.

When he was finished, he put the tissue back in his pocket, and we made our way downstairs. The building was as still as it had been when we arrived. Only the muffled clamor of traffic could be heard.

We had almost reached the first floor when the sound of water splashing in a bucket came from a nearby room. Somebody coughed. Rubber soles squeaked on wet tiles.

Chris laid his hand on my shoulder and signaled with a movement of his head for me to stop. He bent to my ear and whispered, "The cleaning lady."

Paralyzed with terror, I stood still and did not dare to breathe. Any moment, she would come out of the maintenance room and see us. Later, she'd be the one to identify us in a lineup.

"Quick, we'll go the back way!" Chris hissed. Without waiting for my response, he grabbed me by the arm and pulled me along.

Four, five, six steps, then we reached a scuffed-up door and exited into a courtyard. Bicycles, trash cans, a few clotheslines, an old garden chair, and a table with overflowing ashtrays. The windows of the surrounding buildings lifeless and empty.

"Phew," Chris said. "That was close. We have to wait a minute. It's better if we aren't seen. We stick out."

After I recovered from the moments of terror, anger welled up in me. I glared at him. "You mean to say, *I* stick out!"

"Why particularly you?" he asked blankly.

"Don't play dumb. Because of the color of my skin."

"Oh," Chris said. "I guess so. Especially since you're sneaking around with a half-dead zombie like me. We really make a great couple."

I couldn't help but laugh a little, and Chris joined in. Then he went over to the chair to take a seat. He propped both elbows on the table. The skin on his face had a translucent quality. "Just a moment and then we can go," he said.

"Lightheaded?"

Without looking up, he nodded.

I did not know how to help him. So, I took a shot at distraction. "What did you make of all that? On the answering machine?"

Chris drew a deep breath. "This Franzi is obviously our mark. She called a friend, who apparently should have been waiting for her in the apartment. Maybe he heard the message, or maybe he didn't. It doesn't really matter."

"She sounded so happy," I said and observed with relief that color was returning to his face.

"Indeed, she did." Chris sat up.

"Why would she be so happy, just from conducting a stupid interview?"

Chris deliberated a short while before answering. "I have no idea. I guess she must have learned something in the meeting with your Miriam. Something—well, she called it a jackpot, and she sang about diamonds."

I did not like the look in his eyes. "Money? That's all you can think of."

His expression grew cold. "There's nothing wrong with that. With money, you can buy beautiful things."

"Things, stuff—they're so important to you!" Suddenly, the bond that had developed between us lay shattered like shards on the ground. We had nothing in common.

Chris wanted to say something, but when he saw the expression on my face, he only curled his mouth snidely and looked in the other direction.

I turned away as well, walked around a little, and checked out the bikes absentmindedly. One of the two dumpsters was half-open. A big piece of cardboard was sticking out. I lifted the lid and shoved the carton firmly into the container. A little deeper in the bin, a shimmering pink emblem caught my eye. I took out the cardboard box and bent forward. At the bottom of the receptacle, I saw what was left of a laptop. I leaned even farther inside until I could get a hold of it.

"What have you got there?" Chris asked.

I presented him with my find. A normal looking laptop, the monitor cracked, the keyboard smashed. The cover hanging on by a hinge. Decorated with a shiny pink Hello Kitty sticker.

Chris got up and came to my side. "Is that what I think it is?"

"Without a doubt," I said. "I recognize it. Franziska Beck had this laptop with her in the clinic when she interviewed Miriam."

"That's why she was killed."

I looked more closely at the damage. "We'll never find out what was on the hard drive. Someone did a thorough job."

Chris took the laptop out of my hands to examine it from all sides. "Not necessarily. I know a person who owes me a favor, a real genius when it comes to computers. Let's see what can be salvaged. But first, I have to show you something else that I believe could be important."

32

We left the city limits behind us and drove awhile through a forest. Chris slowed his speed to turn onto some kind of private road. After a few meters, we came to a gravel parking lot. Adjacent to it was a long, low building. We got out.

"What is this?" I asked.

"A shooting range," Chris said and waited for my reaction.

"Does it belong to the police?"

"No." Chris shook his head. "It's privately owned. That's why on workdays it isn't busy until evening." As if that were an explanation as to why we were here, he set off walking. I followed.

The entrance was a steel security door. Chris got his keys out and opened it. We entered.

A wide hall with lockers, another door, and we stood on a porch of sorts. In front of us were half a dozen lanes; at the end of each hung a man-sized target in the shape of a hexagon.

Chris went past me to a rail that separated the porch from the lanes. He reached behind his back, drew his pistol, and held it out to me on a flat hand. "A Browning Hi Power nine-millimeter," he said. "Cocked and locked."

"Aha," I replied and glanced with mixed feelings at the ugly monster.

"Look at it very closely. I hope it will never come to this, but this could save your life if the need arises."

I shrugged and acted nonchalant. "Fine," I said. "If you want me to shoot at one of these cardboard dummies, I can give it a try."

"The cardboard dummy, as you call it, is twenty-five meters away. If a firearm is needed, there will be much less distance between you and the assailant."

"So?"

"So, ten meters, maybe less."

"Anyone could hit that," I said.

Chris smiled indulgently. "The assailant has already decided to hurt or even kill you. He needs less than a second to get close enough. Then he rams his knife into your body or smashes your skull with a heavy object."

"A second?" I asked doubtfully.

"He won't need more. That's the time you have. In one second, you have to assess the situation, draw your weapon, and shoot him, or . . ."

"Or what?"

"Or you're dead, like Ms. Beck. Do you remember? Not a pretty picture."

I bit my lip and nodded.

Chris pressed a small button on the railing. A whirring sound followed, and the target moved in our direction. The paper fluttered in the wind.

Chris pressed the button again. The noise stopped. The paper dummy now hung only a few steps away from us.

Although its outline was geometrical in shape, I could easily imagine a man standing in front of me.

"All right," Chris said. "On the left side of the gun at the back of the frame is a lever. The safety catch. You drop the slide safety. Then point the barrel at your target and squeeze the trigger."

"I shouldn't aim first?" I asked.

"No time. You won't be shooting at a clay pigeon."

"And where should I hit him? In a leg or an arm?"

"Forget that rubbish *right* now," Chris said. "You want the assailant on the ground. Not killing you. You shoot him where there's the least chance of missing. In the middle of his body. I'll do it once first. And watch out. It'll be loud." No sooner had he finished his sentence than he had brought the gun into firing position. Three, four earsplitting shots rang out, and I saw the bullet holes cluster together on the target. Stinging gun smoke rose in the air. I blinked.

Chris secured the weapon, turned to face me, and again presented it on an outstretched hand. "You're up."

I hesitated. Then I grabbed the pistol. It was heavier than I had expected. The target stared back at me, menacing. I imagined somebody running toward me. I dropped the safety and shot two times in the middle of the paper. I felt the hard recoil and the hammer biting into the web of my hand. In the upper half of the target, two new points of entry were now visible. So close to one another that a two-euro coin could have covered them.

Chris gave me a contemplative look, took the weapon carefully out of my hand, and secured it. "I think you get the picture," he said.

33

The doorman led us through a veritable maze of corridors until we reached the elevator. Together, we rode to the fourth floor. Down another long hallway. He came to a stop in front of a massive glass door. Black writing on a white sign read "Zacharias and Partners—Consultants, Network Security." He swiped a key card through a slit, and with a hum, the door sprang open.

"From here you should be able to find your way, Inspector Winkler," he said.

Chris thanked him with a slight smile.

We walked past tall dark doors, through which neither a hint of light nor sound passed. Eventually, we came to a stop. Chris knocked and entered without waiting. I followed.

The room was chilly. It smelled pleasantly albeit artificially like lavender. Bluish flickering screens. Beeping, buzzing PCs, computer entrails of every variety, a ganglion of cables as far as the eye could see. Hard drives hot-wired together or standing alone. Audio speakers.

And in the middle of this chaos, a young woman. Twenty-five at most, slim, tall, a model-like figure. And, of course, blond—what else should I have expected?

As soon as she saw us, she smiled at Chris. "Well, look what the cat dragged in."

Only now did she seem to notice me. She threw me a brief perplexed glare before returning her attention to Chris. "Short hair," she said. "Really short. It suits you. You resemble . . . what's that guy's name? He's in those movies."

Chris grinned. "That happens to me all the time lately."

"Damn it," the blonde said. "His name is escaping me right now. His character drives a fast car and is always robbing banks. He saves a Chinese girl, I think. Do you know who I'm talking about?"

"I have no idea," Chris said. "Oh, by the way, this is Alicia Petersen." He turned to me and gestured in the direction of the blonde. "Alicia, may I introduce you to Ms. Plodeck."

"Ms. Plodeck," the blonde aped him. "Since when are we so formal? You used to always call me Saskia, or even something *else.*"

I thought I caught a fleeting hint of embarrassment pass over Chris's mien. But he got it quickly under control. "I need your help, Saskia."

The blonde swept a strand of bright hair out of her face, and a gratified smile danced across her lips. "That's nothing new."

Chris raised the plastic bag that he was carrying, opened it, and revealed Franziska Beck's laptop.

Saskia contorted her mouth. "Yikes. That thing sure is dusty."

"Magnetic powder," Chris explained.

"Oh. You searched for fingerprints."

"Of course. But it was cleaned meticulously before it was destroyed. I didn't even find a partial print."

Saskia took the notebook carefully, set it on her work-table, and opened it. "Cheap gear," she said. "Completely destroyed. Somebody sure wanted to be on the safe side." She bent over and inspected the keyboard more closely. "The hard drive has definitely been trashed."

"There's no chance at all to get at the data?"

"Well," Saskia replied slowly, "I like to think there's the possibility of a chance. If we're lucky, I can fish out one or two pieces of information."

"Lucky?" Chris asked.

Saskia cleared her throat in a self-important way. "Well, luck really has nothing to do with it. More to do with my prowess. But you already know that."

She stared at Chris, obviously pleased with herself. "I need time. And I can't promise you anything. But by noon tomorrow, I should have a better idea."

"That would be great," he said.

Saskia studied him more closely. A trace of wrinkles formed on that beautiful high forehead. "You look tired."

"I am," Chris said.

Saskia checked her watch. "I'm free in half an hour. You can come to me like the old days and *relax*." She empha-sized the word *relax* in a clearly salacious manner, as if I weren't even in the room. What a bitch.

Chris smiled. "Not today."

"Oh." Saskia leaned casually on a cabinet. She pointed at Chris and then at me. "Have I misunderstood some-thing? Are you two somehow . . .?"

Chris remained silent, but I interjected, "No. We're not."

Saskia smiled at me condescendingly. "I would have wondered, honey. You're not exactly his typical prey. You don't look bad or anything. But how should I put it? Just extremely . . . *athletic*. And of course, gentlemen prefer blondes, if you know what I mean."

I was about to tell her what she could do with her opinion, but luckily, I remembered in the nick of time how badly we needed the information that might still be on that computer.

Chris saved the situation. "We'll come back again tomorrow. And if you can restore the data, I'll be tremendously indebted."

Saskia sighed. "Well, that's at least a start."

34

The rolling suitcase contained all the clothes I needed for the next days. Instead of ringing, I used Chris's spare key and entered his apartment. Chris was sprawled out on the leather couch with his legs propped up on the coffee table. His pistol sat alongside an aerosol can of gun oil, a rag, and a fine brush. Obviously, he had been cleaning his weapon.

"You're late," he said.

I stowed the suitcase in a corner and raised the sack that I carried in my other hand. "Chinese. I figured you'd enjoy something like that."

Chris shrugged. "When I absolutely have to . . ."

I went to the dining table, which Chris had already set, and placed the white cardboard boxes in the middle. Their contents gave off an appetizing aroma.

"I've cooled the wine." Chris opened the refrigerator and pulled out a bottle.

I glanced at the label. "White wine? That'll go well."

We sat. Chris poured us both a glass, and I served the rice and duck.

For a while, we ate in silence.

"I was starting to get worried," Chris said between bites.

"About me?"

"To drive to Starnberg and back doesn't take three hours."

I took a sip of wine. "You're right. I spoke with the office manager at the clinic about my leave. That went quickly; Georg—I mean, Dr. Vogt—had already taken care of everything. And then I needed some time for myself."

"Oh yeah?" Chris said reproachfully.

"*Yeah.* I was swimming."

Chris looked at me as if I had a screw loose. "Swimming?"

"I'm training for a race. Long distance. Eight kilometers in the open sea."

Chris poured some more wine for himself. "Sounds interesting. But also demanding."

"You have no idea why I'd do it, right?"

Chris smiled sheepishly. Sometimes he reminded me of a boy. "You're just different."

"Different than whom? Saskia?"

Chris exhaled audibly. "Tastes scrumptious. Is there any more duck?"

I shoved one of the cartons in his direction, and he helped himself to the rest.

"What do you think she'll find on the laptop?" I asked after a bit.

"No idea," Chris said quickly. He seemed happy that I'd changed the topic.

"I can still remember the scene so clearly," I said. "Miriam really didn't want to speak with Ms. Beck at all. She got terribly agitated when she came barging in with that laptop."

"Hmm," Chris said. "Why do people usually get excited? When someone threatens harm or when they're uncomfortable. That entire PhD story from Ms. Beck was presumably just an excuse. In reality, it was about something more obvious—it probably *was* about the banking business."

"Has anyone ever told you that you're fixated on money?"

Chris ignored my taunt. "Maybe it's about extortion. Or revenge. Or both."

"Revenge?"

"Yeah. Falk has been completely wiped out by Dr. Vogt and your lovely Miriam. Professionally as well as physically. If that doesn't provide a motive for revenge ..." He tapped his fork on his dinner plate two or three times. The porcelain protested with sharp clangs.

I grew angry. "You always want to implicate Miriam."

"And you, you're absolutely blind when it comes to her." Chris looked at me. "When people like her direct a huge bank, closing deals of a horrendous magnitude—that just doesn't happen without walking over dead bodies."

"Dead bodies?"

Chris waved his fork in the air. "In a figurative sense. Where wood is chopped, splinters must fall. Miriam might have been super nice to you, but when it came to business, I'm sure she was hard as nails. And I'm almost certain the evidence of that will be found on this laptop."

"Now that we're back on the topic of Saskia," I started in, "she seems to be superwoman. She can give you everything."

Chris's eyes sparkled in the light. "You're right. Saskia *is* fantastic."

I grunted. "Of course, she is. Just as fantastic as that other blonde that slammed the doors at the clinic. Who was that again? Oh yeah. Your fiancée. Or better put, your *ex*-fiancée? You really have a talent for picking rotten women."

A storm broke out in Chris's eyes. "Why rotten? They're both great-looking."

I laughed dismissively. "You said it. They look really good. But they're good for nothing. Gone as soon as you need them. Selfish, superficial tramps. Egotistical bitches."

"Ah! Miss perfect! And you, of course, are completely different!"

I sat back. "Yes, I am."

"You have absolutely no faults?"

I leaned forward with my hands on the table. "Of course, I have faults. Many, in fact. But in contrast to your souped-up Barbie dolls, you can count on me. One hundred percent."

Chris threw his fork on the table. "Wow! You should have been a psychologist. You've seen Saskia and my ex-fiancée one time in your life, and you have them all figured out!" He was leaning forward now too.

"I know this species. Believe me. Great looks, wet lips, trusting eyes, and a heart of stone. I have two half-sisters. They're like that. Cold and calculating."

"Cold and calculating?" A muscle on Chris's face twitched. "And you, you're an opinionated, bullheaded pain in the ass."

I wanted to answer him. But before I could begin, he brought his head closer, wrapped a hand around the back of my neck, and kissed me.

At first, I let it happen. Then I removed his hand and pushed him away.

Chris eyed me with a mixture of surprise and embarrassment.

"I decide who I'm going to sleep with," I said.

Chris cleared his throat. We stared at one another. "I didn't mean it like that," he managed to say, his voice slightly strained.

I smiled. "Oh really?" This time I leaned forward and kissed him. I did not hurry.

When I pulled away, I had the feeling that he'd grown distant. I got up, walked around the table, and stood by him. "What is it?" I asked.

He remained silent and avoided my eyes.

"That's your problem," I said. "Quit brooding over it. Forget the cancer and the chemo. Come to bed. The rest will follow."

He hesitated again. Then he joined me.

Once in the bedroom, we looked at each other. Silently. I gazed in his eyes; their green struck me as being darker than usual. In an instant, I was transported to my Hallig, to the place in the sea where the currents are most fierce. The sea there takes on a nearly identical dark-green color, as if to make people aware of the danger and to encourage them to go back before it's too late.

I grabbed the hem of his T-shirt, and he let me pull it over his head. The skin of his torso glistened, luminous. Despite his sickness, his muscles were firm and defined. They felt good as I ran my hand over them.

He released a subdued sigh. We kissed again. And then it was his hands that went exploring, his touch at first careful and tentative, then incrementally more urgent and demanding.

Tonight belonged to us. This night neither of us would be alone.

35

Sonja, Marko and Sven

Theirs was the only vehicle. The rest stop where they were parked was surrounded by tall pines and offered toilet facilities, overflowing trash cans, and the obligatory benches.

On the nearby highway, the headlights of the cars raced by like a frenzy of comets. The constant droning of the motors enveloped them making the impression of a cocoon.

Sven had lined up two nice and neat rows of fine powder on the vanity mirror. He rolled up a ten-euro bill, lodged one end of the tube in his nostril, and began to inhale the first rail.

"Hey!" snapped Sonja. "What kind of asshole snorts up everything by himself?"

Sven made a grunting sound before he leaned back in the passenger seat. The rolled bill was still stuck in his nose.

"Didn't you hear me? Don't snort it all up by yourself! I've driven all day while you lay in the back sleeping. And then you act like you don't have to share."

Sven's body began to quiver. His skull slammed a couple times against the headrest. "Don't get so excited," he stammered. "There's enough there."

"Enough?" Sonja growled. "I prepared that jet fuel yesterday. One portion for each of us. And you hoard the shit as if Marko and I don't exist."

In the rearview mirror, Sonja caught a glimpse of a car coasting slowly up behind them with its headlights off.

"You know what?" she continued. "That's the problem with you. You don't care about anybody but yourself."

"Me?" Sven said, completely taken aback.

"Yes. You. Marko and I always have to watch after you. Never the other way around."

"But my work . . ." Sven said. He wanted to add something else but had forgotten what they were even talking about.

"Your work. Always your work. I figure out every detail, get the assignments, and procure money and equipment. And what do you do?"

"Money, we have plenty of money." Sven's eyes were glazed over.

"Of course, we have enough money. But that's not thanks to you. I always handle the negotiations. Or do you think these guys would fork over that kinda scratch to you?"

A knock sounded on Sonja's window, and as she turned toward the noise, she saw a woman standing next to the driver's door. Khaki pants, green jacket, a 9mm with a built-in cocking lever secured in its holster. Your typical pig.

Sonja smiled amiably through the window and then slowly rotated her head toward Sven. "See what you've gotten us into? This is all your fault."

The pounding on the window returned. This time more insistent.

With a resigned sigh, Sonja pressed a button, and the window rolled down.

"Hello?" Sonja chirped.

The officer didn't even try to smile. "Is everything all right here?"

Sonja thought for a moment before nodding emphatically. "Sure. Everything's splendid."

The cop was quite young. Maybe twenty-five. Seemed to have a good figure. Obviously able-bodied. And she was bursting with self-confidence. *The police—to fucking protect and serve.*

"What are you doing here?" the pig asked.

Again, Sonja thought long and hard, raised her hand, and waved it toward the windshield. "Well, this here is a rest area. We came from"—she twisted awkwardly in her seat—"there on the highway. And we want"—she turned back around and made a decisive gesture forward—"to go there. You understand? To continue on our journey. But first we're taking a break."

The officer put her right hand on her holster. "And what are you doing in the vehicle?"

Sonja conveyed the impression of wanting to give a serious reply. "Sitting. We are sitting here."

"And the passenger?" The cop kept drilling her. "He's holding a mirror in his hand."

Sonja grinned and in the process winked conspiratorially. "You saw that? The poor guy is terribly vain."

The exhaust of a car thundered one, two times. The blasts were nearly lost in the noise of the traffic.

"I am ordering you to get out of the car now." The officer's voice sounded metallic.

"Get out?" Sonja made big puppy-dog eyes. "Why should we get out? We're happy to be sitting."

"Do as I tell you. My colleague will be here in a second. And then we're going to search your vehicle." Without taking her eyes off Sonja, the police officer signaled to her partner, who was waiting in the squad car, to come back her up.

"I don't understand why you're acting like this," Sonja replied. "We haven't done anything wrong."

Steps were heard as the second cop approached.

At the side of the first officer's head, the barrel of a gun appeared. A shot rang hollow, and the woman's brains splattered across the windshield. Her body crumpled limply to the ground like a marionette whose strings had been severed. No longer a person, just a mound of flesh and bones. And an exceptionally stylish uniform.

Sonja leaned out of the window to have a look at the corpse. Then she lifted her eyes and took a gander at Marko standing next to it.

"Did you handle the other cop back there?" she asked.

"Of course," he answered. "Twice in the face and done."

"Great. *Done*," Sonja retorted. "How many times have I told you that you have to watch out when you blow someone away? Now this stupid bitch's brains are all over our windshield."

In a conciliatory gesture, Marko raised his hand, in which he held the smoking automatic. "I'm sorry, Sonja."

"I'm sorry," Sonja imitated him. "You're always sorry. But now you and Sven are going to wash this mess off the car."

Sonja looked around at Sven. He was sleeping, his eyes half-open. Snoring. And of course, the mirror had fallen to the ground, and the weasel dust was strewn over the floor mats. Sonja angrily kicked Sven several times, but he didn't even notice.

"Well then, move," she said to Marko. "You're gonna clean that up right now."

"Don't get so excited. Of course, I will." Marko hurried to reassure her. "Should I get rid of the bodies too?"

"What for? In less than two hours, they'll find the cop car. Then they'll know exactly what happened, anyway. But be careful and don't forget to collect your bullet casings."

"And the pigs? They'll be hot on our heels. They're sure to find the RV's tracks."

"Marko. Marko." Sonja shook her head sympathetically. "It's nighttime now. Dark. Before the assessment of the forensic evidence gets that far, we'll be long gone and will have already swapped vehicles. They won't find shit."

36

I woke, as always, alone.

Only it was not my bed and not my apartment.

I sat up and searched for my things. They lay scattered throughout the room. A total mess. A lot like what was going on inside me.

I got up, opened the closet, and found a terry cloth bathrobe. I threw it on, fished my toiletries out of my suitcase, and headed to the bathroom. Living room and kitchen seemed quiet and deserted. There was no sign of Chris.

He had one of those ultramodern showers. Water sprayed me from all sides. At first annoying but with time quite pleasant. I toweled my hair half-dry—my frizz didn't require much more attention than that—slipped back into the bathrobe, and brushed my teeth thoroughly.

When I emerged from the bathroom, the smell of fresh coffee hit me like a Mack truck. Chris busied himself in the kitchen. He wore jeans and a light-colored T-shirt. He had set the table. Plates, cups, cutlery, orange juice, and fresh rolls.

I guess I should prepare myself for the worst, I thought.

"Morning," I said.

Chris gave me a smile that almost succeeded in hiding his nervousness.

I looked at the coffee machine. "You know that I can't stomach that black crude."

Chris pointed at an electric kettle. "Ceylon tea, hand cut, top quality."

"Aha." I raised my eyebrows skeptically.

I sat in the same chair as the night before. Chris carried two pots to the table. First, he filled my cup with tea, and then he poured himself a large coffee. Despite my fears, the tea exuded a wonderfully delicate aroma.

We ate in silence. A couple of times, Chris seemed about to say something, but I looked to the side on purpose and acted indifferent. With this technique, I could nip every conversation in the bud. It worked splendidly.

Finally, we finished. I poured myself some more tea.

"I've been thinking." Chris eventually spoke.

"Sounds promising." I grinned. The hint of a blush spread across Chris's face.

"Until we find out what was on our dead postgrad's laptop, we're pretty much at a standstill. So, we could use the time to talk to the professor who was chairing her dissertation committee. If we dig around a little, we'll probably learn why Ms. Beck contacted Miriam in the first place."

"But there are a lot of professors," I said.

"I already thought about that," he said with a somewhat chastising look. "I found four professors in the History Department at the university. Of those, only one specializes in the twentieth century. I think we should start with that one."

"Agreed." I drank my tea and put the cup down. *"And. . ."* I added. Chris looked up at the sound of my voice and eyed me guardedly.

"And," I repeated, "there's one thing I have to make absolutely clear. What happened last night and this breakfast with the expensive tea don't have any meaning."

The spark that had lit up Chris's eyes all morning disappeared, as if it had never even been there at all.

"I'm determined to find Miriam," I said. "And as you've already pointed out, you have your own goals. You're only interested in the big money."

The corner of Chris's mouth began to twitch. I raised my hand reassuringly. "I have no problem with that. Really, I don't. But it's not what I had in mind. So, let me be clear, there is not now, nor in the future, going to be anything between us. And it's better like that. If we are aware of this, neither of us will be distracted by some illusion."

Chris grabbed his coffee. He didn't take his eyes off me. "Last night, I didn't get the feeling that you were uninterested. Quite the contrary."

"Sex," I replied. "I like it just as much as the next guy. And that's why I want to reiterate that we have only recently teamed up, and anything that has happened or might still come to pass means nothing. Although, the tea was a nice gesture."

As I spoke, the expression on his face changed. Disdain replaced uncertainty. "How can you be so emotionless?"

I gathered the plates and silverware. "I'm not emotionless. I'm just being realistic. I need you, because without you, I'll never find Miriam. And you"—I took the cup out of his hand and set it on top of the dirty dishes—"you aren't with me because of my pretty eyes. We're business partners. No more and no less."

37

P rofessor Fembach's office was small. About the size of my dorm room. A window facing the park. Floor-to-ceiling shelves stuffed with books and files along the left wall and a narrow desk with a PC on top. One of those nameplates with interchangeable letters read "Prof. Carla A. Fembach."

Professor Fembach rolled back on her reclining executive chair; Chris and I sat opposite her on uncomfortable plastic stools. The intimate atmosphere of an oral exam.

"It's extremely nice of you," Chris said, "to find time for us, despite your busy schedule."

The professor was a tall, slim woman in her late thirties. Close-cut hair dyed black. Rimless glasses. Pantsuit, white blouse. Superbly manicured but not painted fingernails.

"You work as a detective, if I understood you correctly?" she asked.

Chris nodded. "Ms. Petersen and I are investigating the disappearance of Ms. Miriam Morgenroth. Maybe you've read about it?"

She nodded. "Well, yes. But what does that have to do with me?"

"With you personally?" Chris conjured up a winning smile. "It actually has nothing to do with you. But," he paused dramatically, "Ms. Morgenroth was visited by one of your doctoral students, Franziska Beck, shortly before her disappearance."

"Of course," Professor Fembach said pensively. "Ms. Beck's dissertation."

"Exactly," Chris said. "We want to ensure that Ms. Morgenroth didn't make any offhand comments that might be of interest. Or maybe Ms. Beck noticed something that could be connected to Ms. Morgenroth's subsequent disappearance. You must understand—Ms. Beck was one of the last people to see Ms. Morgenroth."

The professor frowned. "Wouldn't it be better to ask Ms. Beck these questions directly?"

Chris made an apologetic gesture. "Believe me, we've tried. But for the life of us, we can't reach Ms. Beck right now."

Professor Fembach adjusted her glasses and reflected, taking a remarkably long time before she finally sighed. "You've had a similar experience as me. Ms. Beck and I had an appointment yesterday, which she missed without canceling. I've never known her to do this. It's not like her to not at least call if she can't make it to one of our meetings."

"I'm sure there's a good reason for that," Chris said. "But time is of the essence for us. So maybe you could share some information that might help our investigation."

"Like what?"

"The topic of her dissertation, for starters. Why Ms. Beck contacted Ms. Morgenroth in the first place."

Professor Fembach seemed to contemplate for a while. "I don't really know how it could help, but the subject of Ms. Beck's treatise is no national secret. Ms. Beck is doing her doctoral dissertation on Jewish bankers during World War Two."

Chris hid his disappointment. "Jewish bankers and World War Two? What does that have to do with Ms. Morgenroth?"

The professor's smile was meant to appear indulgent. But to me it seemed contrived. "Before the National Socialists seized power in 1933, there were a handful of Jewish banking families in Germany. Ms. Beck's dissertation deals with their fate during and after the Second World War."

"Oh," Chris said. "That's it? More than seventy years have passed since then."

"That's why Ms. Morgenroth represented an extraordinarily rare eyewitness of the period for Ms. Beck. She is one of the few remaining survivors of this terrible tragedy. Ms. Beck was extremely excited when Ms. Morgenroth agreed to speak about that time and her own personal experiences."

"Hearing you describe it makes it sound interesting."

"Academically, highly interesting," the professor agreed. "My secretary can print the rough outline I have of Ms. Beck's thesis. Five pages at most. If you really think it will be helpful."

"Sure, why not. Thank you very much." Chris got up, so I did as well.

He held out his hand. "As soon as Ms. Beck contacts you, I'd appreciate it if you could tell her that she should get in touch with me immediately. You understand. We have to follow up on every lead."

Professor Fembach walked around her desk. "Of course. You can count on it. Are you even certain that Ms. Morgenroth has fallen victim to foul play? I mean, the lady was fairly well advanced in age. And possibly . . ."

"An accident?" Chris picked up where she left off. "I think that's highly probable. Again, thank you very much for your time, professor."

"Don't mention it."

"I always had a much different image of professors," Chris added. "Much stuffier and—please don't take this the wrong way—older."

Professor Fembach beamed. "Thank you for the compliment. In fact, I'm one of the youngest professors to hold a chair at the university."

Chris beamed as well. He pointed to the nameplate. "Carla A. Fembach," he read aloud. "May I ask what the *A* stands for? Anja, perhaps? My sister's name is Anja."

"No. Andrea. Oddly, no one ever called me Carla, as far as I can remember. Although Carla sounds more reputable. It fits better with my position."

"But to your friends you're Andrea?" Chris said. I had never seen him be so charming.

Professor Fembach smiled again. "Half-right. *Andy.* My friends call me Andy."

By then, we were in the front room. Professor Fembach asked an elderly secretary to print out the abstract of Ms. Beck's doctoral dissertation. With the excuse that she had to prepare for a lecture, she disappeared into her office and closed the door quietly behind her.

We waited for the printer to do its job. In the meantime, I looked around the secretary's office. Postcards were pinned to a corkboard next to a sheet of names and room numbers for oral exams. Two orchids sat on the windowsill. In a glass cabinet, under the pretentious title "The Hall of Fame," was a list of donors to the department. Logos from some well-known corporations. A framed picture of an old man. Gray hair, tortoiseshell glasses. Below the photo, an engraved brass plate: "Maximilian Falk, patron and sponsor of the Department of History."

When I turned to Chris, I saw that he too was studying the photograph. I recognized satisfaction on his face. But there was also something new showing: the thrill of the chase.

38

We managed to snag a nice table in one of the many outdoor cafés. The traffic moved sluggishly; the clock already showed well past noon. I finished my sandwich, washed it down with water, and looked at Chris, who heroically fought with a huge Caesar salad.

"Don't ever do that to me," I said.

Chris looked at me questioningly and continued chewing.

"You understood me very well."

Again, the silent, puzzled look from him.

"You manipulate people," I continued. "Find their weakness and then dig at it until they tell you everything you want to know."

Chris speared a few leaves of lettuce and shoved them into his mouth. Again, he said nothing. He swallowed, wiped his lips with a paper napkin, and then laid it next to his plate. "That's my job."

"Your *job*! Is there anything about you that's authentic? Was the down-and-out guy in rehab real, at least? Or was he also just playing a role?"

Chris stared at me intently, but this time he knew that I would not look away. A cold smile crept across his face. "Why do you care? You said yourself that we're merely business partners. I don't understand why you're getting upset like this now."

I laid both hands on the table, maybe a tad too hard. The dishes rattled faintly. "You're just not being honest."

"Honest?" Chris repeated the word as if he'd never heard it before. "I want to explain something to you. People crave to tell you everything that's on their minds. And do you know why? Because no one listens to them. Everyone is only interested in his own crap. The only thing that I do is ask the right questions and then pay attention to how they answer."

What he said did make sense. But it annoyed me all the same. No, it made me downright furious.

Chris sat coolly across from me, observing my reaction. I wouldn't give him the pleasure of watching me lose control. So, I smiled at him sweetly. "We've already established that you have ulterior motives. But we can't do anything about that. So, back to the case. The photo of Falk in the receptionist's office—you saw it too?"

I could tell that my abrupt change of topic took him by surprise. It really threw him for a loop, which I noted with immense satisfaction. Now I could sit back and watch him squirm.

"Of course," he said with some hesitancy. "A man who had every reason to hate Miriam Morgenroth and take revenge on her finances the department of the student who coincidentally interviewed Ms. Morgenroth shortly before her disappearance."

175

"You believe there's a connection?"

"Alicia, I don't believe in shit. Especially not coincidences."

I nodded. "If anything, the professor was lying."

Again, astonishment flashed in his eyes. "That didn't escape you either?"

"It was obvious. The professor's friends call her Andy. And Franziska Beck left a message on her answering machine for an Andy."

Chris raised his nonalcoholic beer to toast me. "A message for her sweetheart. Andy. Only the sweetheart in this case is a she. The professor knows all too well what her girlfriend was looking for at Miriam's. And she doesn't want us to find out, under any circumstances. That's why she let her secretary print out that academic babble, which at best we can use to line a birdcage. Besides that, she's worried because her lover hasn't gotten in contact with her. She tried to conceal her feelings but didn't succeed."

"And? Are we going to let the professor off the hook just like that?"

A wide grin spread across Chris's face before he shook his head. "Absolutely not. Where would the fun be in that? But first things first. We need to see what, if anything, Saskia could rescue from the laptop. Maybe that will give us one or two pieces of useful information. And then we'll go back to our friendly Professor Fembach and rake her over the coals. If my assessment of her is accurate, she won't hold out very long. She's used to having the upper hand because of her profession. When her skin is on the line, and she's suddenly a suspect in a criminal investigation, she'll be quick to cooperate. That you can be sure of."

I glanced across the street at the multilevel concrete block where Saskia worked. "Zacharias and Partners Consulting" shone in silver lettering right under the windows, spanning the entire second floor. Just then, the glass door opened, and a slim blond woman stepped out. She paused and looked around as if she were searching for us. But I knew that in reality she was merely striking a pose in order to stage an unparalleled entrance. Admittedly, she had a lot to offer. Long legs, a semitransparent little summer dress with a plunging neckline. Once she was sure that we had appreciated her appearance sufficiently, she floated across the street in her heels, without squandering as much as a glance at the drivers, who immediately yielded the right of way to her.

She walked directly up to our table. Chris rose, pulled out a chair for her, and Saskia sat down—or better put, gracefully came to rest.

"I didn't see you right away," she lied, and did it poorly.

When neither of us responded, she laid the laptop, which she had tucked under her arm, onto the table. "The notebook is just scrap metal. But I was able to access a few files. Not much." Saskia handed Chris a USB stick. "Everything that I found is on this. I didn't look at the stuff; I imagine that was in your best interest."

Chris took the stick, and their hands touched for half a second. Saskia smiled victoriously.

Clearing his throat, Chris pulled his arm back. "Needless to say, Saskia, I'm tremendously indebted to you."

Saskia brushed a strand of hair off her forehead. She leaned forward in her chair to look deep into Chris's eyes. "You know where I live," she purred. "You can drop by sometime for a visit."

Chris observed her before smiling noncommittally. "Yeah. Maybe."

Saskia blinked in astonishment. "Maybe? I don't make offers like that often. There once was a time when I wouldn't have had to say it twice."

Chris remained silent, and Saskia focused on me. "I've forgotten your name. But that's not important. Anyway, I have to warn you. Chris comes off as incredibly nice, but in reality, he's an egocentric asshole."

Now it was my turn to look into her radiant blue eyes. And I said, "Well then, you'd make a good couple."

39

I sat next to Chris on the couch. He placed his laptop on the small table in front of us and booted it up. In order to see better, we had drawn the drapes. The sun could barely penetrate the thick material; a gloomy dimness dominated the room. Outside it was hot. In here, humid and sticky. I was drinking sparkling water straight from the bottle.

Chris stuck Saskia's thumb drive into the USB port. The file manager opened automatically after a short time, displaying a hierarchy of folders.

"All right," he said. "We'll systematically go through these from top to bottom. Let's see what we find." He double-clicked the first folder.

Images. Vacation pictures. A white sand beach. Blue sea. Chairs with sun umbrellas. A smiling Franziska Beck, tan and sporting a bikini. Once again, Franziska Beck in the water. A sunset. A church. Franziska Beck and the chair of her dissertation committee, Professor Fembach—hand in hand, presumably taken by a random passing stranger. The two looked into the camera, relaxed and in high spirits.

The motifs repeated with different backgrounds. Nothing spectacular, nothing we didn't already know. Franziska Beck and her professor had clearly been a couple. But that didn't make us any wiser. Not one iota.

Chris clicked on the next folder.

A tax declaration from the previous year for one Franziska Beck. Incomplete. Apparently, she had tried to deduct a nonexistent home office.

Next folder, same procedure.

Photos again. This time black and white. A tall wrought-iron gate, on it written in menacing letters: *ARBEIT MACHT FREI.* A picture of prisoners, half-starved, dressed in rags. A guard tower, barbed wire, then a view of a gas chamber from the inside. Corpses, wedged together, frozen in mortal agony. Vacant eyes, parted mouths. Other prisoners, women, then men, and lastly a photograph of children. Unspeakable misery, horrific suffering.

"A concentration camp," I stated.

"Definitely," Chris said.

Outside the window, the afternoon sun beat down mercilessly from a bright-blue sky. And although it had become even warmer in the apartment, I was suddenly freezing. We viewed every photo again before Chris opened the next folder.

Scanned documents. The name Morgenroth appeared repeatedly; only the first names and dates of birth changed. An old passport bearing a Star of David. Inside, a yellowed black-and-white photo of a little girl with blond hair. Staring back at me earnestly. I could sense desperation in her eyes. Miriam Morgenroth.

Chris coughed. Quietly at first. He held his hand in front of his mouth. Then a convulsion shook his body. Beads of sweat formed on his brow, and even in the low light, I could see how his face lost all color, becoming pale and lackluster.

"Hey," I said and nudged him gently.

"What?" he struggled to get the word out.

"I want on the laptop too."

"But—"

"No *buts*. I know my way around computers at least as well as you." Without waiting for his reply, I pulled the laptop to me and put my fingers on the keyboard. "So, if you want, you can sit back and watch me work."

Chris obeyed, with notable reluctance.

I handed him my bottle. "You can have my water. I'm not thirsty."

Chris forced a smile and took a small sip and then a larger one.

I selected the next file.

An extract from a newspaper. On the upper right edge, it was dated "5th of October 1948."

"This should be interesting," I said.

"What does it say?" Chris leaned forward.

"No way," I yelled. "You're going to sit there and relax."

Frowning, Chris accepted his fate.

"Well," I began. "It's entitled 'The Bankers Morgenroth and Vogt Reunited'."

"Sounds interesting," Chris mumbled.

"Doesn't it?" I agreed, before I continued reading the article out loud: "The Vogt Bank, founded by Leopold Vogt and Adam Morgenroth, was owned by the two families for decades. Then the National Socialists came to power. Leopold Vogt relates: *In 1937, the political situation had unfortunately deteriorated so much that I became worried sick for my friend Adam and his family. So, we decided that I would take over the company as a formality and purchase his holdings. In reality, we had agreed that he and his family should leave the country until the villainous Nazi regime was overthrown. I obtained forged documents for Adam and his family and helped them flee. At first, everything went well, but as they were waiting in Hamburg for the ship that would take them to stay with distant relatives in England, they were apprehended and arrested. I later learned they were brought to the concentration camp in Auschwitz. Supposedly, the entire family perished there.*

After the war, I did not want to acknowledge this absolutely horrendous tragedy. I researched incessantly, and to my great delight, I found Adam's youngest daughter, Miriam, sick and destitute in a refugee camp. She is now fourteen and alone in the world. I have taken her in, she is getting the best medical care available, and I will raise her alongside my son. I have already signed over her father's fortune to her and will manage her assets in a trust until she comes of age. That is the least I can do to honor the memory of my good friend Adam. Miriam has returned to her family." I finished and studied the photo that accompanied the article. A stout elderly man in a suit and black overcoat holding a skinny blond girl by the hand. Both smiled into the camera. The caption read: "The heiress Miriam Morgenroth with her foster father Leopold Vogt."

"A moving story," Chris said. "Almost too good to be true."

"Only on the surface. Miriam lost her father, her mother, and all of her siblings back then. No wonder she didn't want to talk about that period."

The next folder consisted of one Word document. I announced the file name out loud: "Assets List Flight."

"What do you think that means?" I asked Chris.

Chris creased his brow. "No idea. The Morgenroths probably took a few things with them when they tried to escape to England. At least that's what I would do. Go on—read it."

I clicked and the document opened, displaying strings of random garbled characters. "Utter hieroglyphics," I said, disappointed. "The data has been corrupted."

I scrolled down. All at once I saw actual words intermixed with the jumble. I read out loud, "Stocks."

Next to this the sum: "One hundred thousand Reichsmarks."

A few lines below this: "One hundred diamonds, flawless, brilliant cut, each two carats."

Chris sat up with a jolt. "A hundred diamonds?" He coughed but ignored it.

"Yeah. That's what it says."

"And how big are the rocks?"

"I told you already. Two carats each."

"Do you have any idea what those would be worth today?" Chris asked. His eyes sparkled.

I shrugged. "Two carats isn't all that big, right?"

"Approximately point four grams."

"Like I said. Tiny things."

Chris snorted. "One diamond of that quality would get a hundred thousand euros. I know that specifically. We had a manslaughter case a couple years back; it was over two or three similar stones. And a hundred thousand multiplied by one hundred—that makes ten million."

"Yeah. Nice," I replied. "Ten million."

"Now you know why the dead postgrad sang about diamonds."

"You mean . . ."

"Right. The Nazis apparently didn't find the stones on the Morgenroths. And our Franziska Beck and her professor Andy were searching for treasure, all these years later. That's why they sought out contact with Miriam Morgenroth."

"Ten million," I repeated.

Chris nodded. "Can you imagine what you could do with that and how much of a motive that is to kill someone?"

40

C hris slept like a log. At first, he had coughed and occasionally groaned. Then his breathing became calmer and more regular.

I sat next to him for a while, monitoring his condition. When I was sure that he was doing better, I went back into the living room. I made myself a cup of tea, took the last roll from breakfast, and returned to the laptop. It had grown dark outside. Even the traffic seemed tired. A nocturnal silence crept in.

I fired up the laptop. Miriam's passport photo greeted me. Maybe four or five years old. A pretty child. Well-dressed. The expression on her face did not fit her age. She was already afraid, knew of the danger that lurked ahead.

Miriam at fourteen. The faded and slightly blurred image from the newspaper. A tall, thin girl. The same blond hair, her expression emphatically happy. What had she experienced in between? The death of her siblings, her parents, and then quasi salvation at the hand of her father's friend. How did she manage to remain positive over all those years? Why hadn't her fate left her haggard and broken?

I thought about the few hours we had spent together. What joy, what radiant energy! And she loved her country, even though it had stolen everything from her. She tried to pass this love on to me. She wanted the love of literature to rectify all the bad things that I had experienced.

I closed my eyes.

The sound of the waves rushed over me. Under my bare feet, I felt the stiff grass on which our animals grazed. I smelled the unforgettable scent of the sea lavender. The sun was blinding. I put my hand up to shield my eyes and looked toward our house. Noises emanated from the barn. My grandmother was working.

I quickly walked up but stopped a few meters in front of the shed's door. A woman stepped out of the darkness. She pushed a wheelbarrow piled high with hay. Her long white hair was twisted into a braid. She did not notice me, kept her head lowered. As she walked past me, she paused and stared up at me. Numerous folds and wrinkles. A scrutinizing, almost reproachful look in eyes the piercing blue of a summer sky.

"Alicia," she said. "Where have you been so long?"

I was startled awake and wiped the hair off my forehead. I wouldn't let Miriam down, as I had done with . . . No. This time, I would do everything right.

41

The music on the car radio hummed softly. I no longer paid attention to it; it merely sufficed as an alternative to the white noise of the street.

I waited, observing the passersby on the sidewalk. Some ambled; others were obviously in more of a hurry. Each was busy with his own thoughts, his own life.

Chris walked out of a building that had a sign that read "Institute of Oncology." He came quickly to the Porsche, opened the driver's door, and got in. Without looking at me, he laid both hands on the steering wheel, lowered his head, and took a deep breath.

I continued to wait.

Finally, he let go of the steering wheel and turned his head toward me. "Do you want to drive?"

"No. Today I'm definitely in the mood to be chauffeured."

"Chauffeured?"

I nodded.

"Do you at least want to know what the doctor had to say? What the results of their tests were?"

I studied the expression in his eyes. "If you want to tell me."

The corner of his mouth hinted at a smile. "Everything was all right. In fact, the doctor was even optimistic. At least for the time being."

"That's marvelous."

Now he nodded and looked forward. "Yeah. It was what I wanted to hear." He paused. "Will we be at Dr. Vogt's on time?"

I glanced at my wristwatch. "We're fine. He said two o'clock—we'll make that easily."

He started the motor; we merged into the flow of traffic. Wind blew through the rolled-down windows. Nice.

We spent the ten-minute drive to Georg's bank in silence. The silence was also nice.

Chris pulled into a parking space and turned off the engine. He started to get out, but I held him back.

"Do we actually want to tell Georg everything?" I asked.

"Everything?" he said.

"Well, you know."

A sarcastic light danced in Chris's eyes. "But of course. We'll tell him that we broke into the postgrad's apartment, discovered a body, and eventually rehid it. Then we'll tell him about how we happened onto the laptop. And what we found on it. I think that will all come off really well."

"A *no* would have sufficed," I said, without succeeding in suppressing my smirk. "But we have to be able to explain the stuff about the diamonds. We couldn't have just come up with that on our own."

Chris shook his head. "Leave that up to me. I've already thought of something."

The same receptionist received us in the foyer. "Dr. Vogt is expecting you," she said with her well-rehearsed smile.

Georg's secretary's workstation was abandoned. He stood in front of a cabinet and flipped through a large folder. When he saw us, he waved us over and tossed the file haphazardly onto the desk.

"Would you care for some coffee?" he asked.

"Please," Chris responded, and I said, "And a water."

"Go on in. I'll just grab those quickly. My secretary is still at lunch."

We entered his office, sat at our customary seats, and soon Georg came in with a tray. He set a coffee out for Chris and took one for himself. He brought a crystal glass and a bottle of Perrier for me.

We drank until Georg finally broke the silence. "I can't wait any longer. Have you found out anything?"

"Maybe," Chris said. "But we need your help. We might have come across a clue."

"A clue?" Georg put his cup down and leaned forward. "Don't keep me in such suspense, Mr. Winkler."

"Ms. Morgenroth was interviewed by a doctoral student shortly before her disappearance," Chris began.

"Her name is Franziska Beck," I added. "You or Miriam—I don't remember which of you it was—said she also met with you."

"That's right," Georg promptly confirmed. "She was studying history at the university. She told me she was writing her doctorate on the Second World War. Specifically, Jewish bankers of the time."

Chris nodded. "Ms. Beck was one of the last people to get in contact with your aunt before her disappearance. We want to question her, of course, but we haven't been able to reach her. We spoke with her professor, though."

"Oh?" Georg said.

Chris nodded again. "Professor Fembach. She was very cooperative, even if she couldn't help us any further with the case. Not directly, that is. But she did give us the rough outline of Ms. Beck's doctoral thesis. And that's where Alicia and I noticed something."

"And what was that?"

"Well, diamonds," Chris paused and then said, "It kept returning to these diamonds."

Georg looked at me and Chris in succession. He leaned back to fold his arms across his chest. "Oh, damn. Those cursed stones!" He paused. "Sorry, but I'd thought I was finally finished with that."

"I don't understand," Chris said.

"Now that you mention it, I remember," Georg said. "I'd probably wanted to ignore or simply to repress it. Of course. This student was relentless; she kept asking me about the whereabouts of those diamonds."

"You wanted to *repress* it?"

"Yes. There's no way you could understand. I have to explain. But I'll have to go way back."

Chris smiled encouragingly. "We have time. Anything that you could tell us would be helpful."

"All right," Georg began. "As you may know, my grandfather started this bank with Adam Morgenroth. Miriam is Adam's youngest daughter. The only one that lived." Georg made a helpless gesture. "During the Nazi era, Miriam's father didn't want to accept the fact that he was in danger. He'd been a soldier in World War One, after all, and thought . . . well, you know. That didn't mean a thing. The Nazis had set out to destroy all Jews, no matter what they'd done for their country. When my grandfather and Miriam's father realized this, Mr. Morgenroth decided to leave Germany for as long as the Nazi reign of terror lasted. But that was highly illegal. At the time, Jews were already under threat of being imprisoned. So, the two men painstakingly prepared for the journey. False documents were procured, money was set aside. An escape route was planned: they were to travel via Hamburg on a ship to England, where Miriam's distant relatives lived and still live today."

"And the diamonds?"

"Adam Morgenroth didn't want to end up destitute, understandably. So, he traded a part of his fortune for diamonds. My grandfather always said there were a hundred of them. Flawless. The best quality. Adam had them with him when he fled."

"The Morgenroth family never made it," Chris said.

Georg shook his head. His expression became serious and concerned. "In Hamburg—the old warehouse district, to be precise—their cover was blown. They were arrested and ultimately ended up in Auschwitz. Miriam was the only one who survived."

"The diamonds were never found?"

"No. The Gestapo searched for them at that time and had no success. If the diamonds really even existed, then they're lost forever. Miriam couldn't remember. She was too small then. No more than five years old. She never saw the diamonds herself."

"And this Ms. Beck, how did she know about the stones?" I said.

Georg threw me a puzzled look. "No idea, Alicia. Maybe she dug it up somewhere. Out of a newspaper or a journal from the postwar period." He went silent and then began again. "But now that you ask me so directly, she repeatedly implied that her professor—"

"Professor Fembach?" Chris interrupted.

Georg shrugged. "She never mentioned a name. She uttered several times that the story with the diamonds and their whereabouts was very important for her thesis. That excuse did make me wonder. I myself have completed academic research and have a PhD. That kind of detail is ir-relevant for a doctoral thesis. And yet she continued to nag me about it." Georg stopped and wiped his face nervously. "Oh my God! You think those diamonds have something to do with Miriam's disappearance, don't you? You're as-suming there's some kind of connection."

Chris took his time to answer. "We can't rule out the possibility at this juncture. Besides, it's our only lead. And no matter how vague, we're going to follow it."

Georg lowered his eyes and seemingly lost in thought, stirred his coffee. "Yes, of course. Do that. Anything that could give us information about Miriam's fate. I'll help you with it in any way I can. My grandfather and my father would have done the same."

Chris gave me a sign with his eyes, and we both rose.

"Do you want to go already?" Georg asked with his gaze anxiously fixed on me.

"Yes," Chris said. "We need to pay the professor an-other visit. Let's see where that leads."

Georg stood up abruptly and held out his hand to wish us good-bye. Then he hesitated. "Oh, Alicia, I have some-thing for you."

He went to his desk, opened a drawer, and took out a small black book. "The clinic sent over Miriam's belong-ings yesterday. And when I looked through everything, this hardcover caught my eye."

Georg came over to me. He held the book with both hands, as if to cling on to it. "I know Miriam read to you from this. The volume of poems has little value in itself; it comes from the twenties. But I think Miriam would have liked to know that you get—" Georg must have noticed the sudden wounded reaction in my eyes. "Keep it for her until you see her again. The book was extremely important to Miriam. She carried it with her everywhere."

He stretched his arm out, and I hesitantly took the volume from which Miriam and I had read together. The leather cover was worn, the edges cracked. I was almost able to hear Miriam's voice as she spoke about the blue flower.

"Thanks," I said. It was all I could get out.

42

P rofessor Fembach's secretary was watering her orchids as we entered. Her purse sat on the desk. By all appearances, she was about to call it a day.

"Excuse me, please, is the professor still here?" Chris asked.

In reply, the secretary looked pointedly at her watch and raised her eyebrows, disapproving.

A voice came from the direction of the half-open office door. "Of course, I'm still here. I have to grade papers until late in the evening. Just come on in."

I followed Chris into the small office. Professor Fembach sat on her swivel chair behind a stack of papers. A red pen lay within her reach. She grabbed its cap and closed the felt-tip carefully. A completely different atmosphere from our first visit.

"Please take a seat," she said.

We pulled up our two plastic stools.

"May I ask again who you are and why you've come to see me?" the professor began.

Chris remained silent, his expression indifferent.

"So, you won't give me an answer?" the professor said, her voice harder. "Imagine, I called the police headquarters this afternoon and asked for Inspector Winkler. And you know what they told me?" Professor Fembach grabbed her pen and pointed it energetically in our direction. "There is an Inspector Winkler, but he's been on sick leave for months. And now I ask myself, how can that be? How can someone who's not fit for duty lead an investigation?" She tapped the pen a few times on the stack of essays. "The way I see it, this is abuse of authority, what you're doing here. And I can press charges."

I glanced at Chris, and to my great surprise, he remained absolutely unaffected. The hint of a cynical smile even appeared on his face. "Bravo," he said with a drawl. "You certainly have a point. But how do you imagine it will sound when a professor—how should I put it?—uses a student and her doctoral thesis to search for lost valuables? And, for the sake of argument, let's call those lost valuables diamonds."

Professor Fembach's complexion changed abruptly. She turned white. A few red splotches appeared. She started in on a vehement answer but stopped herself at the last second. "What do you know about the diamonds?" she finally said.

Chris casually crossed his legs, and his smile grew wider. "More than you might like. Your Ms. Beck didn't concern herself with the Nazi era when she questioned Dr. Vogt and Ms. Morgenroth. Instead, she concentrated on the precious stones and their whereabouts."

"I have nothing to do with that!" the professor erupted.

"Really?" Chris seemed to be thoroughly enjoying the situation. "Then it probably also wouldn't interest you that we've tried to contact Ms. Beck for days with absolutely no success. And when I put two and two together—and as far as addition goes, I'm a whiz—I get the sneaking suspicion that your student has figured out where the gems can be found and has gone to get them all by herself. Without you."

Professor Fembach threw the pen angrily on the papers. The stack began to slide. Some of the essays fell to the floor.

"What a mess," Chris noted calmly.

The professor seemed to register neither the disarray nor Chris's last statement. "That fucking bitch!" she snarled. "She owes everything to me. She wouldn't have passed a single test if I hadn't helped her."

Chris waited until Professor Fembach had regained her composure. "Tell me, how did you learn about the diamonds?"

The professor avoided direct eye contact. "This stays between us," she said finally before she looked up.

Chris nodded. "That I can promise you. How you heard about the diamonds, I will keep private."

"Private?" Professor Fembach shook her head incredulously. "Whatever. Those diamonds," she sighed. "Ever since I started studying history, I've concentrated on the National Socialist era. And I kept coming across stories of how rich Jewish Germans exchanged their assets for precious stones when they fled from the Nazis. I was fascinated with these legends. Then nearly a year ago, I met someone who knew specifics about the huge fortune the Morgenroth family had taken with them when they tried to flee. And that treasure has presumably never been found."

"Who was the person that told you this?" I asked.

The professor threw an uncertain glance at me. "Mrs. Falk."

"The wife of Maximilian Falk?" Chris said.

"The very one. At a fund-raising event, we had a long discussion about the Morgenroths. She told me that her father had always claimed that Adam Morgenroth had embezzled a huge sum. He traded this for diamonds, which he took with him when he fled."

"Miriam Morgenroth's father is alleged to have pilfered the money?" I could not believe it.

"That's what Mrs. Falk said, anyway. I researched it and scoured every available source. Most confirmed Mrs. Falk's statement, at least in regards to the diamonds."

"What happened then? What did you do next?" Chris said.

The professor sighed. "The thing would not let me rest. The more I researched, the clearer it became to me that the Morgenroths actually had the diamonds with them when they fled and must have hidden them along the way. The diamonds, they're out there." She pointed at the window. "Somewhere. Nobody has ever found them."

Chris stood up to go but then turned back to the professor. "You're always going to be stuck in this office with a huge pile of work to plow through. While Franziska Beck, at this very moment, might be sitting on a plane with one hundred flawless diamonds in her luggage. That would be—how does the phrase go?" Chris bent forward, supported himself with both hands on the pile of essays, and whispered, *Isn't it ironic?*"

43

I closed the passenger door. Silence and heat. Chris rolled our windows down.

"Falk," I said. "It keeps coming back to the Falks."

"Hmm."

"Not *hmm*. First off, Maximilian Falk wants nothing more than to see Miriam dead. Then it turns out he's the sponsor of our professor's department. And besides that, Mrs. Falk put that nonsense with the lost diamonds in Professor Fembach's head."

"Hate and money—if that isn't a successful combination," Chris said.

"We have to go back to Berchtesgaden and cross-examine them. Whatever has come of Miriam, Mr. and Mrs. Falk are the key. They're behind the entire thing."

Chris took his phone out of his pocket, tapped the screen, and held it to his ear.

"Who are you calling?" I asked.

He signaled me with his hand to be quiet. "Winkler here, Inspector Winkler," he said after a few moments.

"Good afternoon, Mrs. Falk. Mrs. Falk, circumstances have arisen that make it necessary for us to meet again."

He listened to her response and then said, "No, it cannot be handled over the phone. We should clarify this in person. Just tell me when my colleague and I can visit you in Berchtesgaden."

Again, silence. Then Chris said, "Oh! That works out well . . . Yes, I know it . . . Today, nine p.m.? . . . That suits us. We'll be there." Without saying good-bye, Chris ended the call and stashed his phone away.

"So?" I said.

"Mrs. Falk wasn't very pleased about my call, but we have an appointment with both of them. Today at nine."

"Can we make it to Berchtesgaden by then?"

"As luck would have it, Mr. and Mrs. Falk happen to be in Munich right now. At the Hotel Kempinski."

"How truly convenient."

Chris grinned. "Isn't it?"

"Yes. Because I'm hungry. Let's go by your place first and eat something."

Chris's gaze seemed derisive. "It's a summer evening, the weather is beautiful, and you're in Munich. You're not going home."

"No?"

"On your island, you probably sit around on summer evenings, locked up in your kitchens, and suck down liters of tea before you go to bed at eight thirty. Here in Bavaria, we do it differently."

"And how?"

"Beer gardens."

"And that's supposed to be fun?"

"Cool breezes under chestnut trees, an ice-cold wheat beer, and a platter of cheese and sausage. That has some appeal." Chris grinned again.

"All right. You convinced me. But listen—you haven't tasted really good beer until you're on my Hallig, sitting with your feet dipped in the sea, and looking into the horizon."

"We can try that later as well," he said.

I did not answer.

44

A uniformed bellhop led us to the Royal Ludwig Suite. He knocked softly on the pretentious door, and when Mrs. Falk opened it from within, he bowed almost reverently. "Your guests, madame."

Mrs. Falk answered with a slight nod. The bellboy turned without a word and left us.

"Come in, please," she said. Today she was wearing a dark pantsuit. She looked as if she had just left an official event.

Semidarkness greeted us. The drapes were drawn, the lights dimmed. The armchair, the curtains, even the wallpaper—everything shimmered in burgundy. In the murkiness, the color appeared threatening, almost like blood.

The floor was soft and strangely elastic. Not parquet, not carpeting. It seemed as if it could be leather.

Mrs. Falk took a seat at a round meeting table and indicated our places without saying a word. We pulled up two of the comfortable chairs and sat down.

"My husband is sleeping," she said and gestured toward a closed door.

Silence followed, and then Mrs. Falk said, "How might I help you?"

"Do you know an Andy Fembach?" Chris asked.

"Fembach?" Mrs. Falk seemed a little confused. "The name means nothing to me. Sorry, I can't recall it. Who is it?"

"A professor of history."

"Oh! *Professor* Fembach. Of course, I know her. Not that well, but we've had a few conversations. Why do you ask?"

"Well, this Professor Fembach—how shall I put it?— sent a PhD candidate to Miriam Morgenroth. The student pretended to be interested in the Nazi era. When in fact, the only things that interested her were . . . diamonds."

Mrs. Falk glanced from Chris to me and back to him, genuinely baffled. "Yes, of course. The Morgenroth diamonds."

"Morgenroth diamonds?" Chris repeated slowly.

Mrs. Falk shrugged indifferently. "The jewels that the Morgenroths carried with them when they fled. Back in the Nazi time."

"Did you tell Professor Fembach about them?"

"I believe so. The professor specializes in this era."

"And may I ask what secrets you divulged to Professor Fembach?"

"What everyone in our circle already knows." She frowned, placed her hands over one another on the table, and lifted an index finger. "The Morgenroths fled from the Nazis. They carried diamonds with them. But you must understand that all of the Morgenroths are and always were criminals. The funds with which they purchased the diamonds were misappropriated. They stole their customers' life savings. The Vogts profited from it as well. And boy, did they profit! After the war, they only had to pay back a small fraction of the embezzled money to the bank's defrauded clients. Many of whom were no longer alive. Couple that with a greatly devalued Reichsmark. And then the real estate that the Vogt Bank acquired before and during the war skyrocketed to astronomical levels in the time of the *Wirtschaftswunder.*" Mrs. Falk tapped on the back of her hand with her index finger to drill the point in. "Nine-digit sums were made. Entire city districts were developed. There was profit to no end."

"But Georg—Dr. Vogt—said that the Morgenroths used their own assets to pay for the diamonds," I interjected.

Mrs. Falk gave me a sharp look. "Of course, Dr. Vogt claims that. It would be suicidal for him to say anything else."

"The fact that almost the entire Morgenroth family perished in the concentration camp has no effect on you?" I said, not even trying to disguise my harsh tone. "Are you lacking all compassion?"

Mrs. Falk acknowledged my remark with raised eyebrows. "Indubitably, I have compassion, and I regret that these horrid crimes took place. But"—she lifted her index finger with a resolute movement—"that doesn't change the fact that the Morgenroths and Vogts are criminals. And to top it off, Miriam Morgenroth ruined us as well."

Before I could answer, Chris spoke up. "Back to the diamonds. You seem absolutely convinced that they still exist and are hidden in a safe place. Is that right?"

"Yes. And by the way, Miriam Morgenroth had the same firm belief."

"But Georg—Dr. Vogt—" I started.

Mrs. Falk shook her head brusquely. "My dear child. Stop it with Dr. Vogt. We were more than close friends with Miriam and Georg for years. They were our key business partners. And Miriam always said that she couldn't remember where the diamonds were hidden, because she was too small. However, she confided once that she still possessed a detailed map of their escape route, which ends in the warehouse district. And somewhere on the way between Munich and Hamburg, the diamonds are waiting to be discovered. Isn't that a nice story?" Mrs. Falk smiled bitterly.

Chris ignored the sarcasm in her voice. "You said you and your husband were close friends with Miriam Morgenroth and Georg Vogt?"

Mrs. Falk laughed dryly. "Our families even went on vacations together. It was all very fine and dandy. Until Miriam stuck a knife in our backs."

Chris thought for a while. "I still have one question. How did you come to sponsor the Department of History? Did Professor Fembach contact you or your husband?"

"It had nothing to do with Professor Fembach, if that's what you're interested in." Mrs. Falk had regained her composure. She was sitting as straight as a pin and underlined her words with small hand gestures. "If you have a substantial income, you inevitably have to make donations for tax purposes. And it sounds good when you're associated with a university. It doesn't hurt, anyway." She paused and looked toward the closed door, behind which lay what was left of her husband. "Miriam gave us the idea years ago. She'd always had a soft spot for German poetry, so she donated to the Department of German Literature. We took history. That also has a nice ring to it."

Chris stood up; Mrs. Falk and I did as well. Smiling, he shook Mrs. Falk's hand as we prepared to leave. "Do you know where the escape map is?"

Mrs. Falk looked up, her expression open. "No. No idea. I unfortunately can't help you there." Her reply came so fast that she would not have had time to think up a lie.

45

At first, there were only a few drops that landed as if they had been sown across the windshield. Then the rain knocked tentatively on the roof and finally erupted into a violent thunderstorm. Lightning flashed across the sky, casting garish highlights on the houses on either side of us and turning the puddles on the street a shimmering silver. Thunder roared, at first in the distance and then ever closer, bringing its rolling rumble into the canyons of the city.

When we arrived in front of Chris's apartment building, the storm had already moved on. All that was left behind was the strong rainfall. We waited a bit in the car, in hopes that that too would come to an end, but at some point, we decided that our hopes were in vain. So, we climbed out and ran as fast as we could to the covered entry.

We rushed into the lobby, soaking wet, and beneath the fluorescent lights in the hallway, I noticed how pale Chris had become. Dark circles had formed under his eyes. And he was constantly coughing. In the elevator, he leaned against the wall and didn't speak a word.

Once we were in his apartment, he sat on one of the kitchen chairs. He shivered.

"Tomorrow we'll go back to the professor," he said softly.

"Of course," I said.

He looked up at me, anger sparking in his eyes. Not toward me but toward his condition. "She didn't give us all the information she had."

"Are you cold?" I asked.

"Not terribly." He tried to smile, but his lower lip trembled.

"I think it would be best if you went to sleep now," I said. "It was a hard day."

Without waiting for his answer, I helped him up, steered him in the direction of his room, and pushed him onto the bed. He remained sitting with his chest sunken in. He swayed.

With my help, he got undressed and slid into a lying position. He was still freezing. I pulled the bedspread up and tucked him in, but his condition did not improve. Spontaneously, I slipped out of my clothes and crawled under the covers.

His skin felt ice cold to my touch. He was shaking constantly with the chills. I spooned against his back and laid my arm over him. After a while, he calmed down.

The rain grew stronger. Heavy drops pattered steadily on the windowpanes. The room was dark. All I could see were the outlines of furniture, bulky and shapeless, connected by the night.

Images began running through my head. A little girl in Auschwitz. Chris, approaching the bikers at the rest area, intending to beat them up. Miriam with her small black book of poems. Her piercing blue eyes, loving and kind. The face changed; deeper and harder wrinkles formed. My grandmother looked back at me, and in her expression was boundless disappointment and reproach. The last thing I heard was the breaking of the waves on my Hallig.

I woke up. Somebody stroked my cheek gently. I blinked my lids open and looked into Chris's green eyes.

"Thanks," he whispered.

He stroked my cheek again. He did it with his fingertips, as if he wanted to make sure that I was really there.

"Are you feeling better?" I asked.

"Much better," he said. "The doctor said these moments of weakness are quite normal. A reaction to the chemo. They'll disappear over time."

"Are you sure?"

Chris smiled. "What's ever certain in life?" He bent down to give me a kiss.

I laid my hand on his neck, pulled him to me, and kissed him back.

My hands ran over his body. Between our heavy breaths, I heard him whisper my name many times—hard, raw, and choppy. And when we started to move together, he held me with an intensity reserved for the desperation of a drowning man.

Nothing was certain in this life. Especially not at night.

46

Sonja, Marko and Sven

They had already been sitting in the car for more than an hour when the rain began. Suddenly, it became noticeably cooler, and the funny drumming on the roof briefly distracted them. But only briefly.

It thundered. The first bolt of lightning flashed.

Sven shifted uneasily in the passenger seat. Sonja half lay in the back of the car, her legs bent. She stared forward and sleepily played with a strand of hair. Marko sighed and threw Sven an annoyed look.

"I used to always be afraid when it thundered," Sven said somewhat loudly.

Marko snorted. "You still are."

Sven got angry. "No! Not for a long time."

"Ha!" Marko said. "You're like a child—with your stupid kiddie shows!"

Sven's eyes flashed. "Anime is totally cool. It makes me think a lot."

"What is there to think about?"

"Every creature has a hidden side. If you activate one, you get a huge surprise. Before, you have no idea what will come out."

"What a load of crap! At least people are always the same. There's no surprise."

"You're just jealous because you aren't interested in anything."

Marko turned sideways in his seat in order to look directly at Sven. "But I am. I have a favorite movie."

Sven raised his eyebrows. "Oh yeah? Really? And which one is that?"

Marko hesitated. "I . . . I can't remember the title. But it doesn't matter, anyway. I saw the movie once, and I liked it a lot. It was about this guy who fought against an alien. He was gigantic, at least three meters tall. And invisible."

"The guy?"

"The alien, of course. You idiot!"

"Yeah, and?"

"Then all hell broke loose. The alien had something like dreadlocks and these sharp, crooked teeth that stuck out. And he collected trophies too. Skulls. Loads of human skulls. He polished them. Totally wicked, huh?"

Sven laughed triumphantly. "And that's supposed to have some meaning?"

"What meaning?"

"Well, a good movie, a good series, says something about life."

Marko furrowed his brow. "Like in a Japanese cartoon, where everyone has a hidden monster?"

Sven nodded wildly. "Exactly. Your movie with the alien—what's its message?"

Marko started in on an answer, cleared his throat, and glanced at the backseat for support. "It definitely has a message. I just can't put it into words right now."

"You can't put it into words because there's nothing to say." Sven grinned. "Right, Sonja? Marko's film is pure garbage."

Sonja yawned and swept her dark hair out of her face. "Tell me again what happens in the movie, Marko."

"There's this guy in the jungle, and he runs into an alien that hunts him and wants to kill him. Oh, and the alien is invisible." Marko fell silent and waited anxiously for Sonja's assessment.

"You have to admit the movie has no message whatsoever. It's pure and simple crap," Sven said.

Sonja tried to stretch. "As Marko tells it, the film clearly has a moral."

Sven blinked, dumbfounded. "And that would be?"

"Yeah, exactly. What would it be?" Marko chimed in, resonating hope.

Sonja sighed. "Think for a minute. The guy in the rain forest, he's all alone. Then without warning, a murderous threat appears out of nowhere. Completely deadly. That's right—isn't it?"

Marko nodded.

"Well, you see," Sonja continued, "the jungle is our life. And the things that could really harm us can't be seen. But we still have to deal with them. Or they'll kill us. How does the movie end, anyway?"

"The guy somehow makes the alien visible. And then *bam!*" Marko slapped hard on the steering wheel. "He does him in."

Sven's eyes grew wide. "Do you remember how?"

Marko made a derisive gesture. "It doesn't make a bit of difference. Dead is dead."

Sonja sat all the way up. "You see, like I told you. The movie has a message." She looked down the deserted street. In the meantime, the thunder and lightning had stopped. Only the rain was left.

Up ahead, she could indistinctly make out a small light. It seemed to be approaching.

She raised her arm and pointed in its direction. "Can you guys see that?"

Marko squinted and leaned forward. "Fucking rain. I can't tell for sure."

"We have to be absolutely positive," Sonja said.

"At this hour, in this weather, who else would be out?" Sven said.

Sonja shook her head. "We don't want to get it wrong and have to come back here tomorrow. It was a complete pain in the ass to cover so much ground in such a short amount of time today."

"But that's why we got such a nice Mercedes," Sven said.

"The Benz has to be back tomorrow," Marko stated dryly. "Who knows what kind of heap we'll get then."

Marko brought his face close to the windshield and stared hard through it. "I think it all fits. We're clear to proceed."

He started the engine, and the car rolled at a steady pace.

They drove along the right side. Marko accelerated. On the left, a bicyclist approached. Crouched far over the handlebars, a rain jacket covering the head and upper body.

When they were passing, Marko whipped the wheel hard to the left, and the Mercedes slammed into the side of the bicycle.

Marko brought the car to a stop a few meters away.

"Oh my God!" Sonja screamed with a worried voice. "That didn't really just happen! Sven, climb out and see if the poor lady is all right."

"Why always me?" Sven protested. "It's raining!"

"So what? Do you just want to let the woman lie there? Come on. Get out."

Grumbling, Sven resigned himself to his fate. He opened the door and stepped out onto the road. The rain caught him in the face and on the neck. He pulled the hood of his sweatshirt over his head and hurried the few steps to the victim who lay on the ground next to a completely bent-up bicycle.

"Are you okay?" he asked.

The woman groaned. "My leg . . . my arm."

"We're really sorry. We'll call for help immediately. But first, let me put you in the recovery position." Sven knelt down by the woman and grabbed her gently by the shoulders. He carefully turned her the right way.

"What are you doing?" the woman stammered. "Now I'm lying across the road."

Sven didn't answer. Instead, the tires of the Mercedes let out a shrill retort as Marko stepped on the gas with the hand brake engaged. All at once, the car shot backward. In a fraction of a second, it had reached Sven and the woman. Sven just managed to jump out of the way. One of the tires ran directly over the woman's torso. Her body cracked and crunched loudly.

The brakes screeched, and the Mercedes came to a stop again.

Marko leaned out the window. He grinned from ear to ear.

"Are you completely nuts?" Sven screamed. "You're a fucking asshole! You almost hit me! You just missed me by an inch!"

The back window lowered. Sonja's head popped out. "Is the old hag finally dead?"

"I don't know! Shit, man, look for yourself!" Sven yelled.

Sonja said something to Marko that Sven couldn't understand, and the Mercedes rolled over the woman once more. This time slowly. Again, came that special crunch. Then there was silence.

The back door opened halfway. Sonja leaned out and gestured to Sven. "Don't just stand there. Get in the car. I saw a pizza joint down the hill. You can have one with extra cheese."

Sven started moving. The night shift always made him hungry.

47

A staircase made of concrete. Taped to the walls were posters enticing undergrads to join study trips. Information about exams, used textbooks for sale. First floor, second floor, a glass door, and then the first room on the right.

No one was in the reception area. The door to Professor Fembach's office stood wide open. Chris and I heard noises from within.

"I told you we didn't have to call first," Chris said. "She's here."

"It was just an idea." I defended myself half-heartedly.

A woman appeared in the doorway. Graying hair, maternal demeanor. Professor Fembach's secretary. She carried a huge stack of papers in her arms.

"Does Professor Fembach have a moment for us?" Chris asked.

The secretary opened her mouth and shut it again. She lowered her head and, to my utmost astonishment, sobbed loudly. The papers began to slide precariously. I stepped forward and relieved her of a pile.

"Then you don't know?" she managed to say between sobs.

"What?" I said.

"Professor Fembach . . . She had an accident."

"An accident? What sort of accident?"

The secretary sighed deeply and laid the papers on her desk. She took the ones I was carrying and placed them next to the first bundle with the utmost care. She busied herself for a time aligning the edges exactly. By then, she had gained enough control that she could look up. She tried to smile.

"Please, excuse me." She motioned toward the office door. "I don't know what just came over me."

"No problem," Chris said. "We're concerned too. We spoke with the professor only yesterday. What happened? Has she sustained serious injuries?"

Again, tears welled up in her eyes. She hastily wiped her face. "The professor had midterm papers to correct. She always does that in one go. She gets upset when things lie around unfinished. She worked late into the night and then rode home like she does every day, on her bike. Only this time . . ."

"Only this time . . .?" Chris repeated.

"It had been raining hard. The police said the visibility was extremely poor. And then somebody ran into her with a car."

"Dead?"

The secretary nodded silently.

Chris let a bit of time pass. Then he asked, "And the driver of the vehicle? What happened to him?"

The secretary shook her head. "Hit and run."

"Any evidence found at the scene of the crime?"

The secretary shrugged her shoulders helplessly. "I'm not really sure. But the police said due to the heavy rain . . . that it would make everything all the more difficult."

"I'm so very sorry," I said.

The corners of her mouth twitched, and she lowered her gaze. "I've been in this department for nearly one and a half decades. Professor Fembach came around four years ago, and we immediately hit it off."

"A good boss is rare," Chris said. He paused and then proceeded with hesitation in his voice. "I almost don't dare ask. And it's probably completely inappropriate."

"What is it?" the secretary asked.

"Oh, nothing." Chris played up the embarrassment.

"But you wanted to ask something. There was a reason you came," the secretary urged.

"All right then, if you insist." Chris took a deep breath. "Professor Fembach promised to give us a folder yesterday. A dossier on the Morgenroth family. We desperately need it for academic research. And now . . . now that won't come to pass."

"Professor Fembach promised you?"

Chris nodded without a word.

"Well, I'll look once through her private things. Professor Fembach kept her files in perfect order." She disappeared into the adjoining room and left us in the small outer office. Chris leaned with his forearms on the counter and drummed almost soundlessly on it with his fingers.

It didn't take long before the secretary returned. In her hand, she held a folder bursting at the seams.

"And?" Chris asked.

The secretary shook her head. "Nothing under Morgenroth."

The disappointment was clearly visible on Chris's face.

217

"But," the secretary continued, "a complete file labeled 'Vogt and Morgenroth'. Is that what you were looking for?"

Chris observed her thoughtfully until a warm smile formed on his lips. "Yes, in fact. That is exactly what Professor Fembach promised us yesterday."

48

The sunlight twinkled furtively through the leaves of the large chestnut trees. People sat packed onto countless benches. Individuals of every age. Teenagers, adults, seniors, families with children, businessmen. Large glass beer mugs veiled in a fine mist of condensed water. Platters of food. Garbled voices, not too loud. On occasion the clatter of cutlery. The air was cool and comfortable.

A barmaid in a dirndl set two alcohol-free wheat beers in tall, slender glasses on the table in front of us. In so doing, she leaned just a tad too far forward and showed off her impressive décolleté to Chris.

"Here ya are, ma lord!" she chirped. The stupid cow couldn't even speak correctly.

The foamy white head on our drinks looked inviting. Chris toasted me, and we took long pulls from our glasses.

The beer ran shivers down my throat. It did me good.

The waitress appeared again. Now she carried two plates. On each was a formidable portion of sauerkraut and a multitude of sausages. This time, it was obvious that she was making eyes at Chris. Admittedly, he looked rather attractive today. I checked him out covertly. Broad shoulders, three-day beard. His hair had begun to grow back. You could now see that it was dark brown. It suited him well.

"Does this place have silverware?" I asked the peacock in a dirndl.

She threw me an irritated look, grabbed a jug full of utensils wrapped in paper napkins from the next table, and set it right in front of me.

"Here ya are," she said again. Apparently, she had a rather limited vocabulary.

I watched how she disappeared, swinging her hips between the benches. As I turned toward Chris, I noticed small wrinkles next to his eyes. He laughed furtively. He laughed at me.

"What?" I asked.

"Oh, nothing."

He fished a set of cutlery out of the jug and concentrated his attention on the food.

"How I've missed this." Sighing, he cut off a piece of his bratwurst, piled extra sauerkraut on his fork, and shoved the morsel into his mouth. Then he chewed with great relish. "Now that is a proper meal," he said after he swallowed. He washed it down with beer.

I tried mine. It didn't taste bad. But I couldn't keep myself from saying, "Proper food is fish or lamb. Or even suckling pig on a holiday. But not this."

Chris didn't bite at the bait but merely gave me a smile. I admitted defeat and smiled back.

Our plates were quickly emptied, as were our glasses. Chris made a hand gesture, and as if by magic, two new wheat beers appeared before us. To my satisfaction, we were being waited on by a different server, one who wasn't conspicuously on a manhunt.

The first gulp was again the best.

Chris looked aimlessly around the beer garden. I realized that he was somewhere else with his thoughts. "What are you brooding about?" I asked.

He returned from his sojourn. His eyes focused on me. "I don't want to ruin your good mood."

"You wouldn't be able to do that," I replied. "I'm pretty thick-skinned."

"All right." He took another drink, put his glass down, and turned it between his fingers. Then he looked up. "Miriam Morgenroth has disappeared. And even if this fact hurts you, she is probably dead." He paused again. "The PhD student, Ms. Beck, as far as we know, was the last person outside the clinic that spoke with Miriam Morgenroth. She was murdered. And now her professor, who sent her—she's also dead. She likewise did not die of natural causes. Again, a crime has taken place."

"But a hit-and-run?" I asked, amazed.

"What do you think a hit-and-run is? It's a crime. And if the victim dies, it's manslaughter, at the bare minimum. We can't even rule out full-fledged premeditated murder."

"What would be the point of that?"

"Someone is covering his tracks. Obviously, all three of these women knew things, which sealed their fate."

I frowned. "I don't know. That sounds a bit too conspiratorial. Isn't it much more likely that Miriam . . .?" I could not manage to end my sentence. I changed my approach. "Couldn't Mr. Falk simply have taken his revenge out on Miriam?"

Chris thought a moment. "Certainly. But he's sitting in a wheelchair and can barely speak. In any case, he didn't do it alone. If he called in professional help, . . ." Chris stroked his chin, lost in thought. "But how the other two women fit in there . . ." He shook his head. "Well, maybe they found out something that they shouldn't have."

"What do you mean by professional help?"

"When you have money and need a new bathroom, you call in a contractor who deals with bathrooms. And when you want someone killed, you get a contract killer."

"I thought things like that only happened in low-budget soap operas."

Chris laughed. "When someone is murdered, we search—I mean, the police—in the immediate vicinity of the victim. Cui bono. But if the offender hires someone that has absolutely no connection to the victim, who maybe even travels from another area to commit the murder and disappears directly after. Then it is difficult to identify the killer or the one calling the shots. And rarely, if ever is the connection made—you understand?"

"And who do you think is pulling the strings?"

"Mr. and Mrs. Falk seem to be likely candidates. If we continue to search further, we'll find out if that's true. But ultimately, it's immaterial to me. It's only a means to an end." His tone changed with those last words. He spoke them cold and hard.

Rage surged up in me. "How could I have forgotten? You want to make the big money. Or more precisely, to find the diamonds."

Chris leaned back. "Exactly. And you will learn what happened to Miriam. One hand washes the other. That's fitting."

My beer tasted flat. I shoved it away. "Sure. Fits perfectly."

Chris stood up. "Whatever. First, we'll go through the professor's notes. And then we'll take it from there."

49

More photos from Auschwitz. Children working, children in a barrack. Men with shaved heads, piles of corpses.

Sheet divider.

Behind it, a list of names. Next to the names, mortality data.

I turned the page.

Copies of canceled savings books. Behind that, photocopies of documents. A swastika and some kind of rune. Underneath: "Gestapo." There were many handwritten lines. The script looked antiquated.

"Can you decipher it?" I pushed the file folder over to Chris.

"Old German calligraphy. I can give it a try."

He narrowed his eyes and began to read slowly and falteringly. "Mr. Leopold Vogt, owner of Vogt Bank Munich, appears before the undersigned and gives the following testimony: *As a true member of the nation and possessor of the Golden Party Badge, it is my duty to charge the former co-owner of my bank, Adam Morgenroth, of Jewish ancestry, of embezzling a large sum of money (at least five hundred thousand Reichsmarks) in order to flee the country with his family.*"

"No," I blurted out. "Does it really say that?"

Chris rubbed his neck. "Unfortunately so. But the memo goes on."

I hardly dared to breathe as Chris continued. "*With my statement, I am submitting a detailed escape plan that I came by through my own diligence. I truly hope that the Jew with all of his family is arrested as soon as possible and held responsible for the crimes he committed against the Aryan people and our fatherland.* Munich, the ninth of September, 1938, Heil Hitler, Fritz Oberhauser, second lieutenant of the Gestapo, signed Leopold Vogt."

After Chris had finished, a cold, impersonal silence hung in the room. I closed my eyes and saw the photograph of Miriam as a child in front of me, how she looked at the camera, frightened and lost. Then the pictures of Auschwitz passed before my mind's eye: the forlorn, persecuted people delivered to an incomprehensibly horrific fate.

"Leopold Vogt betrayed Adam Morgenroth and his entire family. He could just as well have killed them himself." Chris sounded perplexed.

I pointed at the copy. "Maybe it's a forgery."

He shook his head adamantly. "I don't think so. Everything looks real."

"How could someone commit such a loathsome betrayal?"

"No idea. But it probably had to do with a lot of money."

"Yeah," I snapped. "A lot of money is the right incentive for greedy pricks."

"I can't help it," Chris said. "I'm just the messenger."

I put my head in my hands and rubbed my temples. "I'm sorry."

"It's all right."

"Was that everything there was?"

"No. Below that is a note scribbled in ballpoint. Apparently written by Professor Fembach. There are the initials *Fe* after it." Chris bent over the open folder and read aloud. "The escape plan was not present in the original files."

"Then this escape map really did exist," I said.

"Evidently."

I couldn't stay still any longer, so I stood up and paced back and forth.

Chris watched me for a time. "What's gotten into you?" he asked me eventually.

I went to the window and looked out at the street, but I wasn't able to focus on anything. "I just have to get out of here."

"Don't do something rash."

I turned to him. "I'm just going for a swim."

Chris forced a smile. "Swimming sounds good. It'll help you clear your head." He reached into his pants pocket and pulled out his car keys. "Here," he said, handing them to me. "Take the Porsche."

"And what are you going to do?" I asked. I grabbed the fob and our fingertips touched for a few seconds.

"I . . ." Chris responded, "I'm going to take a nap. And when you come back, I'll be as good as new. Then we can decide what we want to do next."

50

I climbed out of the water and checked the big clock on the opposite wall. Forty-four laps in exactly one hour. I was getting faster—not that it mattered anymore. This year's long-distance race on the North Sea had taken place last weekend—without me.

I showered, got dressed, packed my sports bag, and headed out to the parking lot. As I opened the Porsche and got in, the eyes of a couple who had just climbed out of an old Golf followed me. Presumably, I did not look like someone who should own a sports car. I ignored them.

Rush-hour traffic had begun; I had to accept the fact that it would take longer to get to Chris's apartment. I waited at the exit of the parking lot for a break. Then I weaved slowly through the streets.

At some point, I glanced down at my wrist. Just five o'clock. Georg would surely still be in his office. Without giving it a further thought, I hit the accelerator and swerved into the opposite lane. Tires screeched; horns protested loudly. But by then, I was already headed in the other direction.

After a few minutes, I pulled the Porsche into the fire lane in front of Vogt Bank. I ripped the key out of the ignition and stormed into the building.

"Is Georg still upstairs?" I asked the puzzled-looking receptionist.

"Yes. He is. But—"

I didn't wait to see what she had to say. Instead, I hurried into the open elevator and pressed Georg's floor.

His secretary's room was empty. I opened the door to his office and walked in.

Georg sat behind his desk. He smiled as he saw me and said into the receiver, "Thanks a lot. She's just come in. Everything is fine." He hung up and looked at me attentively with a hint of concern. "My receptionist," he said and indicated the telephone. "You seem to have frightened her a little."

"Your grandfather, what was he like?" I asked straight out.

Georg made a surprised grimace. "First of all, please sit down."

I went over to his desk and took a seat on one of the client chairs. "What was your grandfather like?" I repeated.

"My grandfather? He was nice. A strict but fair man. He was very supportive of me."

"How did he treat Miriam?"

"Miriam? She was like his own daughter. I never noticed any difference between how he treated my father and how he treated her. They were his children. Both of them." Georg went quiet and looked at me contemplatively. "Why are you asking, anyway?"

"I've just seen a document which clearly indicates that your grandfather was responsible for the arrest of the Morgenroths and their subsequent deportation to the concentration camps."

The expression on Georg's face changed. His eyes lost their luster; the wrinkles became more pronounced. All the color drained from his cheeks. "That can't be!" he gasped.

"But it's true," I replied emphatically. "Leopold Vogt went to the Gestapo and turned in his friend. He also gave the Nazis the Morgenroths' escape plan."

"Escape plan?" Georg creased his brow as if he did not understand what I was saying.

"You must know about that," I insisted.

"Know? Me? Miriam mentioned now and again that one had existed. But I've never seen it myself."

Georg's dismay was clear. His face was open. He was definitely not lying to me.

"In any case, we know how the story ends," I said. "The entire family was deported to Auschwitz and murdered there, with the exception of Miriam."

"Alicia! I cannot believe this!" Georg shook his head, bewildered. "The document must be a fake, created to bring disgrace onto my grandfather and our bank."

"Chris and I aren't experts. But the document came from the university's History Department. And Chris thought it all looked authentic."

Georg stared out the window for a while. He ran a hand over his eyes and turned back to me. "Then there's only one explanation: my grandfather was coerced to file the accusation. They somehow blackmailed him so that he was forced to betray his best friend."

I had never seen Georg like this. He seemed hurt and shaken to his core.

But I could not help him at the moment. "Your theory doesn't shine a much better light on your grandfather, though, does it?"

Georg lowered his head. "No," he murmured. "Not at all."

For a time, neither of us found the courage to speak.

"What are you going to do now?" Georg eventually broke the silence.

"No idea," I said. "I'd love to simply set off and follow the path that the family took back then. I have no idea, why. It probably doesn't make any sense. And we don't even have the route."

"I wish I could help you," Georg said.

"You don't know anything?"

Georg thought for a minute. "Only what Miriam and my grandfather said. The last stop on the escape route was Hamburg. Somewhere in the warehouse district. That's where they waited for the ship that should have taken them to England. And where they were arrested."

"That's everything?"

"Yeah . . . Except for . . . I mean, I have a dim recollection that my grandfather—or was it Miriam herself?— mentioned that they made a stop in Fichtelberg, near Bayreuth."

"Are you sure?"

Georg shrugged with a long sigh. "No, not completely. But my grandmother comes from the vicinity. Her family had an estate there. Well, actually a farm, but she always called it an estate. And if I'm not mistaken, I remember once hearing that they had stayed there overnight."

"And this estate, does it still exist?"

Georg nodded. "Yes. But it's been vacant for years. The building is protected as historically valuable, and the real estate in that area doesn't sell for much. It wouldn't make sense to invest in the necessary refurbishment. So, we write it off on our taxes." Again, he fell silent.

"Can you give me the address?"

Georg turned to his computer and typed something on the keyboard. Shortly thereafter, the printer hummed.

Georg took the sheet and handed it to me. "Do you really want to go there?"

I grabbed the paper, folded it, and tucked it into my pants pocket. "Let's see what Chris has to say about it."

51

C hris wasn't sleeping. Or at least, not anymore. He sat with his arms spread out, resting on the back of the couch. He stared at me. His expression did not bode well.

I let my sports bag fall noisily to the ground, went into the kitchenette, leaned against the counter, and shoved my hands into the front pockets of my jeans.

"Where were you?" he asked.

"I'm not accountable to you."

"But I thought—"

"You thought wrong!"

He opened his mouth, closed it, and swallowed. "At bare minimum, we have some kind of business agreement."

"A business agreement, we have. Well, all right. I was swimming, and then I spontaneously visited Georg."

"And you didn't think it was necessary to tell me first?"

"Nope."

Chris started to reply but then seemed to think better of it. He inhaled deeply, composing himself. "What did you discuss?"

"Georg was flabbergasted when I told him the stuff about his grandfather."

"You actually informed him about the accusation and the document that proves it?"

I nodded.

"That was rather direct, wasn't it?"

I looked into Chris's eyes. He held my stare.

"How come?" I said. "After all, it's his grandfather."

"Exactly. It would be completely understandable if he no longer wanted to work with us because we dug something like that up."

I shook my head. "No, you're wrong."

"Oh? Am I?" Chris sat up straighter.

"Georg was devastated. He desperately wants to get this all cleared up."

"So, he gave you the escape plan?"

"No. He didn't seem to know much about that."

Chris smirked. "So he says."

"I believe him. He wasn't acting. He was completely open, even though he was so upset. But he did remember some details about the escape."

"What?"

"That the Morgenroths were arrested in Hamburg in the warehouse district," I began.

Chris snorted. "We all know that."

"And that the Morgenroths' escape led through a small town called Fichtenberg."

"Fichtenberg?" Chris furrowed his brow. "Never heard of it."

I reached into the back pocket of my jeans and pulled out the paper that Georg had printed for me. I handed it to Chris.

He took it, unfolded it, and read it silently. "Oh! Not Fichtenberg—*Fichtelberg*. An estate in Fichtelberg."

"If that's what it says." I sat opposite him on the armchair.

"Georg was certain about this address?"

I made an indecisive hand gesture. "No. Not completely. It was only a vague memory of his. The property belonged to his grandmother's family."

Chris glanced at the sheet again. "Who lives there now?"

"The house is uninhabited."

"Fichtelberg," Chris mumbled. "That's somewhere near Bayreuth, about three hundred kilometers from here. We could look around the place, but only if there's a real chance of finding something."

"The people who could tell us that are either dead or missing," I pointed out.

Chris stared at me pensively, and then his face took on a determined look. "Not all have gone missing," he said. He grabbed his phone from the coffee table, dialed a number, and held it to his ear.

"Who are you calling?" I asked, but he didn't answer me.

"Good evening, Mrs. Falk. Inspector Winkler again," he said into his cell. "Please excuse the intrusion . . . No. I only have one quick question. I really won't keep you long. Last night, you mentioned that Miriam had talked about the escape route . . . Yes, exactly. The escape plan . . . What I'm interested in is whether the location Fichtelberg was ever brought up? Fichtelberg near Bayreuth? . . . No? Are you absolutely sure? . . . Then thank you very much . . . Yes. That was all I wanted to know. Have a nice evening."

Chris laid his phone down on the coffee table.

"That doesn't prove anything," I said. "Not to mention that we don't have too many other alternatives. Actually, it's the only option remaining. Ever since we started searching for Miriam, we keep coming across the myth of those lost diamonds. They're the unifying element of everything we've discovered. There are no more leads that we can follow up on in Munich. So, it's only logical that we go after the diamonds. And who knows—"

"We're groping in the dark," Chris interrupted. "More than seventy years have passed; it'll be difficult to dig up anything concrete."

"I think we should have a look in Fichtelberg, anyway. It's better than sitting around here. I can't handle it any longer. If you don't want to come, then I'll go without you."

"Not a chance." Chris smiled.

"That's what I thought," I retorted. "You wouldn't miss an opportunity to look for your diamonds."

Chris remained silent. I couldn't gather from his expression what he was thinking.

52

We set off early in the morning in order to get back to Munich by evening. All we took with us was Chris's laptop, the thumb drive containing the data from the murdered postgrad's computer, and Professor Fembach's folder. We chose the fastest route: the autobahn. At first, we listened to a bit of music on the radio, but it gradually got on our nerves, and we turned the racket off. The Porsche glided down the highway; the surroundings blurred into gray-and-green tones.

The GPS, which had been silent for a long time, announced that we should take the next exit. The two-lane highway led through partially harvested fields. Then we came to the forest. Spruces, a few deciduous trees, at first standing alone and then growing denser. The high branches moved closer and closer to the road; the sun had difficulty penetrating the leaf-and-needle roof to reach us. Shadows scurried over our faces like dreams from another life.

The terrain became uneven; the path led uphill. Every time we came across a clearing, I caught a glimpse of knolls, small villages with church steeples, or isolated farms.

Chris stepped hard on the brakes. I must have dozed off, because I was startled awake. In front of us, a large mobile home was obviously having trouble coping with the incline. I looked at the speedometer. Not even sixty kilometers per hour.

"Where did this monster come from?" I asked.

"The RV?"

"Do you see something else blocking our way?"

Chris chuckled. "We're in a tourist area."

"Who wants to spend their vacation here? We're in the middle of nowhere."

"Well, people like these guys in front of us." He steered with his left hand and made a charming circular movement with his right. "Nature, tranquility. You can hike here, tune out. Stuff like that."

Chris drove carefully over the middle line to check for oncoming traffic. "No way," he said. "Way too many curves. Not at all navigable."

"Don't worry about it," I said. "Let's just enjoy the scenery."

"By the by," he said, "did you sleep well?"

"I only dozed off for a second."

"More like forty-five minutes." Chris grinned.

"What do you expect?" I protested. "This is a resort area. And I intend to relax."

"I have no problem with that. You don't talk much, anyway."

"Oh! The gentleman wants entertainment."

"It would be nice."

"Then you should have brought that computer wench along. What was her name again? Scooby? Or Scrappy? Some dog's name."

"Saskia," Chris noted dryly.

"I told you. A great name for a husky. That Saskia would have surely blabbered without end."

The RV in front of us signaled and pulled to the side of the road. Chris heaved a sigh of relief, mumbled "Finally," and hit the gas.

It did not take long before the GPS sounded again. It led us from the two-lane highway to a frontage road. I briefly glimpsed an abandoned rest area that would have been nearly impossible to see from the highway. Every now and then, I saw high stacks of neatly piled timber between the trees.

Again, the GPS came to life. We turned onto a private drive. Chris adjusted his speed. Dilapidated pavement, weeds sprouted out of every nook. No one had been here for a number of years.

A wood gate barred us from driving farther. A sign nailed to its middle stated *Private Property, No Trespassing*.

Chris stopped the car and turned off the engine. I now heard the ripples of what sounded like a small brook. "End of the road," he said. He bent over to my side, opened the glove compartment, and grabbed his pistol. He pulled the slide back, set the safety, and made a move to get out.

"Why the gun?" I asked.

"No one's there. It can't hurt." He climbed out of the car.

When I came around the Porsche, the gun had disappeared, and Chris's shirt had a small bulge in it. He'd apparently stowed the weapon in the back waistband of his pants.

The closer we got to the abandoned farmhouse, the higher the weeds. The pavement had almost completely disappeared beneath them. The midday sun burned hot. The only sound I heard was the chirping of crickets.

The buildings that were now in view had clearly once been a neat farm. A large half-timbered dwelling, behind which stood an attached L-shaped stable and barn. But time had left its mark. The roofs, once tiled in red, were almost entirely overgrown with moss and broken in places. Weathered wood was exposed.

We crossed something that must have once been a fruit and vegetable garden. Tall flowering chives, an overgrown blackberry bush. In the yard in front of the main house, meter-high shrubs, stinging nettles, and wildflowers. The well was surrounded by sandstone blocks; it was covered with ancient timber planks; the iron hand pump brown from rust.

We stepped up onto a kind of patio, whose natural stone was sunken and bumpy. Boards were nailed across the entrance of the house. Chris shook the handle. When nothing budged, he tore down the barrier one piece after the other. The boards splintered. Wood dust trickled to the ground, giving off a moldy smell.

The door's hinges screamed in protest when Chris finally opened it. The interior that greeted us was desolate and dreary. Pressed clay floor, once carefully swept, now covered everywhere with dust, chunks of fallen plaster, and some old bottles. The only piece of furniture was a built-in bread cupboard. Even its doors hung tired and lifeless on their sides.

We carefully made our way across the space that had obviously served as the kitchen. Our passage into the next room was unobstructed. Again, the same desolation inside. Only here, the windows were nailed shut from outside. The windowpanes were either milky or shattered.

"We're not going to find anything here," I said.

"There must be a second story," Chris said.

"We can look later. There's usually only a hayloft up there."

"And you know that from where?"

"It's the same back home."

"Then we'll go to the barn first." Without waiting for my answer, Chris went out.

Left alone, I closed my eyes for a short minute and tried to imagine how it might have once been in this house. A large table with everyone sitting around it for dinner. The smell of freshly baked goods emanating from the bread cupboard. Miriam, then five, with her entire family, frightened, on the run, but here in this room, safe. At least she had thought so. A child could not imagine betrayal.

I had to blink when I stepped outside. The sun was to blame. It hurt my eyes and made them tear.

Chris stood next to the well and fiddled with the pump. "Completely broken, the piece of shit."

"If you don't keep a well properly maintained, it accumulates silt and eventually dries up," I explained.

Chris acknowledged my comment with raised eyebrows, and we fought our way through brush to get to the barn. A heavy sliding door. Chris put his entire weight behind it and shoved it open bit by bit. The air was stuffy. Dust particles danced inertly against the light.

Chris began to cough. "I won't be able to stay here too long."

A former cattle shed with shoulder-high partitions. In one of the stalls, I saw the remains of a large car—the paint faded, the doors ripped open, the hood propped up.

We walked over.

"An ancient Mercedes." Chris coughed once more.

"Doesn't fit with the farm," I said.

"No. This was once a luxury car." Chris's cough was getting worse.

"This has to be the car that Miriam's family drove here."

"Could be."

"They left it behind and switched into something more inconspicuous."

Chris cleared his throat and was once again shaken by a cough.

"What would you think if I examined the car a little more closely and you go back in the house and have a look at the second story?" I asked.

"Sounds good," he said.

"But take care not to fall through. The house definitely doesn't have cement ceilings."

"I'm always careful," he said before clearing out of the barn with hurried steps.

I approached the Mercedes. The motor was no longer there. Loose cables hung haphazardly. Inside the car, there were no more seats. The steering wheel was missing. I jiggled the glove compartment, it gave way with a creak. Empty.

The trunk was closed. Jammed. I pulled up on it until it opened. There was some kind of object in the back left corner. I reached in and grabbed it. A doll—or what had once been a doll. A porcelain face, half-broken, the painted eyes almost completely washed out, same with the mouth and nose. The white arms and legs were yellowed and sewn to a cloth body that lay moth-eaten and brittle in my hand.

I heard footsteps from behind.

"Look what I found, Chris!" I called without turning around.

The footsteps came closer until they stopped next to me.

"This may have once belonged to Miriam," I said and straightened up so I could turn toward Chris.

The blow caught me without warning in the neck. My head slammed against the car. Half-aware, I lurched up. An arm wrapped around my throat and began choking me.

I tried to scream, my body a singularity of pain. A fear stronger than any I'd ever felt filled me. I wanted to free myself but didn't have any more strength. I floundered like a fish does on land shortly before life abandons it.

Just when I thought I couldn't hold out any longer, when I was sure I would die, my assailant let me go. Half-dead and panic-stricken, I crumpled to the ground.

My arms were roughly grabbed and bound together with some kind of wire that cut deep into my skin. A hand yanked my head back by my hair; my mouth was taped shut. Now my legs were lashed to one another until I couldn't move at all.

I heard someone stand up behind me. For a while, I remained lying face down in the dust, arduously sucking for air through my nose.

Then I was seized by the shoulder and spun around. Dirt in my eyes, I blinked frantically until I could see something. A young, scraggy man. At most mid-twenties. Stupid, expressionless eyes. His face covered all over with pimples. On his head, he wore a blue baseball cap featuring an anime monster.

I heard footsteps again. I fervently hoped it was Chris, but at the same time, I felt a deep-seated fear. Nothing was as it had been before. My world fell apart.

A tall man came within view. Massive shoulders, gelled hair, sunglasses. He carried a long stick in his hand. No, scrap that—not a stick. A pistol with a black pipe extending from it. I had never seen such a thing, but I knew that it was a silencer.

He motioned with the gun in my general direction. "Sven, are you nuts? I talked with Sonja on the phone a minute ago and told her where we are and that we have the two. She said just kill them and move on. And you know Sonja."

The scraggy one planted himself defiantly in front of his partner. "But Marko, just killing her means she'll get nothing out of it, and that's not fun at all! Sonja always says that we should have fun."

The sturdy man raised his pistol and leaned the silencer against his right shoulder. "But not on the job, moron!"

The scraggy one danced uneasily in place. "You don't have to tell Sonja. When we meet her tonight, everything will be done. She isn't going to come here and check up on how we did the two in. Main thing: dead."

Brawny stepped closer to us and stared at the scraggy one before he finally said, "Damn. Have you at least tied the whore up good?" He bent down. I tried to squirm away from him, but he caught my arm and threw me effortlessly to the side. Then he pulled on my wrist binding and checked the knot at my feet. "All right. Because it's you. Where's the other asshole gotten to?"

Scraggy grinned triumphantly. "The bald guy went back into the house."

"Okay," the broad-shouldered man said and stood up. "We'll take care of the bald-headed dude. Then you can play with this black bitch."

The scraggy man literally leaped for joy and nearly ran out of the barn.

"But be careful!" Brawny yelled after him. "That bald guy didn't exactly look harmless. Not that he gets one over on ya."

Scraggy did not answer. He had almost reached the barn door when an explosion resounded, then another and another. Scraggy man was hit by an invisible fist in the middle of his body and eddied back. He raised his hand to his face to protect himself. There was one more crack, and his fingers were now just bloody stubs. He let out an inhuman scream. Again, something hit him, spun him around, and threw him to the ground.

He didn't budge any further. Dark liquid gushed from his midsection.

"Fucking shit!" screamed the broad-shouldered man, who had squatted down with the first shot.

I recognized Chris's silhouette in the glare of the backlit barn door. He held his right arm out and aimed at the big man who was still crouched down on the ground. Another explosion. Dust and dirt sprayed up. I tried to crawl away but only managed to move a few centimeters.

I couldn't see the broad-shouldered man any longer, and in the next second, I knew why. An arm reached around my neck from behind, and something hard and cold pressed up against my temple. Putrid, hot breath invaded my nostrils.

Brawny hollered now. I didn't understand him at first. My body felt like ice; my brain was frozen. Then I could make out his words. "Stay put, fucker!"

Chris stood still with the muzzle of his gun pointed directly at me.

"All right!" the man behind me screamed. "Drop your weapon immediately, you stupid bastard, or I'll blow this black bitch away." He leaned forward, his head right next to mine now.

Chris made a face as if he were thinking. Then he said, "No."

The man howled in rage. "Throw your weapon down, or I swear I'll kill her."

Chris raised his eyebrows in amazement. "That would be a good trick."

Another explosion. A fiery lance whizzed by my face. I heard a sound like a hammer hitting a piece of meat. The arm that held me fell limp. I couldn't support myself and toppled backward.

The broad-shouldered man was on the ground, right in front of me. Almost precisely in the middle of his forehead gaped a hole the size of a euro. His eyes glazed bright in a peculiar way, and in one instant, all that light left them. Sticky liquid reached my cheek.

Chris's shoe came into my field of vision. He stopped in front of the dead man and kicked his weapon out of reach. Then he knelt down, took hold of the tape on my mouth, and gently removed it.

I had forgotten to breathe. Gasping loudly, I sucked in air.

"Alicia, are you okay?" he asked.

I wasn't able to answer him.

He helped me sit up. Now I could see both corpses. I closed my eyelids and opened them. Chris's face was directly in front of mine.

"Nothing is okay," I said. "It never will be again."

53

Chris sat by me and held me tight. He wrapped his arms around me, folded them across my chest, and just stayed there. At first, it was uncomfortable. I wanted to shake him off, I wanted to bust free, I wanted to get away and leave behind everything that had happened to me on this horrible day. But I could not. Chris was stronger.

My body began to tremble, despite my attempts to control it. I felt Chris's breath on my neck, felt his warmth.

I cannot say how long we sat next to the two corpses in the dimly lit barn. The silence, the chirp of the crickets, Chris's repetitive cough.

At some point, my heartbeat slowed down, the trembling subsided. Chris loosened his hug and stroked his hand gently over my forehead and hair. I allowed him.

"Are you better?" he asked.

I gave a slight nod.

Chris let go of me completely. He stood up. Without saying a word, he left the stall, and when he was just out of sight, I heard him in the yard, messing with things. Things that screeched and squealed like living beings.

He came back. He pulled a pair of latex gloves on, as he had when we broke into the dead postgrad's apartment together.

Everywhere we went, we ran into death. That was my new life. Death had become our constant companion.

Chris bent down and collected the bullet casings. Then he began to frisk the bodies systematically. He did not even neglect searching underneath the insoles of their shoes. A comb, a pack of chewing gum, some money, a single car key. That was everything.

He straightened up and looked at me intently.

"What did you do out there?" I asked.

"We have to get rid of our two friends."

"Again, no police? No official investigation?"

Chris shook his head.

"And if they're eventually found?" I avoided the sight of the motionless bodies.

"That will take a while. A long while. And if they're discovered, nothing will indicate that you or I had anything to do with it."

"You're sure about that?"

"Trust me," he said. "I'm familiar with forensic investigations."

I mustered all my willpower and pulled myself up, unsteady at first. Taking a deep breath, I tamped down the weakness that wanted to spread through me. "I'll help you."

Chris came closer and handed me a second pair of gloves. I carefully pulled them on.

"We'll start with the smaller of the two." Chris bent over the scraggy one who had been wearing a baseball cap.

It had fallen off, the fabric had turned dark, saturated with blood.

Chris grabbed the young man under the armpits and hoisted him up. I got hold of his feet, which were clad in red suede brand-name sneakers. The soles looked almost new. Together, we dragged the corpse out of the barn.

Chris had removed the wood planks from the well. The rotten timber was stacked neatly in a pile. One of the dead man's feet slipped out of my hand. The body was as soft as rubber, lacking all rigidity. When life left him, it had taken every bit of resistance with it.

We heaved the body up onto the stone ledge encompassing the well. Hard work. Chris and I breathed heavily. Sweat ran down our brows. Sweat that felt cold and foreign on my skin.

I caught another scrutinizing glance from Chris, and then he gave the dead man a nudge. All of a sudden, the corpse disappeared from the stone shelf; a second later, I heard it hit a puddle. That was not the only sound, however. The unmistakable crack of breaking bones was mixed in there.

I felt sick. I fell to my knees, my body convulsed, my stomach heaved. Chris held me by the shoulders as I quashed my nausea. I don't know how he did it. But through his hands, he seemed to transfer the power that I needed to finish what we still had to deal with here.

I stood back up. We headed into the barn again.

Even though the big man weighed substantially more than his partner, we managed to carry the body much faster this time. The circular wall around the well caused us some problems, but in the end, he disappeared too.

Chris's cough got worse. I went into the barn alone. I collected every little thing that could possibly be traced back to the two of them. I carried all of their belongings out and returned them to their rightful owners at the bottom of the dark shaft. I only kept the car key.

While Chris laid the timber back across the opening, I walked one last time into the barn. I found a rusty old shovel and used it to throw dirt, clay, and dust over the traitorous bloodstains.

I painstakingly searched the ground. No evidence remained of what had happened here.

Chris waited for me outside. The well almost looked like it had before. How much time had lapsed since we arrived at this old farm in search of a past that might not ever have been?

We followed the path out in silence. Stinging nettles grasped our legs, like arms that were trying to stop us. We steadily pushed on; we did not look back.

We found our Porsche. The neighboring brook murmured softly. Chris stood still. "We should . . . We have to wash the blood off and clean our clothes as well as possible. Later, we'll get some new things." He went to the creek, stuck his gloved hands in, and rubbed them together. I did the same. Dark reddish-brown streaks broke away from my fingers and drifted off in the clear water. We washed each other's faces and arms. The stains on our clothes and our shoes proved to be more stubborn. We did our best to remove them.

Then we walked on until we reached the road. About twenty meters away stood a mobile home, not unlike the one that had forced us to travel at a snail's pace on our way up. We stopped short. The sun burned down on us; it was a dreadfully hot day. Our clothes had already begun to dry.

"Remember the rest area that we drove past?" Chris asked.

"The one that's maybe three or four kilometers away?"

"I'd guess more like five. That's far enough. I'll drive the RV, and you come after in the Porsche."

"You want to leave the Winnebago sitting in the parking lot?"

"It's not a bad idea. A resort area, an RV on an idyllically situated spot. It'll be weeks before anyone gets suspicious."

"All right," I agreed.

Chris went to the mobile home, put the key into the door, and opened it. "Let me get just a little ahead. You can take off the gloves as soon as you're sitting in the Porsche, but don't throw them away."

I watched Chris start up the RV, turn around in the drive, and follow the narrow street back down. He soon disappeared.

I walked to our car and almost touched the door handle, but in the nick of time, I thought better of it. I stopped, removed my gloves, and stowed them in the pocket of my jeans. We had washed the blood off, but remnants of it surely clung to the thin white rubber. And not only there.

54

S even hours later and four hundred kilometers away from Fichtelberg. I had chosen and applied some decent eye shadow, and now I gave my lashes a second coat of mascara. Afterward, I put a little perfume on. I looked at myself critically in the large illuminated bathroom mirror. The yellow top complimented my complexion. I put my brand-new blazer on over it.

Ready.

I left the bathroom and strolled into our hotel room. Chris sat on a dark chair and studied a colorful flyer. He wore black pants, business shoes that went well with them, and a white shirt opened at the collar. It looked good on him.

"I'm ready," I said.

Chris raised his eyes and ogled me shamelessly.

"And?" I asked.

"Perfect."

He got up, and together we walked out into the hall. We made our way downstairs in the elevator, accompanied by nice soft music.

The hotel lobby was spacious and luxuriously furnished. Several sitting areas spread throughout the room were populated by men and women chatting or flipping through magazines. Staff attended the reception desk; a couple was obviously checking in.

The restaurant was situated just off the lobby. Tables for two, four, and more people. Candles. Obliging waiters scurrying about.

We selected a conspicuous table in the middle of the restaurant. Chris raised his hand for an instant, and a server in black livery was at our side. He gave us leather-bound menus, and Chris ordered red Bordeaux for himself and dry white wine for me. We shared trivialities; sometimes I laughed audibly but never too loud.

Chris had great fun while we ate. He had a medium-rare steak with potato wedges, I a creation of turbot with lasagna and sweet peppers—a slightly decadent mix, but it tasted fantastic. Our dessert comprised a delicious crème brûlée and two double espressos.

All around satisfied, Chris paid the bill. He didn't forget to slip our waiter an obscenely large tip.

We remained seated awhile. Chris enthused about Berlin and the places we had visited that day. Then we threw each other a knowing look, nodded smiling, and rose.

We left the restaurant together arm in arm, crossed the lobby, got into the elevator, and rode to our floor.

Chris used the key card, invited me in with a welcoming gesture, and shut the door behind us.

"Finally," I said and pulled the tight heels off my feet while still standing. "Do you think they bought it?"

Chris leaned against the doorjamb and allowed himself plenty of time to answer. "One hundred percent," he eventually replied.

"We're not your run-of-the-mill couple."

"No?" Chris furrowed his brow. "Don't I look like somebody who could have an attractive girlfriend?"

"That's not what I meant."

"You mean the difference in age?"

"Come on. Cut it out! A practically bald guy and a half African American. We're not easy to forget."

"I'd hope so! That was the whole point—to wangle an alibi." Chris went over to the minibar, opened it, and removed a bottle and two glasses before lounging sideways across the bed. He kicked off his shoes, placed the glasses on the bedside table, and held out the Black Label.

"Should I know that?"

"You will now." He unscrewed the cap and filled each glass halfway.

I moved the wing chair closer to him, took a seat, and grabbed my drink. I tried it. The whisky tasted mild and smoky.

"Good," I said.

Chris leaned his back against the headboard and raised a toast to me.

"Shopping wears you out," I said.

"You're telling me! But we could hardly have checked in here with our old rags."

I thought about the bloodstains that, even with great effort, we'd only managed to get halfway out. And I thought about how the blood got on our clothes in the first place. I drank again. This time more than before.

"We need to get rid of our old things," I said.

Chris nodded. "But not here. They're safe in our new luggage for the moment. When we continue on our way, an opportunity will present itself to dispose of them once and for all."

"And if . . ." I gathered my thoughts. "And if they come arrest us now?"

Chris was perfectly calm. "No one is looking for us. We're two lovers on vacation in Berlin."

My glass was empty. I held it out to Chris, and he poured us both new drinks.

"Who were those men?" I asked. "In the barn."

"I'd be shocked if they weren't hit men."

"Hit men."

"Yeah."

"So that's what they look like in reality."

Chris inspected the whisky in his hand. "For a while there, you were alone with the two. Did they say anything?"

"No." But after some thought I added, "Well, maybe."

"I understand that you wouldn't want to remember. But I'm convinced it's important to try."

I sighed. "You're right. They were talking unintelligibly, some fucked-up shit. The younger one didn't want to kill me immediately, but . . ."

His demeanor became serious. "And anything else?" he asked. "Besides these . . . let's call them threats?"

"The bigger one spoke of a woman. He was saying that she'd sent them. That she'd instructed them to kill us. Something like that."

Chris sipped at his drink. "Did they mention a name, by any chance?"

"Anja or Sonja. I can't remember exactly."

"A woman," Chris said. "What woman would have an interest in seeing us dead?"

"Mrs. Falk," I replied without hesitation.

"That was my thought as well. She blamed Miriam Morgenroth for the destruction of her company. And for her husband's poor health." Chris set his glass down and picked up his smartphone.

"What are you looking for?" I asked.

"I just googled Mrs. Falk." He swiped over the display a few times, found an applicable result, and enlarged it with his index finger and thumb. "Mrs. Falk, given name, Irene."

"That doesn't sound remotely similar to Anja or Sonja."

Chris put his phone away. "Maybe you didn't hear the name correctly. Or she might have used a fake name."

"Yeah. Could be. I'm just wondering how the hit men even found us—out in the middle of nowhere."

"Do you remember when we took that two-lane highway, and you woke up from your snooze? An RV crept along in front of us. That was the two of them."

"Which means that they weren't tailing us but actually knew where they would find us."

Chris slid a little farther down on the bed and folded his hands behind his head. "Mrs. Falk knew that we wanted to go look around Fichtelberg. But so did Georg Vogt."

"Georg?" I said, amazed. "What interest would he have in killing us? He's paying us to do this."

Chris closed his eyes to think everything over. I noticed how tired he was. "The murderers were heading in the same direction as us, but it took them awhile to track us down. So, they must not have known the exact address. That points more towards Mrs. Falk."

"She wanted to prevent us from finding Miriam," I said.

"Ludicrous," Chris said, sounding sleepy. "She wants to ensure that we don't find the diamonds."

I was about to respond to that, but Chris's breathing indicated that he had fallen asleep. His chest rose and fell at regular intervals.

I rested my feet on the bed and made myself more comfortable on the chair. I closed my eyes and thought about sparkling diamonds and Miriam. And about the blood that flew out of the back of the bigger man's head when Chris shot him. My heart began to beat wildly, and I concentrated as hard I could. The gruesome image disappeared. Wind whipped up against me, the smell of salt rose to my nose. I saw the spray of the surf and the blue of the sea lavender as I approached my island.

I fell asleep.

55

A noise woke me. Light was shining through the half-open bathroom door. A bright fissure in a gray world. Chris slept soundly, completely relaxed. A peaceful image.

He had probably just turned onto his other side, and that was what had woken me. I quietly stood up, took the blanket from the foot of the bed, and spread it carefully over him.

I've been doing this quite a lot lately, I thought.

I went over to the window and pushed the curtain to the side so I could see out. Your typical big-city street. Tall buildings, dark windows—only the displays of the stores on the first floor were illuminated brightly. Little traffic, a few pedestrians, among them couples strolling by arm in arm.

I shot a glance at Chris. No, we were not like that. We had nothing in common. Fate had simply brought us together. We would travel the same path for a little while. Nothing more.

Was I sure about that? I pressed my forehead against the glass, closed my eyes, and listened deep inside me. No. I had no feelings for Chris. I cared for him because he did not have anyone else. And because I needed him.

And what about him? Without hesitating, he had shot a man who had a gun pressed against my temple. Had Chris just barely missed, it would have been my corpse now lying in that cold well.

What did that prove? Nothing. The question was: Would he have been able to shoot if he cared even the slightest bit for me? I didn't know the answer.

In any case, we were too different from one another. Chris wanted to be rich, travel to distant lands, laugh it up, and lead a life without commitment.

And where did I fit in? What was I actually expecting out of life? I thought about my prison cell, where I had spent a year, and about the nurses' dorm in Starnberg. About my work in the rehab clinic. Did I really want to go back there? Should that be my life?

Absolutely not.

But then what?

My home had died with my grandmother. I could never return. And as soon as we found out what had happened to Miriam, I would never see Chris again.

And then?

Nothing came to mind.

Okay, I thought, *this is a wonderful depression.*

I tiptoed to my purse, which was hanging on the coatrack, opened the clasp, and took out the book of poems Miriam and I had read together. In the opposite corner of the room stood a small desk. I sat on the chair in front of it, switched the reading lamp on, and opened the book.

On the first page a dedication—written in pencil, in scrawling handwriting:

For my favorite blue flower,
Miriam Morgenroth.

I had to smile. An appropriate name for Miriam. Her blue eyes, her wonderful nature. Everything about her reminded me of the delicate and yet extremely strong sea lavender.

I turned to the title page.

German Poetry

Federation of Book Lovers, Wegweiser Publishing House GmbH, Berlin, 1926

How many times had Miriam held this volume in her hands? In what places and under what circumstances? The book was printed long before the Second World War. Did her family have it with them when they fled? Had it also accompanied Miriam to the concentration camps? Wasn't every possession taken away there?

I definitely have to ask Miriam flew through my head, followed by a feeling of vast emptiness, because it suddenly hit me that, like my grandmother, I would never see Miriam again.

I quickly turned the pages until I came to the poem about the blue flower.

I search for the blue flower,
I search but never find it,
I dream, that in that flower
Happiness would bloom for me.

I had been searching for Miriam for a long time. But—how had she put it? It's not the finding that's important but rather the path taken.

With every passing day, the probability that I would be able to save my friend waned. But had I ever expected anything different? Had I actually ever expected to find Miriam safe and sound? Or had I always been on a search for the corpse of a woman who had entered my life only to disappear after deeply touching my heart?

I closed the book. Lost in thought, I ran my fingers over the worn leather jacket. It was not original but a protective covering that was added later. I gingerly removed the left cover flap of the jacket from the book and then the right. The backside of the leather was tanned lightly. Someone had painted black words and lines on it. Names of locations, addresses, kilometers, times. There was even a title:

Escape Plan.

56

Sonja

A gray Toyota drove slowly over the pavement. An inconspicuous car—just right if you did not want to attract attention. The half-rotted wooden gate blocked the entry. The brakes squeaked, and the car came to a stop. The window was rolled down on the driver's side, and a woman with long dark hair stuck her head out. She squinted in an attempt to read the sign: "Private Property, No Trespassing."

Sonja swore under her breath. "Fuck! Fuck! Fuck! Those stupid fuckers! I told them in plain words where to meet. And what do they do?" She slapped the steering wheel with her palm.

Delicate mist hung over the small brook and the gate. The sun was just rising, and its rays had not yet gained the power to make the white haze disappear. Birds were chirping. Their song blared in Sonja's ear.

"Shut your face!" she screamed and rolled the window back up.

But the problem remained. Marko and Sven had not shown up last night. They had just left her sitting there. And they couldn't be reached by phone. That was not a good sign. But if the cops had caught them, uniformed men would be crawling all around the place. And there weren't any.

Where were those two cocksuckers? They had probably gotten comfortable somewhere and were lying around in the mobile home, completely wasted. And if the pigs found them like that, all three of them would be screwed.

Sonja stepped on the accelerator, the front wheels spun. She flew in reverse and turned back down the road. Marko and Sven had finished their job. Maybe they'd even had some fun while doing it. And afterward, they would have been completely amped, as they always were. So, what would the idiots have done? They'd have found a cozy spot to park the mobile home. They had a couple bottles of Coke and a few bags of dope—everything they would need for a great night.

They would be surprised when she found them so fast. And what she had in store for the two of them, they would not soon forget! Sonja flashed an evil grin. A harsh punishment. What must be, must be.

She sped off at a breakneck pace. At this early hour, the road was deserted anyway. On her left, she saw a sign. It took a few seconds before its significance sunk in: "Rest Area."

Sonja slammed hard on the brakes. The Toyota pulled fitfully to the left. The tires protested loudly as she skidded over the rough asphalt. Then the car came to a stop.

Sonja turned the steering wheel as far as she could, did a one-eighty, and drove to the entrance of the rest area. She signaled according to regulation and let the car roll in at a snail's pace.

Bingo! Her intuition had not led her astray. The mobile home stood in the farthest corner, so it could not be seen from the road. Marko, that dipshit, thought that he could actually get away with this.

Sonja parked the car, climbed out, and approached the Winnebago. No noise, not even the slightest movement, emerged from the vehicle. As she had expected—Sven and Marko were so wasted that they could no longer move.

She tried the side door. Locked. Well, at least they were cautious.

She dug the spare key out of her pocket, unlocked the door, then climbed inside. Empty. No sign of the boys. The interior looked as it always did: dirty dishes, food remnants, and empty wrappers on the floor.

There was no one in the cab either.

Sonja opened the side compartment, where the pistol with the silencer was usually stored. It was gone. So, Marko had the gun.

After she had another look around, she got out, gingerly shut the door, and locked it back up. She returned to the Toyota and sat behind the wheel.

"Those dumbasses," she hissed quietly. "How often did I tell them, get away from the scene of the crime as fast as possible? A thousand times! But these guys are so fucking stupid, I can't believe it. They actually stayed on the farm and are still playing with the winners."

It did not take long before she pulled herself together and turned back onto the narrow road. She soon reached the decrepit old gate a second time.

Meanwhile, the fog had dissipated. Bright-blue sky, yet still comfortably cool. Sonja took her pistol out of the bag, ensured that there was a cartridge in the chamber, and set the safety. She rummaged around the interior of the car and found a flashlight, which she also grabbed. You never know.

She set off. Weeds everywhere. When she looked closer, she could see that they had been trampled down in places. Evidence that people had been here not all that long ago. The stems were bent in one and then the other direction.

The farm was a veritable ramshackle hut. Not even fit for rats. The door had been nailed shut. Someone had ripped out the boards and left them scattered about. The rooms were empty. Footprints covered the dusty floor; they did not belong to Marko or Sven. No sign that anything out of the ordinary had taken place here.

Sonja returned to the courtyard, letting her eyes wander. A covered well, tall grass, weeds, and farther back, the barn. Some kind of trampled path in the middle of the yard, coming from the entrance—this time wider, left by more people.

Sonja made her way to the shed, whose door stood half-open. She peeked inside. Nothing. The room was filled with musty air, still cool from the previous night. No one to be seen.

But the tracks clearly led to this spot. What had happened between her boys and the victims in here? She pulled the flashlight out of her jacket and turned it on. The harsh beam flitted over the filthy walls.

Sonja directed her attention to the floor. Rotten straw, dust, spiderwebs, dirt. Two, three, no, four blotches that looked different. Someone had cleaned up. With what? An old shovel was leaning against the wall. With that!

Sonja stood in the middle of the barn. On her left was a large area with fresh-looking dirt. She stuck her foot into it, wiped it back and forth. When she pulled it out, the tip of her shoe was dark. Blood.

What happened here? Farther in front, there was a similar spot. Relatively large. Bloodstains from two people. Judging from the amount, they had both been liquidated. No one survived when liters of blood gushed out of him. At that point, anyone would die. Her boys had done a good job.

But what had they done with the bodies? And again, where the hell had Marko and Sven gotten to?

The bodies were not in the mobile home. So, they hadn't hidden them there. But also not in the main house and not in the stable.

Sonja left the barn. The trampled brush in front of her led directly to the well. Of course! Perfect! She marched over to it, placed her pistol carefully on the stone ledge, and began pulling up the boards. It went easier than expected.

She bent over the hole and was confronted with a dark, gaping void. Farther down, she saw the silver reflection of light off of water. She distinctly recognized the outline of at least one body.

Sonja took the flashlight out and shined it below. Marko's lifeless white eyes gaped back at her. He had a circular hole in the middle of his brow. Next to him lay Sven, legs broken. They were twisted at a grotesque angle.

Sonja screamed, the sound amplified by the walls of the well.

57

Sonja

The burger was topped with crispy bacon, extra cheese, and tomatoes. The sauce tasted a bit strange, but it somehow still fit. Sonja took a long sip of her Diet Coke through the thick straw.

The fast-food restaurant was bustling. Families with children, workers who had taken an early lunch, truck drivers. The gray Toyota stood in the shade under a tree. The windows were up.

Sonja wiped her hands clean on a paper napkin and let it fall carelessly. She fished out a cheap burner and dialed a number with her fingertips before she put the phone to her ear and waited.

"You are the biggest asshole," she said, instead of her usual greeting. "Why? No one told us that the two we were sent to knock off were some kind of fucking Rambos. At any rate, they laid my two men out cold."

Sonja listened to the reply. She laughed aloud. "No. They couldn't have ratted. They didn't have any infor-

mation to divulge, because they never knew where the contracts came from in the first place. That was entirely my
job."

She paused, grabbed a couple fries, chewed, and swallowed. "Of course, I'm going to finish the job. By all
means. You don't need anyone else. That you can be sure
of. I'll do it myself. Just tell me where to find the stupid
fuckers."

Another load of fries landed in her mouth. "What? You
have no idea? . . . They must be somewhere! You said you
know the two of them. So just give them a call and ask
where they are, and then I'll come along and take care of
the rest."

Sonja had a look-see in the fry box. It was empty. "No?
You don't want to call? . . . But you must know something!
Where could they have gone? . . . Either Munich or Ham-
burg? That's great. They're so close to one another."

Sonja made a pained expression and observed her grimace in the rearview mirror. "And if you had to bet? . . .
So, Hamburg. Good. But Hamburg is big. Really big. A lot
of people . . . Do you happen to have an address? . . . Once
again, no?"

She exhaled impatiently. "In the warehouse district? . . .
Yeah, I know it. I've been there before . . . If these two
show up, I'll find them. One black and one bald, they'll
stick out . . . But just so we understand each other correctly, this will cost you extra. Those were two really good
people I lost because of you. And it'll take some time before I can replace them."

At the reply, Sonja's expression hardened, as did her
voice. "No. Not double. Triple . . . That won't kill you.
And while you're at it, you can write off the RV, as well.
There's going to be a fire. The thing was utterly filthy, anyway."

58

The light timidly crept through the thick curtains into the room. The contours of the objects dissolved into the black of night. The new day did not have enough power yet to assert itself against the obscureness. Indecisive, virtually lost, it fought the dark.

Chris's face emerged from the dawn. The pastiness of his cheeks, the shadow of his three-day beard.

Without warning, his eyes opened. They glowed translucent with a shimmer of green.

"I had a dream," he said. It sounded like he was surprised by this.

"Oh yeah?" I said.

"Sun. And sand. I believe I was in the desert."

"Did you like it?"

Chris thought a moment before he answered. "Like it? I felt safe. Secure."

"Ah," I said.

"You can't sleep?"

I shook my head. "I was excited. I had to do something to distract myself."

"Did you have any success with that?"

"Yes." I took the leather book cover, went to the bed, and climbed in next to him.

"What do you have there?"

"Do you remember the book that belonged to Miriam, the one she read to me?"

"Of course. Dr. Vogt gave it to you."

"Exactly." I switched on one of the lamps. Warm yellow light.

Chris blinked.

"And look," I continued, "what I found on the inside of the jacket."

I opened up the leather cover and showed Chris the map.

"The escape plan," he whispered. He stretched out his hand and followed the painted, partly faded line with his index finger. "Munich, Fichtelberg . . . I can't make out the next stop. And at the end, Hamburg. The warehouse district."

"Do you see?" I asked him. "At every location an address is noted, a street name, a house number. But not in Hamburg."

Chris studied the map intently. "Just a marking." He pointed again, this time at a seemingly meaningless scribble. "I see three gables whose roofs are rather oddly shaped. And look, there's something scratched next to them: 6-3."

I examined it more closely. "That appears to have been added later. You think . . .?"

"If we find the building with those gables, we'll be where the Morgenroths' journey ended. The place where they were arrested. And precisely where . . ."

"Where the diamonds are hidden?"

Chris smiled. "Who knows?"

He took the leather cover out of my hand, gave it one last look, and laid it on the bedside table. He turned to me. Our faces nearly touched. "I have no idea what will be waiting for us in that building."

"Miriam," I mumbled.

"Maybe the diamonds remain as lost as your Mir—"

Before he could finish the end of his sentence, I kissed him. Long and full of desperation.

He gently pushed me away. "You're deluded. You want to find something that you know can no longer be found."

"That means I'm in good company," I retorted. "You—and your lost diamonds."

Chris observed me seriously. Then the hint of a loving smile crept onto his face.

"Exactly," he said. "Me and my diamonds." He pulled me to him.

And as the sun's rays began to grow stronger, we made love. But this time, it was my arms that latched onto him and did not want to let go, because they knew that our time together was drawing to a close.

59

In the last kilometers before Hamburg, it started to rain. Fat drops pelted the Porsche's windshield. Chris turned on the wipers. They slid over the glass and left wet streaks.

The GPS guided us from the autobahn into the city through extremely crowded streets, past the harbor, where enormous ships were being loaded and unloaded by gargantuan cranes.

We penetrated deeper and deeper into the tangle of buildings. I lost my bearings and no longer knew which direction we were even traveling—quasi-aimlessly we drove on and flowed with the stream of busy traffic.

The navigation system incessantly gave out instructions, ordering us to make right and left turns at the next intersection, to switch lanes here or there, to follow this and that alteration in the direction of the street. The computer voice became meaningless background noise to me. Vapors huddled delicately on the inside of the glass. The surroundings disappeared as if behind a soft-focus filter.

A jolt went through the car, and Chris switched off the motor.

"Alicia," he said. "We're here."

I sat up, unbuckled my belt, and then leaned forward. "It's still raining," I said, as I looked doubtfully out the window. It was warm in the car; I felt snug and secure. The thought of getting out was deeply unappealing, not only because of the weather.

"I can go alone," Chris said.

"No, no," I hurried to answer. "You'd like that, wouldn't you? I'm coming with."

A little bit too overzealous, I opened the door and climbed out. I was greeted by a mild gust of mist. Countless tiny water particles sprayed me in the face. It smelled fresh, as it does anywhere after it has just rained. Then another note mixed in, ethereal and almost undetectable; the Elbe carried a delicate hint of the acrid scent of the sea with it.

In front of us stood virtually endless rows of impressive multi-story brick buildings. Dark red and powerful, they blocked every view of what lay behind.

Chris paused to look around. "So, this is the famous warehouse district?"

"Yes."

Chris seemed as though he wanted to launch into a lengthy response, but he merely said, "Impressive."

We started off. The old cobblestones felt bumpy under-foot and, due to the recent precipitation, slippery. The fine drizzling rain grew stronger. Light gusts swept wisps of wa-ter against us.

We crossed a bridge connecting two rows of ware-houses with one another. Brown, seemingly brackish water stretched between them, its surface inert and lifeless.

We took the street along the dock—past large wooden doors, company signs, and dark windows, some with advertisements hanging in them. And everywhere, we encountered that deep-red brick.

A café, a restaurant, a museum. Then once again companies, warehouses. Entries without any markings.

Every now and then, Chris stepped to the side to examine a building we were passing more intently. Each time he shook his head.

When we were almost to the end of the section, Chris came to a standstill and hooked his thumbs in the belt loops of his jeans. "We can't continue like this," he said.

"This does take a while. The warehouse district is huge."

"True. But also, from here we can only see one side of the buildings. Maybe those gables need to be spotted from the waterfront."

"Maybe," I agreed. "But how do you intend to get there?"

Chris grinned. "Like everyone else." He pointed diagonally downward at a boat that was moored at a dock. A group of people waited in an orderly line in front of it.

"Those are tourists," I said.

"The way you enunciate that, you make it sound like something vile." Chris was still grinning. "May I invite you on a romantic boat ride?"

"In this weather, it's anything but romantic."

"Just the two of us and the ship. What more do you want?"

"That's not a ship! That's a barge."

"Barge?"

I shook my head. "You wouldn't understand."

We went to the dock, bought two tickets, and walked on board across a gangplank. The other passengers took seats in the covered interior. We sat on a bench on the open stern. We were caught in the rain here, but the view was substantially better.

The gangplank was removed, the lines brought in. A diesel below us began to chug, and the barge set off.

We moved along the narrow channel, passed a bend, and the waterway widened. We entered a veritable gorge. The clouds above us appeared impenetrable, the light wan and illusory. In the slight wake that the bow of the barge produced, I could detect traces of raindrops.

Warehouses rose to the left and the right of us like stone guards, mercilessly locking us in. Their walls appeared as if they would draw near and squash us. The neo-Gothic-style architecture towered immovable and cold high up into the sky—timeless, at rest, like a piece of strange nature, not man-made but rather self-propagating.

We slid by innumerable windows, whose black and dusty panes denied any glimpse inside. After a while, the indistinguishable buildings seemed to lose their substance. They transformed into shadows silently gawking at us.

A strange feeling took hold of me. I wondered whether I was really here—if the time in which I lived truly existed or if, as at the movies, I was a voyeur spying on a foreign world.

The small barge that carried Chris and me seemed imaginary. The rotund voice of our tour guide, who babbled various banalities about the origin and history of the warehouse district, sporadically reached us from inside the compartment. The passengers had pushed the windows open and repeatedly leaned out. Diffuse flashes flared occasionally as the tourists tried to capture the silent beauty of the location with their cameras.

We came to another bend. A new row of warehouses, a new gorge.

In the middle stood a warehouse with three irregularly shaped gables.

We had found the last sanctuary of Miriam's family.

60

Another bridge, again cobblestone. The rain had stopped; only the wind remained, and it had increased in intensity over the past half hour.

Chris paused in front of a building. "This must be it," he said.

"Are you sure?"

"Absolutely. I counted the warehouses when we were on the boat."

"You mean on the barge."

"Precisely."

The customary wood gate had been replaced with an extravagant glass door. *Oasis and More* promised a wrought-iron inscription that hung above it.

We climbed a few steps and entered the restaurant. The entire first floor was gutted; a half dozen exposed cast-iron columns supported the ceiling. On the left ran a mahogany bar, behind it stood spices, coffee beans in silver canisters, tea in porcelain vessels. An intense, pleasant aroma.

On the right side there was a typical café, done up in finished wood. Comfortable round tables for two to four people with a view of the canal. We sat down.

Chris glanced around. "It all looks relatively new," he said.

"It doesn't seem so to me. Everything is still authentic," I replied.

"Authentically *refurbished*. A lot has changed here over the last years."

A server arrived. We ordered coffee, tea, and two pieces of apple pie. In no time, the young woman came back and set her fully loaded tray on our table. She began distributing.

"This place is beautiful," Chris said.

"Yeah. Isn't it?" the waitress smiled with a certain amount of pride.

"The renovation must have cost a fortune."

"You can see that?" she asked.

"I'm an architect." Chris sounded so convincing that I nearly believed him myself.

"During the Second World War, this block was virtually destroyed," the waitress explained.

"Is there anything left from that time?"

"I can't say exactly." The server shrugged as she let her eyes wander. "But I believe the columns, part of the ceiling, and the paneling on the rear wall comes from back then. They're original. I think everything else is fake."

The waitress left us, and we ate our pie with a hearty appetite—giant slices, still warm and spiced with cinnamon, just like it should be.

"This paneling"—I pointed with my fork across the café at the checker-patterned wall—"is definitely old. The waitress was right about that. The wood is almost black. But as an architect, you already knew that, correct?"

Chris smirked. "Dark, smoked, dried. With that, my knowledge is exhausted."

We laughed.

"The wood paneling reminds me of a big Battleship board," I said.

Chris furrowed his brow.

"You know—A7, you sank my battleship."

The smile disappeared from his face. He narrowed his eyes and pondered. "You mean like a coordinate system?"

I shrugged. "If you want to call it that."

Chris went silent again before he said, "Can you get Miriam's book out? I have an idea."

I took it out and put the volume on the table.

Chris gingerly removed the jacket and studied the markings. "Six three," he whispered. He looked in my direction, but his gaze passed right through me. "It can't be that simple," he said more to himself than to me.

"What do you mean?"

"The coordinate six three. That could indicate one of the squares on the paneling. It's easy to find, if you know what you are looking for."

I discreetly followed his gaze and studied the wall. "I doubt it. That's a real long shot."

"But we should check it out all the same."

"Now?"

Chris shook his head, smiling. "No. It would come across as a little strange if we start knocking on and prying at the wall. The tourist disclaimer wouldn't cover that."

"So, what do we do?"

"First, let's find a hotel in the vicinity with a nice, comfortable room. We'll rest a few hours, eat, and come back here later tonight."

This time, I grinned. "And of course, we have a key."

Chris smiled back knowingly. "As you recall, I don't need a key. We'll snoop around, and then we'll have our answer."

He made a small gesture, the waitress came over, and we paid.

As we were leaving, Chris opened the door for me to go out first. But at the same time, a tall young lady was entering the establishment. She accidentally bumped into me. She stopped in place and threw me a vacant glance. The woman was thin with a strikingly pale face. She wore her dark hair long and sleek.

"Excuse me," she said.

"No harm done," I replied and left the restaurant with Chris.

61

Darkness. The silhouettes of the warehouses and the night coalesced into one. No moon in the sky, the stars obscured by the cloud cover. Every now and then, a lonely lamp kept vigil; its shine merely cut a circular hole out of the dense black.

The wrought-iron *Oasis and More* sign was backlit by two spots. Their pale white light projected contours on the restaurant's walls. Inside the tavern, the blue luster of the emergency lighting glowed dimly.

Three o'clock in the morning. The café had been closed for a while. No one in sight.

Chris walked up to the entrance with me and began to fiddle with the lock. Just a few seconds later, the door opened, and we slipped into the restaurant.

The counter, the tables, the goods on the shelves—everything appeared as it had a few hours earlier, only now lonely and deserted. Asleep in the twilight.

Chris cast an exploratory eye about. "I'll take care of the wall, and you—"

"I can help you," I said.

Chris shook his head. "No. I'd rather you keep watch to make sure no one comes. It wouldn't be unusual to have security guards patrolling the area."

"Stand lookout," I said. "I've always wanted to do that."

Chris patted me on the shoulder and headed toward the paneling.

I turned to the window and stared out, trying to see something beyond my immediate surroundings. While doing this, I heard Chris behind me, moving a few pieces of furniture to the side. Then a light knock sounded as he inspected the wood wall.

"Six three." The thumping grew louder. "Shit!"

"Is everything all right?" I asked without taking my eyes off the road.

"Not really. It's completely solid. No hidden chamber."

"Maybe we read the numbers wrong. Can you try six eight or six nine?"

Chris knocked again. "No. Not there either."

"Just try every square," I suggested. "Who knows, maybe a piece of the wall is missing, and the numbers are off."

Chris went back to work. The pounding of his knuckles echoed dully through the café.

For a split second, I thought I caught a movement outside. I squinted and tried to reassure myself. Nothing. I was mistaken.

Chris stopped knocking, and a wooden creak tore into the ensuing silence.

And then Chris said, "Damn" and whistled quietly through his teeth.

Without thinking, I left my post and hurried back to him. He stood in front of the wall, which now revealed a square indentation. An identically sized wood panel lay on one of the tables.

"Did you find anything?" I asked breathlessly.

Chris nodded. He reached into the hollow space, pulled out papers covered in a thick blanket of dust, and spread them out next to the wood panel. Three, four, five thick bundles of banknotes. Ten thousand Reichsmarks each, banded with currency straps. Chris returned to the cranny and carefully felt around in it. He took out five booklets and handed them to me. I flipped the first one open: a passport belonging to a man named Peter Schmidt. The third document was for a small girl with light hair who was earnestly looking into the camera. Miriam—only here her name was Clara Schmidt.

"False passports," I said.

"They'd prepared for everything. Thought out every detail."

"But they hadn't planned on betrayal." I almost didn't dare to ask my next question. "And the diamonds?" I finally said.

Chris sighed and shook his head. "None."

"Not a single stone?" I glanced at the worthless money, at the unused passports. "We came all this way for nothing. You have no diamonds, and I . . . I don't have the slightest idea where Miriam is. It was all pointless."

Chris ran his fingertips over the spread-out papers. "Actually, I didn't expect to find anything."

A pane of glass broke with a clatter. An object slammed loudly against a table. Instantly, meter-long flames shot across the room.

We spun around. A second object exploded at our feet. Fire sprayed over Chris, eating away at his clothes, licking up his body.

I screamed and threw myself on him. We fell hard to the floor. I squeezed my weight up against his. Then I let

281

go, tore off my jacket, and used it to smother the last of the flames on him.

A noise, a rumbling filled the whole café. The bar, the floor, the wall that had concealed Miriam's passport—everything was becoming a sea of fire. Thick black smoke billowed over us.

Chris coughed and writhed in pain. Retching, he tried to dive below the smoke. His cough became stronger, fitful. I held him tight; the fumes made my eyes tear and started scratching my throat.

Without warning, Chris collapsed, unconscious.

I grabbed him under the arms; flames were close at his feet. I dragged him toward the exit.

The door stood open; wind swept in. We had almost made it.

A woman appeared in the doorway. Tall, slim, dark hair. Her face ghostly white. In her right hand, she held a large glass bottle out of which protruded a piece of fabric. *Molotov cocktail* shot through my head.

The woman realized that I had seen her. With her left hand, she flicked a lighter and a small flame jumped up. In the red-yellow glow of the fire, her eyes appeared ecstatic and full of passion. The hand holding the lighter closed in millimeter by millimeter on the gasoline-soaked rag sticking out of the bottle.

I dropped to my knees next to Chris, found the pistol in his waistband, and pulled it out. I flipped the thumb safety and shot. The bullet hit the woman above the left hip, and she spun around like a doll. She fell to the ground, her hand opened, and the bottle rolled out of harm's reach.

I stuck the pistol hastily in my belt, grabbed Chris, and dragged his unconscious body outside, down the stairs, and away from the building to the opposite side of the street.

I doubled over, breathing heavily.

The woman in the café screamed.

I left the pistol with Chris and then hurried back up the stairs. In the doorway, I stood still and scanned the sea of flames.

The woman had crawled out of the immediate danger zone, as far as she could manage. Blood oozed from her wound; she had raised herself halfway up to a sitting position.

"Get me out of here, you fucking bitch!" she hollered.

I lowered myself onto all fours and crept closer to see her better. Her face was contorted in pain, her eyes full of fury and hatred, directed at me. Dense, pungent smoke rolled over both of our heads.

"Why did you do it?" I yelled over the roar of the flames.

She did not seem to understand me.

"Why did you start the fire?" I said.

Her expression changed to raging anger. "You bastards killed my partners! And left their bodies to rot in the well."

"It was self-defense."

The flames were moving closer and closer to us. I could feel the relentless heat on my skin.

"Get me out of here!" the woman moaned again.

I shook my head. "This all has something to do with Miriam. With Miriam Morgenroth."

"I don't know her."

I took my time. "An elderly lady. White hair, blue eyes, from a rehab clinic in Starnberg."

"Oh, her! What do you have to do with that old hag?"

I couldn't hold myself back any longer. I grabbed her collar with both hands and dragged her up until her face was only centimeters away from mine. "Tell me what happened to her. Or I'll let you burn to death in the flames."

The woman tried to free herself from my grasp. "What should have happened? We drugged her and carried her away."

I shook her. "And where is she now?"

Amusement flared in her eyes. "Where do you think? She's dead. Died quickly."

"And her body?"

This time, she actually laughed out loud. "Torched. In some forest. The rest we buried. You fucking bitch! Help me out of here!"

The wood ceiling creaked ominously. Blue, then yellow, and finally red shadows raced across it.

I shook the woman again. "We don't have much time! Any moment everything will collapse. Who hired you?"

The woman coughed, laughed, and coughed again. "It doesn't matter. The old hag stays dead."

I hit her in the face. "Who was it? Come on—say it!"

"Some old geezer wanted to save his company. His name is . . ." Out of the corner of my eye, I saw a flash. A motion as fast as a blink. The woman had pulled out a knife, whose blade slashed into my upper abdomen. The pain seared through me.

I fell over backward. The woman lurched up. Kneeling, she swung the knife again.

I slid away from her until a wall stopped me. I tried frantically to push myself up. The woman came closer—and with her, the fire.

My fingers felt a hard object. I grabbed the bottle that had fallen out of the woman's hand a few minutes earlier. I flung it at her. I missed. The bottle crashed against a post, the glass burst, gasoline sprayed in every direction. It ignited already in flight, rained down on the woman, and engulfed her in a flaming cloak.

She screamed again. Earsplitting.

Someone grabbed me hard by the arm, dragged me heedlessly over the floor, down the stairs, across the cobblestones until I was in safety.

Chris bent over me, his face blackened from soot. "Can you stand up?"

I attempted a nod. I do not know if I succeeded.

"We have to go," he urged. "The fire department. I can hear the sirens."

62

I squeezed the cloth slowly and steadily. Silvery drops beaded out, fell on the burned skin, and coated it with a transparent film.

"Ow," Chris cursed.

"You have to get through this," I said, as I dunked the cloth in a plastic bowl full of water until it was soaked again.

"Isn't there some kind of ointment you can just put on it?"

I returned my attention to my work. "Trust me. You have second-degree burns. I'm sure it's extremely painful, but in three weeks, the worst will be over."

"You really know how to bolster a man's courage."

"That's me. Stretch out your arm. The fire caught you there as well."

Chris obeyed without argument. He was careful to stay on the towels that I had spread out under him so as not to drench the hotel bed.

After I had cooled his wounds, I wrapped a sterile bandage around his chest. Not too tight but snug enough to last through the night. I was afraid to hurt him and paid attention to my every move. He flinched several times, but instead of groaning like any other normal human being would have done, he smiled, completely self-composed. Macho man—I let him have his fun.

"Done," I said when I had finished. "Tomorrow morning we'll do it again. The bandage has to be changed regularly."

"I can hardly wait," Chris quipped. This time, however, I could see perfectly well that he was acting. He was in a lot of pain.

I took two tablets out of the first aid kit lying on the bedside table and handed them to him.

"What do I need these for?" he asked.

"You have to sleep. And without help, you won't be able to."

"I'll take the tablets but only with a whisky."

"Of course," I said. "How could I have forgotten?"

I grabbed the water bottle and poured a glass to the top. I held it out to Chris. "The finest scotch," I said.

Chris wanted to protest, but he saw my determined expression and sighed. He put the pills in his mouth and washed them down with the water.

I took the glass out of his hand. Our fingers touched momentarily.

"I had almost forgotten what a merciless caregiver you were."

"Consider yourself lucky."

Chris became serious, his smile pensive. "Yeah. You got that right," he said. "By the way, how are your injuries?"

"Nothing serious. Just a scratch. I stuck a Band-Aid on it." I stood up. "You're going to get tired now. When you wake up, you'll feel much better."

"You're lying."

The drugs began to take effect. Chris relaxed; his eyelids drooped shut. "Will you stay?"

"You know I will."

"Good," he mumbled, and when I thought he was already asleep, he added, "Take the pistol, just in case."

I waited on the chair; in front of me on the coffee table lay the weapon, its barrel shimmering midnight blue. A feeling of security.

I listened to Chris's regular breathing pattern. I tried to remember the tall dark-haired woman who wanted to kill Chris and me. For a moment, I heard her screams, right before she croaked. Now she was dead. And I wasn't the least bit sorry.

I quietly stood up, grabbed Chris's smartphone from next to the gun, and disappeared with it into the bathroom, shutting the door gingerly behind me.

I sat down on the edge of the tub, searched the contacts for a particular number, and pressed "Call."

I heard a series of rings. No one answered.

After an eternity, I got the voice mail. I spoke slowly and articulately. "This is Alicia Petersen. Mrs. Falk, I now know the truth. You and your husband took out a contract on Miriam Morgenroth. I have proof of this. And you also wanted to kill us. I have proof of this too. If you would like to prevent me from going to the police, you should contact me immediately."

63

C hris attempted to button up his shirt without assistance. He was sitting in the chair now, an improvement from yesterday when he was still in bed.

"Let me. You can't do it alone," I said and helped him.

Finally, I collected the dirty bandages and stuffed them into a plastic bag. As I had done on the previous day, I would later dispose of the bag in a random trash can on the street.

"And?" he asked.

"Your wounds? No infection, it's coming along," I said. "You just need to be patient."

"You should talk."

I said nothing, picked up the cereal bowl from the table, and sat across from him on the corner of the bed with the intention of feeding him.

"Stop it!" he said. "I still allowed that yesterday. But as of now, I'm going to do it myself."

"I thought it was easier for you; it's no big deal for me."

"That's not the point." He took the bowl from me and began to eat. "You've taken care of me since I left rehab. I have to slowly start becoming self-reliant."

I grinned. "At the latest, you have to be fit by the time your world tour begins. You'll definitely have to manage without me then."

"Exactly," Chris said, and in one word, all lightheartedness left the room.

Chris ate in silence. Now and again, he glanced up at me.

"You look sad," he said after a while.

I wiped my eyes and shook my head. "That's hardly surprising. Miriam is dead. I couldn't save her, nor will I ever be able to visit her grave."

Chris put his spoon down. "At least you can be sure what happened to her wasn't your fault."

"That's not much of a consolation. I failed miserably. We didn't even find your stupid diamonds."

Chris looked at his leg and nodded slightly. "Yeah."

"It will hit Georg hard when I tell him about Miriam," I said.

Chris raised his eyes. "Waiting longer to have that conversation won't make it any easier."

I took the bowl out of his hands and put it back on the table. "You're right."

I grabbed the phone and looked indecisively at the display.

"You have to inform him. We've left him in the dark long enough. If it's too hard for you, I don't mind taking over," Chris said.

"No," I said. "I owe Georg that much."

I placed the call. Two, three times Georg's phone rang, and then I heard his voice. "Alicia?"

"Hello, Georg," I began, but then I couldn't find the words to go on.

"What's the matter?" he asked. "Did something happen? You sound so . . . different."

I walked over to the window, pushed the curtain aside, and leaned my forehead against the glass. "I promised to inform you as soon as I found something out."

Georg remained silent for a while. "Should I prepare myself for the worst?" he asked finally.

"Yes."

I heard him inhale sharply. "Okay."

"Miriam is dead."

Again, silence. Then he said, "Are you absolutely sure?"

"Yes."

"Oh my God," he said quietly. "How did she die? Did she fall? Or did she have a stroke? What happened?"

"She's been murdered."

"Murdered?" Georg shouted. "How can that be? I don't believe it. Who would've . . .?"

I closed my eyes. "Hired assassins," I said. "Two men and a woman. I can't even tell you where you can find her remains."

"Miriam! You must be mistaken. She's a good person. She's interested in literature, is well-read, and . . . *hit men*?"

"I'm afraid there's no doubt about it."

"Then you have the identities of the murderers? We should have them arrested immediately. We can't just let them get away with this. I need to know where Miriam is. I want to be able to bury her."

"That won't work," I replied as gently as I possibly could.

"Why shouldn't that work? Of course, it'll work! We live in a land of laws. Ask Mr. Winkler, your partner."

"Miriam's murderers were also after Chris and me." My throat was dry. I swallowed. "Anyway, as far as the killers go, we definitely won't be able to prosecute. I'll tell you about that later, in person."

Georg was breathing heavily. "How about you and Mr. Winkler? Are you okay?"

"Nothing happened to me," I assured him. "But Chris is injured. He'll need some days before he's recovered."

Georg seemed not to have heard my last words at all. "I'll never be able to give Miriam a decent burial. I won't get to say good-bye. The last time I saw her, I was in a hurry because I had a meeting regarding some insignificant business matters. If I had only known . . ."

I couldn't hold back the tears any longer. They ran hot down my cheek.

Georg was the stronger of the two of us. He pulled himself together more quickly. "You spoke of hired killers. If we can't get our hands on the gunmen, we need to punish whoever ordered this insanity."

I nodded. Then I realized that Georg could not see me. "You're right," I said. "Whoever's calling the shots is walking around free."

"And you know who it is?" All of a sudden, Georg sounded calm and collected.

"Falk," I said quietly. "Maximilian Falk."

"Do you have any doubt about that?"

"Not the least," I said. "But I can't prove it. Not yet."

"Max Falk. I can hardly believe it. If it really is true what you say, it'll be difficult for us to prove that he did it."

"Why?" I did not understand.

"Maximilian Falk committed suicide tonight and, from what I heard, did it without warning and without leaving a last note."

I wanted to say something, but Georg continued. "Miriam is no longer here. What should I do now? I can't imagine my life without her. And our bank . . . I can't do anything but wait until she is officially declared dead . . . Alicia? Where are you? I'll come right now, and you can tell me every detail. Maybe . . . maybe you're missing a small clue that we'll discover when we talk about everything, and we can find Miriam's remains . . . A funeral, dignified closure, she deserves that . . ." He broke off.

I swallowed fresh tears. "I think it's a good idea that we meet. But let's wait a few days, until Chris is back on his feet. I'll call you as soon as he's doing better."

"Promise?"

"Yes, I promise," I said and hung up.

I stood at the window for a while, turned back around, and sat down on one of the chairs.

"That wasn't easy," Chris said.

"Georg took it harder than me," I explained. "He wanted to come to us immediately, but I told him it would have to wait."

"I picked up on that. I definitely need a day or two before I'm fit again."

"More like a week."

"A whole week?"

I shrugged. "We'll see. A few days, at any rate."

"And what do you want to do in the meantime?"

"Life goes on. There's a swimming pool nearby. The distraction will do me good. And besides that . . ."

"Besides that?"

"Aside from that, I wanted to visit my mother."

Chris listened in astonishment. "Your mother lives in Hamburg?"

I tried to smile. "My stepfather is a big shot around here. And I haven't seen my mother for quite a while."

64

The automatic glass door shut quietly. Agreeable, well-tempered air greeted me—the result of a perfectly adjusted air conditioner. A young lady sporting a platinum-blond pageboy sat at an enormous desk, pretending to work at a computer.

"May I help you?" she said breathily.

"I have an appointment with Mrs. Vossen."

The young woman furrowed her brow. "Mrs. Vossen has a private engagement."

"Exactly," I replied. "With me."

"*You* are Alicia Petersen?"

I nodded.

"Ms. Petersen, of course. Mrs. Vossen will be back any minute now. She asked me to have you wait in the gallery lounge. I can show you there if you'd like."

"No, that won't be necessary. I can find my own way."

"As you wish." She had risen halfway up and now sat back down. She invitingly motioned to a large passage into an adjacent room. "Just a few steps. Help yourself to a drink."

"Thank you," I said.

The soles of my shoes squeaked with every step on the floor, which appeared to be made of marble.

I walked into a windowless room—actually, it was more like a hall. Indirect light, an unobtrusive scent that was reminiscent of frankincense. Before me, an oversized white couch, two matching armchairs, an immaculate glass table with a variety of beverages and sparkling clean tumblers.

And I was not alone.

Dozens of faces stared at me, stark and austere. Fingers, hands, arms extended in my direction. Along a lily-white painted wall stood one sculpture after another. Wood statues on pedestals and platforms, in fabricated niches and on stone benches. Artful images of saints, all different sizes and poses—hand-carved, skillfully painted, and embellished with gold leaf. A reticent legion of devout figures.

I contemplated whether I wanted to sit down or not, but I couldn't bring myself to and instead nervously walked back and forth. I studied one of the pieces more closely. Almost life-sized. The wood was rough and crannied, the eyes painted light blue. A black varnished arrow protruded from his side. The blood that flowed out of the wound had faded over time.

Real lacerations look different shot through my mind. I reached my hand out and ran it across the saint's chest at the spot where he was mortally wounded.

"Saint Sebastian," a voice behind me said.

I slowly lowered my arm and turned. A middle-aged woman stood in front of me. Still very attractive. Her hair flaxen, probably colored, but done so professionally that it looked natural. Her pantsuit discreet, ostensibly minimalistic, but actually painstakingly tailored to accentuate her body's best assets. Piercingly blue eyes like those of my grandmother—with one fundamental difference: unlike my grandmother's, hers were hard and without any semblance of feeling.

"Hello, Mother," I said.

"Alicia," she said, making it sound like an accusation. I could not manage to move, so my mother came to me. Only then did I notice she carried a brown file in her hand. Without setting it down, she hugged me briefly, ensuring that our faces did not touch. Then she pushed me quickly, almost abruptly away.

"Alicia," she repeated, "let's sit down." I went to the couch and took a seat. My mother chose the chair opposite me.

For a moment, no one said a word. Then my mother cleared her throat. "You can't believe how surprised I was when you called me yesterday. That was really . . ."

"It made you happy," I said.

My mother inhaled deeply. "Sure. Happy."

Again, that silence.

"I was in Hamburg," I explained. "And I thought . . . we haven't seen each other for so long . . . and it would be nice if we . . ." Now I was the one who couldn't bring her sentence to an end.

My mother raised her eyebrows. "Alicia. Quit beating around the bush. You can't make me believe that after five years, you just show up here without a reason. What do you want from me this time?"

"Well, you're mistaken. I just wanted to say hello."

"Good. You've done that. Now what?"

"You're selling antiques?" I motioned toward the holy relics.

"A hobby. Björn said that as a senator's wife, I should find myself an occupation. And the gallery has become one of the hottest addresses in Hamburg's art scene."

"You can make money with artwork from churches?"

My mother threw me an indulgent look. "Yes. Imagine that. These statues fit exquisitely in a private spa, in front of a sauna, or in a conservatory. But what am I saying? What's with you?"

"With me?"

"You look splendid. You're surely together with some good-for-nothing guy again."

At first, I didn't know what I should say. Then I nodded.

"And? Is it serious this time? Is there a future in store for the two of you?"

I avoided her stare. Then I shook my head.

"You see, it's just like it always was."

"But—"

"No, Alicia," she interrupted me. "Now I'm talking. Years ago, I chose to have you. That was the worst decision of my life. You've only brought me worry and sorrow. To have a baby is one thing, but dark skinned . . ." My mother exhaled. Her mouth made a bitter line. "When I met your stepfather, I had to leave you with my mother. That wasn't easy, but it wouldn't have worked to have you, with his social circles. You would've inevitably destroyed our relationship, and after all, I deserved a little comfort as well."

"I was two years old then," I reminded her.

"It had nothing to do with your age. I certainly always provided optimally for you. You lacked nothing. But you . . . you only ever made problems. Nothing but trouble. You never fit in anywhere. I gave you everything, put the world within your reach. The most expensive private schools, money, the best upbringing. None of it interested you. As soon as you entered puberty, you were in love with one no-good loser or the next. And then you had to start getting in trouble with the law. Did you ever even think what that meant for me and your stepfather? How difficult

297

it was to constantly have to cover that up? It would have ruined your stepfather's career and the lives of your two stepsisters with it."

"I've never asked you for anything—or ever betrayed that I was related to you." My voice echoed dully through the room. I looked to the faces of the saints; they looked back, unmoved.

"You never asked?" my mother snapped. "Do you think I didn't care what would become of you? Every effort I made to help you, you pushed away or trampled upon. No one can get along with you. You're like your father. He didn't want to fit in anywhere either."

The blood that trickled out of Saint Sebastian shimmered dark in the artificial light. "Grandmother got along with me. *She* loved me," I said.

"Oh really?" My mother twisted her mouth contemptuously. "Should I tell you something about your *beloved* grandmother? When it was coming to the end, we had to take her to a clinic. I visited her every day. And always, *always* when I was with her, she said, 'Today my Alicia is going to come. She won't forget me.' And you know what happened?" My mother looked at me questioningly and smiled. It seemed cruel.

I couldn't take it anymore, lowered my head. Tears welled up in my eyes.

"You don't want to answer? Then I will. You couldn't come, because you were in prison. You forged checks from me to pay your debts. You took drugs and sold them too. And you were violent. Your grandmother didn't see that; she didn't know about it. I hid everything from her. And with the help of our attorney, I even managed to get you a special leave weekend so that you could visit your dying grandmother. Everything was worked out. But what I hadn't counted on was you, right? Do you still remember?"

I remained still.

"I'll give you a little hint. On the day before your leave, you picked a fight with another inmate and beat the hell out of her." My mother snapped her fingers. "That was it for your visit."

"But—"

"No *buts* about it," my mother interrupted again. "Now, I'm talking. Your grandmother is dead, and she constantly waited for you. You never arrived. All the people that cared for you, you have forsaken. No one can depend on you."

A feeling of emptiness came over me. I tried to fight against it, but I did not succeed. I thought about what my mother had just accused me of. I thought about my grandmother, who had wistfully hoped to see me one last time before her death. And I thought about Miriam and about my desperate attempt to at least get it right with her. Once again, I had failed. My mother was right. No one could count on me.

My mother reached for the folder that she had placed on the table during our talk and straightened it. "Thanks to our connections, I got you that position in Starnberg. I'm sure you'll find a way to lose it. If you cared about keeping it, you wouldn't be running around here during your probationary period. That's why I've made a decision."

I looked up at her blurry outline and wiped my eyes.

"A very painful decision that really isn't easy for me," she continued. "Today, here and now, we are meeting for the last time. It doesn't make sense anymore. I need to admit that to myself. You'll never change. You'll always be a loser without any prospects."

I tried to say something, but my mother raised her hand to silence me. "Your grandmother left me the Hallig. I was her only daughter, and Kronsoog is mine now. Of course, we immediately thought to make use of it. It really is a beautiful piece of land. Your stepfather had the grandiose idea to fix it up for an exclusive clientele. Far away from the bustle of the city, next to the sea. With its own helipad and an apartment complex. In short, an unrivaled spa experience." She shrugged dismissively. "But those damned environmentalists ruined our plans at the last minute. Even with your stepfather's extensive contacts, nothing could be done about it. The island can only be used for agriculture, and that's not financially interesting—at least, not for us."

She leaned forward and pushed the brown folder in my direction. "Maybe you could lease Kronsoog out. Then you could get a few euros every month." She pointed to the file. "I've prepared all the paperwork and signed over the island to you. This is the last thing you will get from me and the last time that we will see one another. You have to take control of your own life. We're finished now."

I looked at the file that she was pushing a little closer to me. Brown cardboard with a white label that read "Kronsoog." Nothing else.

It was difficult for me to bring myself even to move. Then I grabbed the file and stood up under the scrutinizing look of my mother.

"I should take control of my own life?" I asked her and without waiting for a response added, "Now I will tell you something. I have always been in control of my life. I have always been on my own. My mother was only interested in her own personal advancement. And my sisters were ashamed of me. I learned very early and very astutely how to get along on my own."

I left her sitting, turned around, and headed toward the door. Her voice stopped me. "Alicia!" she called. This time, she sounded different: human, almost tender.

I stayed put. For a minute, I toyed with the idea of turning around, going back to her, and telling her what I never had the opportunity to tell her before. The folder in my hand suddenly became heavy. I squared my shoulders and walked on.

When I was about to enter the reception area, I saw Chris—pale with hollow cheeks. But the worst was behind him. The burns were healing. He leaned on one of the walls near the entrance. I walked right past him and the platinum-blond saleslady. The glass door opened automatically for me.

The Porsche was not locked. I sat behind the wheel and placed the file on the backseat. A moment later, the passenger door opened, and Chris sat next to me.

He looked out the window and studied the façade of the art gallery.

"My mother is an amazing woman," I said. "She actually gave me my grandmother's island, just because she likes me so much."

"Ah," Chris said, without looking at me.

"Yeah. She'd also like to get to know you. But she has so much to do." There was the remnant of a tear in my eye. I resolutely wiped it away. "My stepfather is an important figure here. She said we can stop by anytime we like all the same."

Chris flopped the glove compartment open, removed a packet of gum, and offered me a stick. I forced a smile and helped myself.

"You have your own island now? I'd like to see it sometime," he said. "I think a couple days' vacation would do me good, before I go back to Munich."

"A couple days?" I said.

Chris took a stick of gum. "A week, maybe two."

"Sounds great," I said and started the Porsche.

65

The sea was as smooth as a mirror. The clouds, the fog resembled thick cotton. The diesel engine worked quietly, and the small cutter fought forward bravely and with surprising speed. The visibility was lousy. The hint of the powerful vortex that the motor left behind us disappeared into the mist after a few meters. The air smelled of salt, algae, and silt. How I had missed this!

Fiete stepped out of the cabin and came up to me on the stern. He wore the obligatory rubber boots, blue overalls, and yellow parka on top. An obviously hand-knitted cap covered most of his shaggy blond hair.

"Well, Alicia," he said. "How does it feel?"

I grinned. "Simply fantastic, you know that."

"Doesn't it? And we've got perfect weather for our little voyage."

"It's so nice of you and Biane to take us along," I said.

Fiete scratched himself sheepishly under his cap. "Forget it. You already thanked me earlier. I was going to my Hallig anyway, so dropping you off on Kronsoog along the way is no big deal. Only a little detour."

I leaned to the right and tried to look out past the cabin.

"Terrible visibility," Fiete said. "You can't make out your home yet. But if I'm not mistaken, it's going to clear up soon."

I tipped my head back and stared up through the thick billows. "Yeah, you're right."

"You can hardly wait to get to your Hallig." Fiete stuck his hands in his pockets and stood with his legs akimbo.

"Is it that obvious?"

Fiete sighed. "I don't want you to be surprised when you get there, though. Since your grandmother left, a few things have changed on Kronsoog."

"Really?"

"First off, we collected all the animals. There was no one left to look after them. Your mother sold them to us before she sent for the contractors, who pretty much wreaked havoc."

His words practically strangled me. "Is the house still standing?" I asked. I squinted, trying to see anything. But the fog was forming an impenetrable wall.

Fiete nodded. "They were actually planning on ripping it down and building an ultramodern tourist complex. But they weren't able to get that far." A glimmer of pride coupled with satisfaction showed on his face. "We put an end to that."

"You've done a great job," I said. "I can't thank you enough."

Fiete glanced at his shoes. "I thought it would make you happy." He turned around and then also looked out over the railings. "And what are you going to do?"

"The Hallig belongs to me now," I said to his back.

"Nice," he said after a while. "Will you lease it?"

I had not yet thought about what I would do when I returned home. But the minute Fiete asked, I knew the answer. "I'm going to stay on Kronsoog."

Fiete turned back to me. He wore a sincere smile. "If you grow up here, you can't live anywhere else. When I'm on the mainland for two or three days, I start to feel totally lost and have to get back. The noise, the cars—it all drives me crazy."

"Isn't that the truth," I said, and we both fell silent.

Fiete motioned toward the cabin. "What's with your friend?"

"He had an accident not all that long ago and wants to rest a little on Kronsoog."

"Will he stay here as well?"

I shook my head. "Only a couple of weeks. Then he'll leave."

Fiete nodded almost imperceptibly, as if he had guessed as much. "If you want to live on Kronsoog, you're going to need money to get your farm running again."

"Money?"

"Of course. Livestock, feed, fertilizer, food—it doesn't come cheap."

I shrugged. "It'll all work out somehow."

Fiete patted me on the shoulder with his big paw. "Don't you worry. The rest of us from the Halligen, we'll chip in and loan you what you need. And when you're on your feet again, you can pay us back."

"You'd do that for me?" A lump formed in my throat.

"Definitely. There aren't too many of us. We have to look out for one another."

A cool breeze reached my face; a soft wind set in.

"You really think that I belong here?"

Fiete straightened his cap. "Well," he began slowly. "You are a bit of a misfit. But you belong here—there's no doubt about that. Don't you worry. Together we're gonna make it."

The boat began to lurch. Fiete countered the movement by slightly bending one knee. "Biane!" he bellowed in the direction of the cabin. "Pay attention—here comes the current! Give it all it's got!"

The roar of the engine grew louder.

The cabin door opened, and Chris staggered out. The fishing boat shifted uneasily once more, and Chris was nearly slammed into the doorframe. He caught himself with lightning reflexes. "What's the matter?" he asked.

"It's nothing," Fiete replied. "Just the current off Kronsoog. It's really strong. It can become unpleasant."

Chris joined us on the stern. "What do you mean by unpleasant?"

"Well, if you're not careful, it'll unequivocally drag your ass out to the big green sea. And it takes a long time to come back."

"Don't exaggerate," I said.

Before Fiete could answer, the wind picked up. Really intensely. And all at once, the sky overhead became blue.

A faint silhouette emerged out of the sparkling mirror of the sea. A flat island with a small dwelling mound in the middle: the terp. Kronsoog. I could see our house, our barn. The green of the meadow grew denser the closer we got.

Then our little levee came into view, built from dark, almost black granite blocks, followed by the narrow wooden footbridge that led to our Hallig. As if on cue, seagulls appeared to greet us, screeching.

But no matter how hard I searched, I couldn't detect a trace of what I had missed most: the delicate blue of the flower.

"Where is the sea lavender?" I asked. "It should be in bloom."

Fiete also stared at the small piece of land that seemed to be waiting for me in the distance. "I told you. The developers wanted to turn the island inside out. They started to build a helipad. The machines plowed over everything. It'll take time before the sea lavender comes back. But don't you worry. The sea lavender is like us—you can't beat it down with a stick."

The noise of the motor changed again. Out of the constant hum came an almost distressed chugging as Biane cut the throttle. The vessel lurched, and the stern broached off the port quarter. The granite wall, which my grandmother had always proudly called the Kronsooger Wharf, jutted massively out of the gray water.

The cutter continued to slow down, and the waves pushed it closer to the stone fortification. Fiete left Chris and me, grabbed a large red fender, and climbed sideways past the cabin. With somnambulistic skill, he placed the fender between the boat and the granite wall.

A dull roar sounded, and we were properly shaken one last time. The diesel died. Fiete threw a thick line over a wooden post that served as a bollard, and moored the boat.

Biane joined us. He was the spitting image of his brother, equally tall and big-boned. But he was the silent one of the family. Even now, he only acknowledged us with a slight nod before he and his brother helped us to unload our luggage and supplies. Soon, several white plastic crates and our suitcases were stacked on the edge of the dock.

I could hardly wait and jumped on the platform. Chris climbed after me.

"Should we help you carry the things off the jetty?" Fiete asked.

"We'll manage, thank you," I said.

Fiete showed his irregular teeth through his smile and then actually snorted. "Yeah, you probably don't want us around when you celebrate your reunion with your Hallig."

"Is that terrible?"

"No. In a week, we'll come by with some supplies. Then you'll have to invite us in for a rum."

"Deal," I promised.

Biane disappeared into the cabin, as silently as he had appeared. The diesel fired up. Chris unhooked the line and threw it to Fiete, who caught it adroitly. The vessel set off sternway and came about.

Fiete waved good-bye to us. "See you soon!" he yelled before following his brother into the cabin.

I inhaled audibly and looked up toward the terp. The house's old brick glowed in red tones.

"What are you waiting for?" Chris asked when I didn't move.

"I don't . . ." I said and fell silent.

"You're afraid that everything has changed?"

I nodded.

"I know you; you'll whip it back into shape in no time."

I looked at him to make sure that he meant what he had just said. His eyes were calm and full of confidence in me.

"Well then, let's go," I said. I grabbed my suitcase and walked up the narrow pier toward my home.

66

A wooden footbridge connected the pier to the rocky shore—just wide enough to drive a handcart across. Thick oak boards, warped and cracked over the years, offered a clear view of the gray water below as I walked. Only a roughly built handrail on the left. Nothing fancy—but when the wind whipped up or it really stormed, it offered firm support.

The path to the house was paved with construction waste. Broken bricks, gravel, and pieces of concrete pressed into a layer of clay served as a subgrade. At first, the land was level; the meadows were flat with the occasional crevice. The tracks of the construction equipment were inescapable. Big tires, chains, had ripped up the turf and left deep scars. The plants had warily repossessed their old habitat, but it would take years before it fully recovered.

I swallowed hard and searched desperately for a sign of the delicate blue. On either side of the path, only green. I was just about to give up, and then I discovered it. Here and there, in isolated spots, I saw remnants of sea lavender. Timidly peeking its blue flowers out of the grass surrounding it—too few to be seen from a great distance but still alive and determined to stand its ground. Fiete was right. Even the sea lavender would come back. It just needed rest and relaxation. I took a deep breath.

My eyes fell on countless rusty brown rebar stakes. They marked off my mother's construction plans. Many had red and white plastic bands stretched between them; some of these were only fastened at one end. The candy-striped ribbons fluttered frantically in the wind, producing a rattling whistle. I quickly made up my mind that they would be the first thing to go.

We continued up the path, which now had a slight incline to it. The house on the terp came closer. The weight of my suitcase tugged on my arm, and I switched hands. Chris walked next to me. From time to time, he would throw me a sidelong glance, and I had the distinct impression that he liked the Hallig.

Our farm consisted of a thatched cottage with a stable and a freestanding barn. The straw on the roof was covered with moss. The mullioned windows were filthy and opaque. I tried the doorknob—locked.

"Normally the house is open," I said to Chris.

"Doesn't make much sense to lock yourself out," Chris responded. "I would think the number of burglaries in this area is rather small."

"Nincompoop," I said and smiled.

The area in front of the entrance was covered with cobblestones. I bent over and eagerly counted the stones, grabbed the seventh one, and lifted it after wobbling it back and forth several times. Underneath lay a tin box. I freed it from the ground and picked it up. Over the years, it had rusted, and it took quite an effort before I could get it open. A small, oil-soaked rag was wrapped around our spare key.

With fingers, whose trembling I could not suppress, I unlocked the door.

An unadorned hallway. The entry on the right wall led to the stable. I opened the door on the left, hesitated, and then walked in with Chris.

Our kitchen. The old coal stove, next to it the ultramodern electric oven from the seventies. The sink. A buffet with dishes, a cupboard with pots, in the middle of the room a large dinner table, around it six scuffed-up wood chairs.

I closed my eyes for a moment and saw my grandmother coming out from the living room, scrutinizing me discerningly, and then giving me her beaming smile.

Chris set his suitcase down on the floorboards. "Nice," he said as he let his gaze wander.

I tore myself away from my memories. "Do you really like it?"

"Once you've cleaned it up, it will definitely be homey." Chris grinned.

"Homey?" I repeated. "And I should clean up? What about you?"

Chris's grin grew even broader. "I'm the guest. But I can already see where this is going. Vacation on the farm, right?"

"You got it. And of course, the guest chips in. That's what gives it its charm."

"Charm," Chris muttered with mock horror, and we laughed.

It was almost like it used to be.

67

As always, I swam to the wall of broken stones, pulled myself up, and climbed out of the water. For a late summer day, it was pleasantly warm, easily above seventy degrees, and the wind wasn't really cold yet. I had left a towel on the wall and dried off with it before I put it over my shoulder and slipped into my flip-flops. As I crossed the meadow, the hard grass scratched at my ankles. On the path, I made better time.

A muffled hammering could be heard.

As I got closer to the terp, I could see Chris struggling with the fence. Actually, for a city dweller, he had proved to be surprisingly skillful. Our vegetable garden was nearly completely fenced in again.

As soon as he saw me, Chris took a break from his work and straightened up. He was only wearing jeans. His shirt was hanging on one of the posts. By all appearances, he had gotten hot while working. He looked good standing there. Broad shoulders, well-defined muscles. And over the past two weeks on my Hallig, he had gotten some color. His zombie-like pallor had given way to a healthy brown.

I waved to him and walked into the house. As soon as I had shut the door behind me, the hammering started up again. I showered, put on some fresh clothes, and went into the kitchen.

To my utter surprise, Chris was standing in front of the stove and busying himself over two frying pans.

"What's going on here?" I asked.

"Lunch," he said. "What do you think?"

"Don't you want me to—"

"No. You sit down and marvel at my work."

I took a seat on one of the stools and supported my chin on both hands. "What's for lunch?"

Chris turned his back to me. "Fish."

"We have fish?"

"Caught early this morning. While you were still sleeping. I don't know what it's called, but it's big, and I have three of them."

"Long or flat?"

"Looks like carp."

"*Carp?* They live in fresh water." I rolled my eyes. "Let's wait and be surprised."

"Served with fried potatoes, like every day."

"We had noodles yesterday," I said.

Before Chris could respond, his phone rang, obtrusively ending our conversation.

"Can you get it?" he asked.

I grabbed the cell. "Petersen."

"Ms. Alicia Petersen?" I recognized the voice. I put the speaker on and placed the phone on the table.

"Yes, this is she," I said. "Good morning, Mrs. Falk."

Chris set the skillets on the stove and came over to me while wiping his hand on a tea towel.

"Whether the day will turn out good remains to be seen," she said. "I am inclined to doubt that that is going to be the case for you."

"Oh?"

"Don't act so innocent, Ms. Petersen. You know exactly why I'm calling. I heard your message on my voice mail, and it was the greatest effrontery I have ever experienced in my life. I didn't respond sooner because my husband passed away. But you can rest assured that there will be legal consequences!"

Chris threw me a questioning look, but I just shook my head and concentrated on the conversation.

"Mrs. Falk," I said. "You can level as many threats at me as you like. But I know what I know. And I'll repeat it once more. Your husband is responsible for Miriam's death."

"Are you completely delusional?" she shrieked. "You met my husband yourself, shortly before he died! He was a crippled, severely handicapped man. Without my help, he couldn't even leave the house. And you think this wreck of a man killed Miriam Morgenroth?"

"Not personally," I said. "He hired someone to do it."

"*Hired?* What a load of nonsense! Did the honorable Dr. Vogt put you up to this?" Her voice cracked. "Surely, he did! That scumbag! His family and the Morgenroths were always sleazy. They've never done an honest day's work in their lives. A veritable band of thieves, as my father always called them. And he knew exactly what he was talking about."

"Georg didn't say a word to me!"

"Go ahead and protect him. I don't care. I know his lot! And I've finally had enough of this slander. I won't allow the memory of my husband to be dragged through the dirt anymore. You claimed to have proof. And you're going to need it. I will sue you for everything you're worth. I will destroy you!"

Before I could say anything, she hung up.

I rubbed my forehead and looked at Chris.

"What was that?" he asked. "What did she mean when she said *slander*?"

I did not answer him but stood up and went to the stove.

"Alicia!"

I stopped and turned around. "The night of the fire. After you fell asleep, I called Mrs. Falk and left a message on her voice mail that I had proof that she and her husband had Miriam killed and wanted us killed as well."

Chris's eyes flashed angrily. "Are you out of your mind? Why did you do that? And on her voice mail? There will be no end to this shit."

I crossed my arms. "I thought it would draw her out. And it has."

"Great way to lure her out! She's had enough time to destroy any evidence that would have pointed in her direction. Her husband is dead. With that, she's off the hook. She can put everything on him if she needs to. And you'll never be able to prove she's lying."

"It was worth a try," I said, defending myself.

"Mrs. Falk will come after you. I know these people. She won't let it go; she'll never give up. We have to prepare for that."

"But how?"

Chris stared out the window and thought it over. "She's repeatedly spoken about her father. That he knew the Vogts and Morgenroths and considered them criminals. Maybe there's more to this hostility than meets the eye—something that we haven't yet realized."

"And how are we supposed to find that out here on Kronsoog?"

"We could go through Professor Fembach's and the student's files one more time. Who knows, maybe we've overlooked something."

68

Outside, twilight had set in. The grandfather clock tolled eight times. Then it ticked remorselessly on. My eyes were watering, I had a headache, and I felt as if I had been run over by a bulldozer.

"I can't anymore," I said.

"What's the matter?" Chris asked without lifting his eyes from the screen, which displayed a file he'd just pulled up.

"We've been hunkered down here for hours," I said. "You've looked at every detail of these frickin' records at least a thousand times. How do you do it?"

"Do what?"

"This mind-numbing research that leads nowhere."

"Studying files?" His voice sounded mocking. "That's the backbone of any good police work."

"But I'm not a cop. I'm an aspiring farmer."

Chris looked over at me. "We're almost finished. Just a few more photos and a couple lists."

"And we haven't found out anything. The whole effort was an exercise in futility." I stretched and yawned.

"You don't have to stay here," Chris said. "I can see it through to the end."

I got up, went over to the sink, and let the hot water run. I hated doing the dishes, but anything was better than poking around in those files.

"These pictures are appalling," Chris said after a while.

I began to dry the dishes. "The concentration camps were unimaginably horrible."

"Yeah. They took the last remnants of human dignity away from the inmates before they murdered them. Like all the prisoners, Miriam Morgenroth had a number tattooed on her arm, and from that point on, she was no longer an individual but just a row of digits."

"135763," I said quietly.

Chris leaned forward and stared at the screen. "No. Where did you get that from? Miriam's number was 438891."

"I'm absolutely sure." I put down the plate that I was drying and walked over to Chris. "I applied ointment on Miriam's tattoo a bunch of times. She had some kind of eczema. And I can still see her number clearly in my head. I'll never forget it. 135763."

"Maybe the tattoo had faded. Or you're just mistaken."

"Definitely not," I insisted. "The file must be wrong."

Chris clicked through more documents. A never-ending list of names and numbers. Men, women, and children—all murdered. "Miriam's name appears often in these lists. And always in conjunction with the sequence of digits that I just mentioned."

"Maybe it's a mistake."

Chris shook his head emphatically. "These criminals were all overtly meticulous—compulsively so. There would've been no room for a mistake like that."

I looked at him, bewildered. "Do you have another explanation?"

"No idea. I'm also not sure if it matters."

"We could ask Georg," I suggested. "If someone knows about it, it would be him. Miriam and he were pretty tight. I could call him."

Chris furrowed his brow, thought about it, and then handed me his phone. "All right. Do it. It can't hurt."

I selected *Recent*, clicked on Georg's number, and waited as it rang.

"Vogt." His voice sounded hollow. I could hear noise in the background. Obviously, Georg was in his car and talking on speakerphone.

"It's Alicia," I said. "Is this a bad time?"

"Alicia! No, not at all. I'm on the autobahn, there's little traffic, and I'm very happy to hear from you."

"It's nice to talk to you too, Georg."

"How are you? And how is Mr. Winkler doing?"

"Great, thanks. Chris has recovered and looks as good as new."

"That's fantastic! What's up? Why did you call? Can we finally get together?"

"Sure, but first I have a question for you."

"Shoot."

"It sounds a bit absurd, but Miriam had a tattoo on her arm, a number."

"Yes. The number she received in the concentration camp."

"That's why I'm calling. It doesn't agree with the documents that we have from the professor."

"Which documents?"

"From Auschwitz. They kept painstaking records of every prisoner, and Miriam is listed in several places with a completely different number than she had on her arm."

For a time, I could only hear the noise of the motor. Then Georg said, "Strange. Do you have any idea what that could mean?"

"No. That's why I'm calling you."

"Who knows? Maybe a mistake, an error in the registry. I would guess something like that. Why are you digging around in this old stuff, anyway?"

I sighed. "It's complicated. It has less to do with Miriam than it does with the Falks. You know, we wanted to have something on them."

"I can't imagine how Miriam's number could help there."

I sighed once more. "Well, yeah. It's just that it's all we could find."

Again, only the sound of the motor. "I think it would make a lot of sense if I came by to see you guys. Remember, I've known the Falk family for years. If I look at the documents, maybe I'll catch something that escaped you."

"Of course," I hastened to agree. "We'd love to have you over. But Munich is rather far away."

Georg laughed. "Go figure! It just so happens, I'm right outside of Hamburg. I have an appointment tomorrow morning in the Hanseatic city. Which hotel are you in? As soon as I'm finished, I'll come by and see you."

"We're not in Hamburg anymore."

"Oh? Then, where are you?"

"We're on Kronsoog."

"On your Hallig?"

"Exactly."

"Well, that's only a stone's throw away from Hamburg. Should I come out?"

"That would be great, Georg."

"All right. I'll get my business over with and join you in the afternoon. Then we can talk about everything at length. And I'm looking forward to seeing you again too, Alicia."

I had to smile. "I feel the same. How about if I ask my neighbor Fiete to pick you up in Nordstrand with his cutter?"

"A cutter? What do you take me for?" Georg laughed. "I've owned an ocean-worthy yacht for years and enjoy sailing across the sea on my own. I'll just rent a small motorboat in the harbor and take it out to you."

"Kronsoog is pretty far away from the mainland. You will need at least forty-five minutes if you come out in a little tub."

"I can hardly wait!" Georg laughed again. "This will be a nice change. Should I bring anything?"

I glanced at Chris. "Georg is visiting us tomorrow. Is there anything we could use?"

Chris grinned. "Coffee and scotch. I can't look at another cup of tea—or rum, for that matter."

69

I grabbed one of the irregular stone blocks and picked it up. The wall on which I stood had clearly seen better days. The tide had left its mark over the past few years.

"Now what?" Chris asked.

"You have to find a spot where it will fit in best and then . . ." I didn't finish my sentence but rather let the stone slip down into a large cavity. It canted out just a bit, so I placed my foot on it and forced it with my whole weight into the opening.

"See?" I said. "That's how it's done."

"Like a three-dimensional puzzle," Chris said.

"Yes. A gigantic puzzle," I agreed. "The breakwater prevents the sea from carrying off the island. The water tries its best every day. The North Sea easily rips the stones out of the wall. And then . . . well, yeah, then the shore is next."

Chris bent over and picked up an extremely large boulder. "And we don't want that," he said.

"Absolutely not." I grinned.

Chris glanced around, decided on a location, and rammed the stone powerfully into a wide hole. It fit perfectly.

"That method also works," I said.

"Doesn't it? I learn fast." Chris was in high spirits.

We worked long without a break and forgot about the time. The sun climbed ever more; its rays burned on our skin, but the cool sea breeze provided relief. At some point, I squatted on the levee and observed Chris briefly. He went without stopping; he seemed to never tire.

"Wow," I said. "It's well past noon. We can skip right to our afternoon tea."

Chris placed his last stone in the shoreline stabilization, stood straight, and wiped the sweat off his brow with his forearm. "Cut it out with your tea. I want coffee—or better yet, a beer." He removed the heavy-duty work gloves and came over. He sat down next to me, and together we looked in the direction of the shore. The sea shone like a mirror today, as if a Titan had smoothed it out with a giant trowel. A light haze had risen on the horizon, obstructing our view.

"How far did we get?" Chris asked.

"A good twenty meters."

"And how much more do we have?"

I grinned. "You don't really want to know."

"It's fun," he said, "but incredibly strenuous."

"That's our motto out here on the Hallig," I said, and we laughed. "It's been years," I continued, "since anyone has properly tended to the breakwater. That takes its toll."

"But now you're back. Your Hallig can breathe a sigh of relief."

"Exactly."

The haze that had approached from the mainland seemed to get denser. Gradually it changed colors. A washed-out gray mixed in and got noticeably darker.

I started sweating and rubbed my face on the sleeve of my T-shirt.

"It's hot today," Chris said. "And now the wind has stopped."

I squinted my eyes and stared over the lead-gray surface of the water. "There's something brewing."

"Oh, come on. Blue skies far and wide, not a cloud in sight, sun shining. You may be one with your Hallig and all, but this time you're mistaken. This is your normal boring hot summer's day. If I were in Munich, you'd find me in a shady beer garden with an ice-cold wheat beer—or maybe even two."

The gray band of clouds made itself more apparent and grew in size. All at once, the wind returned—not friendly and cooling like before but instead smacking us hard in the face. Whitecaps appeared out of thin air, waves rose up, slapping, at first timidly and then violently, against the wall on which we sat. The sun lost its power; its rays petered out before they could reach us. A fine mist enveloped us. I could feel it damp on my cheek.

Chris went, "Uh oh!"

"You can say that again." No sooner than I had spoken, there was a sudden flash of light on the water, closely followed by an admonitory growl.

"Thunderstorm?" Chris sounded astonished.

"Just a few kilometers away." In response to my reply, another flash zigzagged across the sky, and the thunder that followed rang in my ear. "It's approaching quickly."

The waves that rushed toward us now were almost a meter high. As if all that was not enough, it began to rain.

"What's this?" Chris yelled in horror and protected his eyes with his hand. "Since when does it rain horizontally? All respectable rain falls downward."

"We definitely need to call Georg to keep him from setting out. If he gets caught up in this thunderstorm, he won't have a chance in a small motorboat. It'll inevitably capsize."

Instead of answering, Chris held his arm out and pointed to the raging sea. "That warning would be a bit late."

I looked in the direction he indicated, and recognized a small dot dancing back and forth on the agitated water.

"I don't think my eyes are deceiving me," he said.

"No," I confirmed. "That's definitely a boat."

The rain drenched our clothing and dripped from my eyelashes. Lightning flashed unremittingly; the crashes of thunder layered over one another until they coalesced into one infernal blast.

"What's he doing?" Chris screamed, and even though he was yelling at the top of his lungs, his voice was almost absorbed by the roar of the thunderstorm.

The boat was now clearly visible. A small tub with an outboard motor. Just right for a Sunday tour in nice weather. But completely inadequate for a storm like this. The boat bounced between the raging swells.

"He's doing it exactly right," I screamed back. "He's riding on top of the waves, using their power."

The boat came within a few hundred meters. It repeatedly seemed to sink in the water, only to immediately rise on top of a white crest.

I could make out a lone man sitting at the helm, piloting the small craft.

"Hopefully he can handle the current," I yelled. "During a storm, it's even stronger than usual."

Spellbound, we watched how Georg's boat was thrown back and forth, almost spinning on its own axis in order to dash to the next mountain of waves. It would disappear from our sight momentarily and emerge as swift as an arrow in a calmer spot of the sea. Then the surge pushed angrily again, grabbing after it in an attempt to turn it over.

Once more Georg changed directions, sailed parallel to the surf, then abruptly maneuvered the little boat around, and on the last stretch, he shot almost straight toward us.

For a finale, he pulled the wheel hard over. His boat was pressed up to the granite jetty of our little harbor. Although the tide slapped against the rocks there, the sea was calmer in that spot.

As if given a secret signal, Chris and I took off together—across the meadow, over the footbridge to the pier.

Georg had already managed to lodge two fenders. He threw us a line. On the second attempt, Chris succeeded in catching the wet rope. Together, we lashed the boat down tight to one of the wood posts.

Georg stood in the wobbling tub and handed his sports bag over to us. We stretched out our arms to him, and with a unified effort, we pulled him up onto the pier.

Georg glowed. "That was magnificent. I feel ten years younger."

70

"The bath is yours," I said to Chris as I slipped into a zippered hoodie.

"Took long enough," he said, smiling while he squeezed past me. The hallway was tight, and our bodies grazed each other. He laid his hand on my hip and tried to pull me even closer, but I pushed him away.

"Later," I said. "We have a guest."

When I entered the kitchen, the scent of wonderfully aromatic coffee hit me. Even though I didn't like the stuff, I had to admit it smelled pretty darn good.

Georg, who had been the first to shower, stood in front of the stove and poured boiling water into my old porcelain teapot with the blue strawflower pattern.

"I'm almost ready," he said over his shoulder. "Then we can talk."

"Don't rush," I said. "On the Hallig, everything takes its time."

"I've noticed." Georg laughed. "Everything about this place is different."

"Do you think?"

"It seems like time stands still here."

"That's especially noticeable in the kitchen equipment. It all dates back to the seventies." I grinned.

"Well, it all continues to work perfectly."

I opened the cupboard, took some dishes out, and brought them to the table. The storm that raged outside had lost nothing of its fierceness. It rattled the shutters. Over and over, deafening claps of thunder sounded. Rain pelted the windows incessantly, and the wind howled around the house.

"Do you have enough light? Or should I switch on the floor lamp as well?" I asked Georg.

"No, it's fine," he said. "It's original. I didn't know that you even had electricity out here on the Hallig."

"I'm not Robinson Crusoe or something!" I responded with mock indignation. "We have electricity and running water. And sometimes, when the wind blows just right, we can even use our cell phones."

Georg laughed and sat down on one of the chairs. He motioned in the direction of the bathroom. "It seems that the stay has done your partner, Mr. Winkler, some good. Not a trace of that sickly pallor. You'd think he was a completely different person."

I picked a seat across from Georg. "Yeah, the change in environment seems to have done him well."

"Only the change in environment?"

I felt myself blushing involuntarily.

Georg reached over and patted my hand. A trusting, almost intimate gesture. I sensed it came from the heart.

For a time, we did not speak, and then Chris walked in. "Do I smell coffee?"

Georg rose. "Coffee, and besides that, I brought something else along." He turned to the sideboard. There stood a green whisky bottle with a gold label. He grabbed it and placed it in the middle of the table.

Chris sat down and studied the label. He whistled through his teeth. "Boy oh boy. Twenty-five years old."

Georg laughed. "You have to spoil yourself some-times." He took our cups from the table, went with them to the stove, and poured us coffee with his back to us. "The perfect weather for Irish cream—coffee and whisky," he said.

He handed me two cups for Chris and me, brought his own to the table and sat down.

Chris uncorked the whisky and served first Georg then himself a substantial shot into the black brew. As he went to pour some into mine, I placed a protective hand over the cup. "No thanks."

"No? You don't like whisky?" Georg asked, astounded.

"Yes, but"—I stood up and got myself a glass—"I don't like coffee."

Georg looked at me, bewildered, and Chris raised his eyebrows apologetically. He poured me a shot, and we toasted each other.

The whisky brought a subtle taste of vanilla and caramel to the front of my tongue. Even its finish was extremely mild. "Marvelous," I said.

Chris nodded in agreement, and Georg seemed satis-fied.

"I think it's about time we stop addressing each other so formally." Georg raised his cup and held it out to Chris. "My name is Georg."

Chris clinked his cup against Georg's. "It's a pleasure to make your acquaintance. My name is Chris."

A dazzling light flashed through the room, immediately followed by a jarring blast.

"The storm is directly above us," I said.

Georg stared transfixed out the window. It had become even darker outside. "Real adventures in nature. Like Theodor Storm," he said. "Miriam would have enjoyed it."

"Yes, she would have," I agreed. "And she would have especially loved the island. Normally, this time of year, the entire island is covered with blue flowers. With sea lavender. She would have loved that. Unfortunately, not too long ago there was some construction work going on here. The heavy machinery has done a lot of damage. But the blue flower will make a comeback."

Georg drank from his coffee, set it down, and added a little more whisky. "I wish Miriam would also come back. I miss her so much." He paused. "As difficult as it may be, I need clarity. Alicia, on the telephone you promised you would tell me in person how you found out about Miriam's murder."

I put my glass down on the table and turned it between my fingers. "Three people," I said. "A woman and two men. When Chris and I tried to reconstruct Miriam's escape route, the men tracked and found us. They attacked us and clearly meant to kill us."

Georg's eyes twitched nervously. "What happened to them?"

I looked out the window into the storm and shook my head silently.

Out of the corner of my eye, I could see Georg transfer his perplexed stare from me to Chris, where he also received no answer.

Georg cleared his throat. "That's why you said they couldn't be prosecuted. Okay. You also said there was a woman involved."

"We found Miriam's escape plan. It's in her book, the one you gave me, on the inside of the leather book cover."

Georg opened his mouth, closed it again, and in the dim light of the room, I could see the color leave his face. "Oh my God! I never even considered that. It was in my hands the entire time."

Without paying attention to his outburst, I kept going. "We went to the warehouse district in Hamburg, to the exact address where Miriam's family had hidden and where they were arrested. We even found their fake passports there."

Georg listened attentively. "What about the diamonds?"

"No diamonds." Chris butted into the conversation. "Only old passports and a few bundles of dusty Reichsmarks. The story of the diamonds was a fairy tale."

Georg nodded, lost in thought. "A fairy tale," he slowly repeated.

"The woman who I mentioned earlier," I continued, "was obviously the boss of the three. We walked right into her trap in the warehouse district."

"And?" Georg's eyes shifted from me to Chris and back and forth again.

"She liked fire," Chris said bluntly.

"Liked fire?"

Chris took a drink from his coffee. "In the meantime, she's also not to be counted among the living."

Georg waited for more details, and when we didn't supply him with any, he said, "But then, who gave you the information about Miriam's murder?"

"The woman did," I said. "Before she died, she told me quite a bit."

Georg became deathly pale. Another bolt of lightning made his face appear ghostly white. "How was Miriam . . .?"

"How Miriam was murdered?" I swallowed my tears. "The woman didn't describe the particulars. She only said that they abducted Miriam from the clinic, that she died quickly, and that they burned her body and buried the rest somewhere in a forest."

Georg leaned back on the chair, his arms hung down limply. "She didn't tell you anything else?" His voice sounded hollow.

"She talked about who had hired her. She admitted that she and her two partners had been paid to murder Miriam."

Georg looked startled. He seemed hypnotized by my narration. Chris leaned forward and observed Georg's reaction with a pensive alertness.

"And the name of the son of a bitch who hired her?" Georg burst out. "This is essential."

"She spoke about an old man. Verbatim, she said, 'Some old geezer wanted to save his company.' She didn't need to mention the name. I already knew who she was referring to."

Georg was spellbound, hanging on my every word. "You still suspect Max Falk?"

"Of course. He really didn't want to lose his company."

Georg looked down, placed his arms on the table, and clenched his hands into fists. "Max. I didn't want to believe it. I had my doubts, which got stronger ever since our telephone call, although ultimately, I wasn't convinced. But you're right. He's the only one it could have been."

"I'm afraid," Chris said in the ensuing silence, "Alicia didn't resist the temptation to call Mrs. Falk and tell her that we had evidence against her and her husband in our possession. We only learned from you later that Max Falk committed suicide. And now, Mrs. Falk is threatening Alicia with legal measures."

Georg needed some time to process everything. Then he nodded. "It all fits together now. And now I see why you're still digging. It's no longer just about catching Miriam's murderers. You need to find evidence against the Falks."

I nodded silently while Georg continued, "I'll help you, of course. And Alicia, don't you worry about a thing. In the unlikely case that it goes that far, and Mrs. Falk really takes legal action against you, I'll supply the best lawyers available."

Chris emptied his glass in one slug, set it on the table, took the whisky bottle, and poured himself another. "You're absolutely right, Georg. Everything is crystal clear, and it all fits together." He sipped his drink and looked directly at Georg. "I just don't understand why the killers would have abducted Miriam."

Georg pursed his lips. "They had a contract to murder her."

"Murder. Precisely. But they dragged her away, killed her somewhere else, burned her body, and hid the rest in such a way that she wouldn't be found anytime soon. That's a lot of trouble."

"Who knows what goes through a hit man's mind," Georg replied.

Chris nodded contemplatively. "We always assume that murderers' thoughts are complicated. That since killers behave differently than us, they must also be wired differently. But Georg, I have to say that isn't so. When murderers do something, they always have a good reason for it."

"They probably didn't want to attract attention in the rehab clinic," I said.

Chris furrowed his brow. "It's at least as difficult to kidnap someone as it is to kill her. It would have been much easier to just—please forgive me, Georg—press a pillow against Miriam's mouth. She was old. She wouldn't have resisted long. No, there must be another reason."

Georg forced an uneasy smile. It seemed to be hard for him to make himself talk about Miriam's last hours. "It's true what you're saying, Chris. I can't give you an answer to your question either. But maybe when we bring charges against Mr. and Mrs. Falk, maybe then Mrs. Falk will tell us the truth. After all, she despised Miriam from the bottom of her heart because of the collapse of her company."

Chris lifted his cup and then set it down without taking a drink. "That doesn't change the facts. Mr. and Mrs. Falk would have just as soon had Miriam murdered in the clinic, if it were a mere matter of revenge. And why did they wait so long to have it done?"

"So as not to raise suspicion," Georg said immediately. "And maybe . . . maybe the plan was first conceived when Max Falk got seriously sick, and he and his wife started brooding day and night over their fate. At that point, it became virtually essential for them to find a scapegoat for the bankruptcy. And who was more suited for this role than Miriam?"

Chris yawned. "If you look at it that way, it seems logical." He rubbed his eyes.

"Hmm," Georg said and exhaled.

"But still," Chris started again. "Why burn Miriam's body? They could have just buried her remains straight away if they hadn't wanted to murder her in the clinic."

"Who knows?" Georg raised his hands ineffectually.

"Let's assume for a minute that there was something more behind the murderers' choices."

"Okay." Georg leaned forward attentively.

"Why would you abduct someone, kill her, and then burn her body?" Chris tapped his index finger on the table. "To get rid of the corpse."

"And? What would be the purpose of that?"

"That's precisely the question. For weeks, I've been racking my brain over it. And then, by chance, we stumbled across the fact that Miriam's tattooed concentration camp number doesn't match the number in the Nazi's registry."

"Oh, right." Georg turned to me. "Alicia, you said something about that yesterday when we talked on the phone."

I was about to answer, but Chris said, "Georg, what could that mean?"

"That the numbers don't match?" Georg shrugged indecisively. "Why are you asking me? I would guess a mix-up in the bookkeeping."

Chris rubbed his eyes again. "Yeah. A mix-up. But not in the bookkeeping. I've figured out a different story. And like the diamonds, it's a fairy tale. Do you two want to hear it?"

Before either Georg or I could answer, lightning flashed, and it thundered two, three times in close succession. A truly deafening racket, and suddenly we were sitting in the dark.

"Power outage," I said and stood up to fetch the old storm lantern out of the cupboard. I lit it and placed it in the middle of the table. The flickering light threw red-yellow tones onto our faces and into the corners of the room.

"Nothing out of the ordinary. It happens sometimes," I said and motioned to the overhead light. "It'll come back on in an hour or two."

Chris stretched and yawned. "So, where was I? I was telling you a fairy tale. Once upon a time, there were two bankers. They were very rich and very good friends. However, when the wicked Nazis came to power, one of the bankers sensed an opportunity to get the money from his friend, who also just happened to be Jewish. The first banker supposedly helped his Jewish friend escape with his family. However, in reality, he betrayed the second banker to the jackbooted Nazi thugs, who tracked him and his entire family down, stuck them in a concentration camp, and ultimately murdered all of them."

"Not all of them. The entire family didn't perish," Georg hurried to point out. "As a result of some act of God, Miriam survived. And my grandfather didn't betray the man because he was consumed with greed—"

Chris raised his hand. "Let me tell the tale to the end. This banker, who murdered his friend and his friend's family, hadn't thought about one thing. The Americans came and chased away the wicked Nazis. All at once, the political situation changed entirely. And the enormous fortune, which he already considered his own, would now have to be given to his friend's heirs in faraway England."

"Only hypothetically." Georg bit his lip.

"I told you that it's merely a fairy tale. If I understand right, half of your grandfather's bank, half of his property, would have been lost in one stroke. I can imagine how desperate he must have been to wangle a solution. And then an incredible twist of fate saved the day." Chris motioned to Georg. "Your grandfather found among the concentration camp victims a little girl. Miriam Morgenroth. She inherited everything. He took her into his family, managed her assets. And the distant relatives in England were left empty-handed."

Georg blinked, ran his thumb and index finger over the corners of his mouth, and said, "What are you getting at?"

"I needed a while before I realized it. The concentration camp numbers don't match. The little girl that your grandfather took in after the war was Jewish, she had been in a concentration camp, but she wasn't Miriam."

"What a load of nonsense! Who would she be?"

Chris smiled knowingly with a trace of sorrow in his expression as well. "Some other girl, whose entire family was also murdered and who was left all alone in this world. This child had even coincidentally met Miriam. For all I know, maybe they were even kept in the same quarters. The real Miriam read to her out of her book of poems at night, and they became very good friends in the midst of that hell. That would also explain why this little girl had the volume of poems. But in any case, for our rich banker, it only meant that he could keep his entire fortune intact without any restrictions. And that went on just fine for decades. Until . . ."

"Until what?" I said, torn between the desire not to believe him and the realization that he was speaking the truth.

Chris twisted his face into a grimace. Maybe he was trying to laugh. In the lantern's weak light, he appeared drowsy and physically spent. "A history professor heard another fairy tale. The tale of the Morgenroth diamonds. She sent her girlfriend, a PhD student, to go off and find this treasure. The two posed many questions, pored through innumerable files, and researched everything available about the Morgenroths. And . . ." Chris wobbled, supported himself with both hands on the table, tried to stand up, and fell to the ground.

"Chris," I screamed. I jumped up and started to rush to him.

As fast as lightning, Georg lunged across the table and seized my wrist with an iron grip. "Sit down!"

I tried to free myself, but he held on tight. "What's gotten into you?" I sputtered, horror-struck.

Georg waited until I stopped struggling. "Sit down," he repeated with an ice-cold voice, a tone I had never heard from him before.

As if in a trance, I obeyed. His clutch loosened. Then he let me go. He motioned to Chris. "Don't worry. Only a sleeping pill."

He observed me closely, a somewhat apologetic look on his face. "A really smart guy, your friend. If it had ever come out that Miriam wasn't who she claimed to be, I'd have lost a vast fortune. We managed to keep the secret for three generations. Miriam was happy to be with us. You see, the Nazis had sterilized her: she couldn't have any children. Her own family had been completely eradicated, without exception. We had given her a home. In her will, she named me the beneficiary to her fortune. And everything was taking its course. Sometime in the next few years, she would have died of natural causes, and everyone would have been happy and satisfied. But no! The confounded history professor had to go looking for lost diamonds. She forced me to take action."

I was seized by a fathomless terror. "You hired the killers!"

Georg laughed coldly. "Alicia, you're so naïve! I didn't have to hire the killers. They already worked for me. When someone makes real estate transactions the size of which we deal in, sometimes it's necessary to use unorthodox methods. Tenants, for example, can be extremely stubborn. And our fine country of laws, our strong so-called renter's rights, reinforce their position even further. You saw the model of the new city district when you were in my office. Those who have vision must be prepared to fight for it."

"But Miriam," I stuttered. "How could you do that to her?"

Georg's face softened momentarily, and he sighed. "I really loved Miriam like a true member of the family. And she was also downright useful when it came to forcing competitors out of business. Or did you truly believe it was she who smeared the Falks' reputation? No, that was me. She didn't really have any idea about business. She preferred to read books. It's too bad about her. But when our entire company was suddenly at stake, my money, my fortune . . . No." He slapped his hand on the table. "I couldn't let that happen. After Miriam's disappearance, everything went perfectly, until you two stuck your noses in. But I was still convinced that you would never find out."

Chris moved slightly on the floor. My throat felt dry. I could barely speak. "Let me see to him," I begged hoarsely.

Georg threw Chris a sidelong glance. "Your friend will easily sleep a couple hours longer."

"But when he does wake up"—my voice was more of a whisper, barely audible above the roar of the storm—"he will talk, and you . . . you will pay for everything that you've done."

George laughed mockingly. "Oh yes! He could tell a lot. He could tell about my grandfather and his betrayal of his friend, Adam Morgenroth. The money that disappeared back then—the Vogts appropriated it and acted as if it was the evil Jew Morgenroth who had embezzled it. You have to admit, a super chess move." Georg's eyes bore into mine—steadfast and firm. "But no one will ever know. Your friend will never speak again. Neither will you. Unfortunately, you don't drink coffee. That would have made things easier for you and for me." An affectionate smile spread across his face.

Without further thought, I grabbed for the whisky bottle. I jumped up and swung it in his direction. I caught him in the head, the glass shattered. Shards flew through the air and across the floor. Georg screamed. He was bleeding. He reached up and pressed a hand against the wound on his forehead. His eyes settled on me. A nearly inhuman expression came across his face. Suddenly, he rushed at me.

I turned quickly around and stumbled through the kitchen, Georg close behind.

I hurried down the hallway to the door, ripped it open, and ran out into the violent storm.

71

I ran through the darkness. Rain lashed my face. Wind fought against me, slowed my progress. Whenever the lightning cut the sky, I could recognize my surroundings for a fraction of a second. The path of compressed rubble, the meadow. On the horizon, the sea reared up in enormous, white-capped waves.

My heart pounded like crazy in my ears. My eyes stung. I didn't risk closing them even for a moment. I scrambled forward as quickly as I could, without stopping, without knowing where I was, without knowing if Georg was still chasing me. I stumbled, fell hard on one knee, and sprang right back up. I had lost all orientation; maybe I was running toward the shoreline, or maybe I had strayed into the pasture.

The blow caught me off guard. A remorseless fist cracked against my neck. I collapsed to the ground. I was hit over and over again. Methodically and mercilessly. My body became numb. It no longer obeyed me.

Georg grabbed me by the collar of my jacket and dragged me through the underbrush. Grass, stones, sand scratched and cut at my clothes, my skin, until they reached my flesh.

I tried to scream, but no sound escaped my throat.

I sensed that Georg was pulling me up steep footing. We had arrived at the jetty—the oak planks, the platform that served as our dock. In a last-ditch effort, I reared up. Bolts of lightning flashed repeatedly across the sky. Georg stood over me. His fists struck my unprotected face. The back of my head pounded into the granite. Everything swam before my eyes in a foggy gray.

Next, I felt myself being rolled to the side. For a moment, I was in midair, and then I fell hard between the seats of a boat. Georg climbed in after, messed with the rope, and started the motor.

I lay on my back, breathing heavily, painfully, and stared up at the rain. The daylight timidly returned. The clouds ripped open. Gloomy lead-colored light pushed through to me. The boat danced wildly on the waves—up and down, to and fro—apparently without any purpose. But I knew better; Georg fought once again through the waves, used every opportunity to move forward.

The motor died.

Georg bent over me to haul me up. Our faces nearly touched.

"No," I wheezed.

"Yes!" Georg brayed. "I'm going to drown you, and then I'll do the same with your partner. He would have been better off if the cancer had taken him."

I kicked my legs in a futile attempt to free myself. Georg laughed. A strong gust of wind hit us. The boat careened straight up. I slipped out of Georg's hands and slid to the side. I gripped the rail. I held on tight and shifted my weight so that I was hanging half out of the boat.

"No!" This time, it was Georg who bellowed the word, before he came rushing over to me. He grappled around my waist once more in an attempt to pull me back into the boat.

We flipped over.

Ice-cold water. We sank. Salt water in my throat.

Georg still clung on to me. I thrust my elbow backward once, twice, three times. He let go.

I tried to reach the surface, but something kept me down: Georg had grabbed my hoodie. I managed to slip my arms out. I propelled myself up. My head breached the surface, and I gasped desperately for air.

A few meters away from me, Georg popped out of the water. He moved in my direction with powerful strokes. I turned and swam. For months, I had been training. My body knew what it had to do. It operated like a machine. I began to take deep, even breaths.

The storm was letting up. The waves were still as strong as before, but the thunder had quit. The rain became weaker, and then it stopped completely. Whenever a wave lifted me up, I turned my head. I saw my Hallig and Georg, who tirelessly pursued me.

Georg swam well. Like a world champion. I didn't have a chance against him. He kept gaining on me. I was almost five hundred meters away from my island. The current—it was just ahead. I dove like I always did. Down under the water, there were no waves; there were no sounds.

And again, Georg followed me. He got very close. Deeper and deeper I dove, and yet I could not escape him. He grabbed me by the ankle. I kicked at him with my free foot but missed.

Georg was above me now. He tried to clasp on to my waist. I rammed my knee straight up and hit him hard— presumably in the face. He let go of me for a second.

The current, I thought. Even the best swimmer wouldn't have a chance. The North Sea showed no mercy when it came to any kind of weakness. She'd abduct her victims and never return them.

Death pulled on me with its icy fingers. Tighter than ever before. I could feel it. It lay in wait for one mistake, one thoughtless move.

With my last vestiges of strength, I shoved Georg as hard as I possibly could and actually felt him being ripped away from my side.

Silence. Peace.

Georg would not be coming back.

The North Sea had carried him away.

72

Almost two weeks had passed since the big storm. The summer was nearly over. The mornings already smelled like autumn.

I climbed out of the sea, toweled myself dry, and slipped into my bathrobe.

I looked around. The rain had been good for the meadows. The grass was lush and high. Next spring, sheep would graze here—perhaps even a cow or two.

Occasionally, I could make out scattered spots of another color in the green. Little blue flowers. Sea lavender.

As always, the door of my home wasn't locked. I walked through the corridor and entered the kitchen. Chris leaned over one of the chairs and was just about to close his suitcase.

I stopped and folded my arms in front of my chest.

He straightened up and looked me directly in the eyes. "You knew this day would come," he said.

I did not answer.

"Fiete will be here any minute now," he continued. "I'm going with him."

Again, I remained silent.

Chris inhaled deeply and tried to smile. He didn't succeed. "You realize if I don't go now, I'll stay forever. Every day it's getting more difficult for me to leave. And even now, I can just barely manage."

"Your decision," I said. My voice sounded vacant to my ears.

Chris nodded, as if I had said something important. "I have my dreams. I want to see the world. And actually . . . the cancer might relapse. I don't know how much time I have left."

"Nobody knows how long he has," I said.

Chris lowered his gaze briefly before he looked at me again. "But you do understand that I have to leave now."

I didn't want to make it that easy for him. But still, I said, "However you fare out there, you should know that Kronsoog is waiting for you."

Chris took his suitcase and went to the door. "Will you walk with me to the jetty?"

I shook my head. "I don't think that's a good idea. Farewell scenes don't sit well with me."

"I understand." He opened the door, stepped outside, and closed it behind him.

I heard footfalls in the corridor and the door latch shut. Then I was alone.

I leaned against the wall; I tried to breathe calmly and regularly. Tears poured out of my eyes. There was no need to harness my emotions any longer. Nobody was here to hear my sobs.

Eventually, I stopped crying and wiped my face.

Miriam's book was lying on the kitchen table—opened facedown with its dark cover made out of leather. I walked over and picked it up, so as to close it.

Dozens of little stars shone up at me. Radiant and sparkling in the light. Diamonds, lying on my white tablecloth. Each of the stones was as big as a fingernail. Next to them, a folded sheet of paper.

I put Miriam's book down, grabbed the piece of paper, and opened it.

The diamonds weren't a fairy tale. I found them by the passports.
You are entitled to half of them.
Chris

I let the paper fall and touched the stones with my fingertips. They were beautiful in a timeless way, yet cold. How many people had died because of them? Without thinking further, I left the room, my house, and went toward the dock.

Soon, I could make out the cutter. Chris stood at the stern, talking with Fiete.

I started running.

Now the engines of the cutter fired up. I took a few more steps before I stopped. I wanted to call and scream. I wanted to wave, to draw Chris's attention. To talk to him one last time.

The diesel revved up.

I let my arms sink and made an effort to turn away. Behind me, I heard the cutter set off, chugging loudly. Gradually, the noise of the engine grew fainter.

I began to move toward the house—only to stop again. Something was holding me back. Involuntarily, I turned around.

The cutter was already fighting against the current on its course.

I glanced at the dock. A big man with broad shoulders was standing there. He carried a suitcase. He was looking steadily in my direction.

I smiled at him through tears, lifted my arm, and waved. He waved back and started to walk toward me.

Dear Reader,

We hope you have enjoyed MISFIT GIRL – DEATH OF THE BLUE FLOWER, and you were able to spend some exciting hours with Alicia and Chris.

On the next page is a list of our English novels.

Sincerely
Yours

Roxann Hill and Paul Wagle

ENGLISH NOVELS BY ROXANN HILL AND PAUL WAGLE

Roxann Hill and Paul Wagle

Wolf and Gutenberg Psychological Thrillers

- MOONSLAUGHTER
  Wolf and Gutenberg, vol. 1
- DARK SCAR
  Wolf and Gutenberg, vol. 2
- TAINTED MIND
  Wolf and Gutenberg, vol 3

Dr. Evelin Wolf und Alex Gutenberg will return!

Roxann Hill – translated by Paul Wagle

Misfit Girl Suspense Thriller Series

- MISFIT GIRL: DEATH OF THE BLUE FLOWER
  Misfit Girl, vol. 1

THE AUTHOR

Roxann Hill

Roxann Hill is one of the most successful thriller authors in the German-speaking world. Her novels have delighted millions of readers and are regularly among the top titles on the bestseller lists. Her books have been translated into multiple languages.

Born in Brno/Czech Republic, the author lives with her family and two large dogs in Middle Franconia.

THE TRANSLATOR

Paul Wagle

© Frank Peters

Paul Wagle was born the youngest of twelve children in Wichita Kansas. After graduating with a Philosophy degree from the University of Kansas he served in the United States Peace Corps in Ecuador. He moved from South America to Europe where he resides in Berlin with his three children.

Made in the USA
Las Vegas, NV
18 April 2024

88828497R00208